I LIKE IT LIKE THAT

Damn. No wonder she hadn't wanted to rush into any other man's bed. Cary turned her, hauled her into his arms, and kissed her. Not a gentle kiss this time, but one of hunger and need and possession. He hurt for her and wished for some way to erase those memories from her mind, even while he sought a way to claim her.

She wasn't really kissing him back, but her hands clutched his shoulders and he could feel her fast breaths. "Give me your tongue."

She parted her lips, shyly did as he ordered—and Cary was lost. He drew her soft pink tongue into his mouth, sucked gently, teased with his own and followed her tongue back into her mouth, licking, tasting. Hot. Damn, she was hot.

The kiss went on and on, sharing, taking, giving. It required all his concentration to keep his hands on her waist and not lift them to her breasts, or drop them to her bottom. It was enough that he could feel her skin, wet from her swim, warm from the summer day.

Slowly, before he pushed too far too fast, he pulled back. She struggled to get her heavy eyelids lifted, then her gaze locked with his and her tongue flicked out, tasting her lips. "I liked that."

She wasn't helping his self-control, saying things like that. He cupped her face. "You'll like everything I do to you, I swear. We'll be incredible together, Nora."

from "Some Like It Hot" by Lori Foster

BOOK YOUR PLACE ON OUR WEBSITE AND MAKE THE READING CONNECTION!

We've created a customized website just for our very special readers, where you can get the inside scoop on everything that's going on with Zebra, Pinnacle and Kensington books.

When you come online, you'll have the exciting opportunity to:

- View covers of upcoming books
- Read sample chapters
- Learn about our future publishing schedule (listed by publication month *and author*)
- Find out when your favorite authors will be visiting a city near you
- Search for and order backlist books from our online catalog
- Check out author bios and background information
- Send e-mail to your favorite authors
- Meet the Kensington staff online
- Join us in weekly chats with authors, readers and other guests
- Get writing guidelines
- AND MUCH MORE!

**Visit our website at
http://www.kensingtonbooks.com**

PERFECT FOR THE BEACH

Lori Foster

Janelle Denison

Erin McCarthy

MaryJanice Davidson

Kayla Perrin

Morgan Leigh

KENSINGTON BOOKS
KENSINGTON PUBLISHING CORP.
http://www.kensingtonbooks.com

KENSINGTON BOOKS are published by

Kensington Publishing Corp.
850 Third Avenue
New York, NY 10022

All Kensington titles, imprints, and distributed lines are available at special quantity discounts for bulk purchases for sales
promotion, premiums, fund-raising, educational or institutional
use.

Special book excerpts or customized printings can also be
created to fit specific needs. For details, write or phone the
office of the Kensington Special Sales Manager: Kensington
Publishing Corp., 850 Third Avenue, New York, NY 10022.
Attn: Special Sales Department. Phone: 1-800-221-2647.

Kensington and the K logo Reg. U.S. Pat. & TM Off.

First Trade Paperback Printing: June 2004
First Mass Market Paperback Printing: June 2005
10 9 8 7 6 5 4 3

Printed in the United States of America

CONTENTS

SOME LIKE IT HOT

Lori Foster

Chapter One

Harsh sunlight found its way through the miniblinds on the window in exam room four. Though it was well after six, there were no clouds and no breeze to offer relief from the ninety-degree day. Saturday and Sunday promised to be just as stifling. Cary Rupert peeled off his requisite white coat, loosened his tie, and opened the top button of his dress shirt with a sigh.

Maybe the heat could account for his adult patients being so cranky, as well as the incessant whining of his younger patients. Appointments had run two hours over; nothing serious—a summer cold, sunburn, poison ivy rash. Cary was more than ready to head home. He wanted an easy chair, a cold drink, and a smiling, willing woman.

Hell yeah, he'd take all three. Didn't matter where he got the first two, but the third was a specific craving for one elusive woman. Maybe today he'd finally get lucky.

Leaving his office assistant and two nurses to lock up, Cary stepped outside, a man on a mission. Immediately, he was struck with a wave of hot, humid air. He reached into his breast pocket and fished out his reflective sunglasses for the short walk across the lot to the complex next door, where his best friend, Axel Dean, had an office and where the woman of his dreams worked.

Last year he and Axel had leased space side by side in the new medical complex. As a general practitioner, Cary saw patients of all ages, with just about every ailment under the sun. Axel had specialized as an OB-GYN, so he had only female clientele with the occasional husband or boyfriend stranded in the waiting room. A few spaces down were an ENT and a plastic surgeon. Other various businesses unrelated to medicine filled the complex, and not too many yards away, a Hooters restaurant kept a packed parking lot.

There were no men waiting in Axel's outer office on this late Friday. Cary had no sooner removed his glasses and taken a breath of the air-conditioned lobby air before Axel stuck his head out. "I'll be out of here in ten minutes. You wanna do dinner?"

In doctor mode, Axel was a different person. Serious. Concerned. Attentive to his patients' every word.

Away from the job, he became a complete hedonist, hysterically funny, and the world's biggest ladies' man. Cary liked him a lot. "Sure thing." Cary cleared his throat and tried to sound casual. "I'll just gab at Nora till you're ready."

Axel rolled his eyes as if he'd expected no less. "She's filing papers in the back," he said, then pointed a finger. "Don't distract her too much. She needs to finish up before she heads home." He ducked back into the hallway and disappeared into an exam room.

Cary's heart beat a little faster in anticipation. From the day he met Nora Chilton eleven months ago, she'd always had that effect on him. She stood five feet, six inches tall, had light brown hair, and kept her soft brown eyes shielded behind librarian-type glasses. Physically, there was nothing to drive a man into a frenzy of lust. But . . . sometimes these things didn't make sense, they just were.

He'd been frenzied from jump, and it just kept getting worse, not better. When she smiled, his abdomen clenched as if accepting a punch. Once she'd assisted a pregnant woman to her car, and her gentleness had his pulse tripping. Seeing her in quiet conversation with an expectant father made him tense in what felt too damn much like jealousy. And watching her work, her head bent in just that way, her brows puckered in concentration, caused a slow burn. He loved the way she moved, the gracefulness of her hands, her studious expression behind her glasses.

Five times now he'd asked her out. Five times, she'd declined.

He wanted her, damn it.

She wanted to remain friendly associates.

Sooner or later, Cary knew he'd wear her down, but until then, his life had been filled with frustration of the sexual *and* emotional kind. Lately, he'd turned down so many other women that Axel was starting to give him funny looks. But he didn't want anyone else. He wanted Nora.

Hands deep in his pants pockets, Cary approached the room where his quarry worked. Nora wasn't alone. Before he'd reached the open doorway, Cary heard her chatting with another female. He stuck his head inside and noticed an older woman running a fax machine.

"Hello."

Both women looked up. The older woman smiled. Nora flushed. "Dr. Rupert."

"Cary," he told her, a little peeved that Nora continued to insist on such formality when they were in the office. For crying out loud, there were no patients around, no one to be offended by the fact that they knew each other. Even as he scowled at her, he absorbed her every word. He loved her voice. It was deep and sexy, and she had this crooked way of smiling when she spoke . . .

Nora turned to her coworker to make hasty introductions. "Liza Welch, this is Dr. Rupert. He has an office next door." And with a mere glance at Cary, "Liza started with us a week ago."

Liza reached out. "Nice to meet you, Cary."

He smiled. At least *she* got it right. "Same here, Liza."

She started to say more, but Nora adjusted her glasses and stepped forward. "Can I help you with something?"

Cary stared into those big brown eyes and was lost. He'd meant to just chitchat. He'd meant to just visit her. Instead, he murmured low, "Have dinner with me."

Nora blinked at his husky tone, blushed—and shook her head. "No, I can't. I have work to do."

"Axel's a slave driver." He took two steps into the small room, his gaze glued to hers. "You have to eat. I want the company. *Your* company." And then softer, coaxing, "Have dinner with me."

Her lips parted. Her breath stuttered. And a file slipped right out of her hands, scattering papers everywhere.

Cary backed up a step.

"Oh damn!" Frantic, Nora dropped to her knees to gather the papers. Cary stared at the top of her head. Her hair was cut in short wispy curls that look adorable and exposed her nape—a nape he wanted to touch and kiss. She was dressed in a shapeless white nurse's uniform, and somehow even that looked sexy, despite the rubber-soled shoes.

Jesus, he had it bad.

He knelt down to help.

At his nearness, Nora rushed into speech, turning him down once again. "Really, Dr. Rupert." She snatched a paper right out of his hand. "I'm so busy and I don't have time to talk right now. It's going to take me forever to sort this again."

Insulted, Cary pushed back to his feet. She stood, too, the mangled papers clutched to her chest. She looked pugnacious and put out and so damn cute, it irritated him.

"I'm sorry I interrupted." In a huff, he stalked out.

To hell with it. He wouldn't ask her again. Of course, he'd told himself that before, but whenever he saw her, the invitation just came out of his mouth, without his permission, without coherent intent from him. She muddled him and made him hot and destroyed his ego with her persistent cold shoulder.

When he didn't hit on her, she was as pleasant as could be. But let him even hint that he wanted more than friendship, and she shot him down real fast.

Cary had his head lowered, chewing over his turbulent thoughts, when he literally ran into Axel.

"Whoa." Axel, tall and strong and equally stubborn, stumbled back into a wall. "Where the hell are you going?"

Cary slashed a hand through the air. "Out."

"Out?"

Shit. He didn't want Axel in his private business, privy to his turmoil. They shared a lot, but not that, not rejection. Axel never got rejected, which guaranteed he'd find Cary's situation entertaining and fodder for endless prodding.

Cary thought fast and came up with a lame but plausible excuse. "I'm going to start my car so it can cool off. It must be like an oven inside with this damned heat wave."

"Great idea." Axel thwacked him on the shoulder, hard enough to be retaliation for the way Cary ran into him moments earlier. "Grab my keys out of my office and start mine, too, will you? I'll be ready in just a couple of minutes, I swear."

"Why not?" Cary turned around and retraced his steps to reach Axel's office. He was glaring toward the room where Nora and the other woman worked when, as he got closer, he heard their voices, and this time the conversation was much more . . . titillating.

"Why in the world would you turn a stud-muffin like that down?" Liza demanded.

Stud muffin? Cary flattened himself against the wall beside the door.

"I have to work."

"Yeah, right," Liza said. "And I'm a nun. You'll have to tell that tale to someone younger or dumber than me, because honey, I've been around the block."

Cary could hear the smile in Nora's tone when she replied. "You're only fifty, not a wizened hundred."

"Fifty is a lot of years to watch human nature. That young buck scares you."

"No."

"Yes," Liza insisted. "And I'm nosy enough to want to know why."

He scared Nora? Ears cocked like a bloodhound, Cary waited to hear more.

Nora's sigh of exasperation was extreme. Papers rustled, the fax machine dialed. "I'm widowed."

Widowed! But she was in her mid-twenties—too young to be married, much less widowed.

Liza snorted. "I know, but you're very much alive."

How come Liza knew, but no one had ever told him?

"And," Liza continued, "given the way Cary was looking at you, it's for sure you'd have a great time if you just gave him a chance."

"A good time, maybe. But I want what I had. A husband, not a lover. The promise of home and hearth, not just sex." Nora sighed. "And I want kids."

Chuckling, Liza said, "Now, I may have just met him, but that young man looked more than potent enough to give you a dozen babies if you want them."

Cary's eyes nearly crossed. Babies? With Nora? He thought of her pregnant, maybe breast-feeding, holding an infant that looked like him or her or both.

"Capable, sure, but willing?"

Hell yeah.

"Maybe you should ask him," Liza suggested.

Yeah, ask me. Ask me.

"No need. If you'd ever heard the way Cary goes on about children, you'd know how he feels on that subject. After a long day of treating them, he makes it clear how glad he is *not* to have any of his own."

Liza was undaunted by that fact. "So until you meet this paragon of husband material, why not have some fun with the willing doctor?"

Cary held his breath. The silence stretched out so long, he almost suffocated himself.

Then, in a small voice, Nora said, "What if I fall in love with him? No, Liza, I'm serious. I'm not the type to have an affair. I was a virgin when I married, and I haven't been with anyone since."

"You're kidding, right?" Liza's tone sounded disbelieving. "When did your husband die?"

"Two years ago. We were married only six months. Not long enough. I miss him still."

Heart in his throat, Cary moved to stand in the open doorway. Liza had just reached for Nora and embraced her. "Shame on me for bringing it all back up. I'm sorry."

Cary stared at Nora and said, "I'm not."

The file fell out of her hands again.

Liza laughed and shook a finger at Cary. "You've had your ear to the wall, haven't you?"

"More or less." He wouldn't lie about it. He may have been a reprobate—almost as bad as Axel—but he would never lie to Nora.

"Well, you two go on and talk it out." Liza winked at Cary. "I'll get this file put away."

Before she could react to that suggestion, Cary wrapped his fingers around Nora's upper arm. She was stiff, silent. "Good idea."

"No." Belatedly, Nora found her voice, although it was

little more than a whisper. She pulled back, but Cary al-
ready had her through the doorway. He'd been headed
to Axel's office, so he continued on his way there, urging
Nora inside and shutting the thick door behind them.

He turned to face her, considered everything he wanted
to say. But she was just standing there, her arms folded
over her middle, her soft mouth trembling, her cheeks
hot. And he jumped the gun.

He kissed her.

Nora didn't have time to react. She'd done her best
to block out his warm masculine scent, to ignore how
fine he looked with his shirtsleeves rolled up and his tie
loose. His visual appeal got to her every time, but she'd
been resisting it for almost a year now. His brown hair,
shades darker than her own, was immaculately trimmed
but always disheveled in a very boyish way. His green
eyes were teasing and they made her feel both light-
hearted and needy.

She'd been prepared to hear his coaxing voice, to
withstand the intensity of his warm appraisal.

But she hadn't even considered a kiss. At least not
now, not in the office. God knew she'd spent too many
nights imagining what it'd be like, but she'd assumed
it'd never happen.

It happened now. And the second his warm, firm
mouth touched hers, coherent thought evaporated.
Her mind felt sluggish, her skin far too sensitive, while
her heart pounded fast and hard, making her struggle
for breath. Mercy!

It wasn't an invasive kiss. It was gentle and sweet, soft
and lingering. Her toes curled.

Cary hovered so close she didn't dare open her eyes
or she'd be caught. They shared breath. His scent
wrapped around her. His body heat added to the heat
of the day and her own turbulence.

"Nora," he whispered, and his big hand curled around her nape, caressing, keeping her close. His palm was hot, too. Everything about the man sizzled. "Kiss me back."

She drew a stuttering breath. "I . . ." *Don't know how.* No, she couldn't say something that stupid. But it had been so many years, the memories of kissing had long since faded. The need remained, but the mechanics were vague. "I'm sorry."

His forehead touched hers, displacing her glasses. "I'm not giving up."

She almost laughed. For the length of time she'd known Cary, he'd been gently persistent, crawling under her skin and into her dreams, and not a day went by that she didn't think of him. During the week, he found one reason or another to come to the office and talk with her. At every social event, he sought her out. "I know."

"I do so like kids."

That sudden disclosure startled her. "What?"

He raised his head, gave her a long look, then straightened her glasses with a small smile. "When I bitch about it, that's just exhaustion talking. If I didn't love kids, I wouldn't work so hard to keep them healthy."

Heat rushed into her face. "You said plain as day you didn't want any."

He rolled one shoulder. "Men say that crap all the time. It's nothing, just hot air meant to bloat our images as bachelors." Then, more firmly, "I want kids. *Someday.*" And softly, "With the right woman."

Why did he have to look at her like that while saying such a thing? Nora tried to back up, but her shoulder blades were already touching the door. "Your *someday* is probably ten years away."

Eyes narrowed in consideration, Cary looked her over. "Will you go to dinner with me tonight?"

She almost swallowed her tongue at the quick change in subject. "What does that have to do with you and kids?"

There was that small smile again, teasing her senses, melting her heart. "I can't start figuring out when someday will be until I start making headway with you."

Nora dropped back against the door; she needed it for support. "You just want to have sex."

"With you? Damn right." He braced his hands on the door at either side of her head. "Bad."

Somehow, her heart was up in her throat, choking off her breath. She stared up at him, and got snared.

Cary brushed a kiss to her chin. "Knowing you've been celibate two years just honed the knife." He kissed her cheekbone beneath the armature of her glasses.

"Knife?" she squeaked.

"The one that cuts me every time I think of lying down with you." His breath warmed her neck, then his mouth was there, damp, gently sucking.

"Oh." She literally panted. Without really considering it, she put her hands up against his chest—and froze at the delightful feel of solid muscles beneath fine linen. She could feel his heartbeat, too—hard, slow, and steady.

"I want you bad enough that it hurts, Nora. Tell me yes."

He kissed his way up to her ear, leaving a damp, molten path behind on her neck. His tongue touched her lobe, prodded just inside, and her knees almost gave out. *"Yes."*

Grasping her shoulders, Cary lurched back to see her face. "Really?"

Uh-oh. Nora blinked fast, bringing herself back to reality. What had she said? "Ummm . . ."

His hold tightened. "No, never mind. I heard it." His grin stretched from ear to ear. "Tonight?"

Tonight. Tonight. "No, I, uh . . . I'm beat, Cary. I just want to go home and take a swim and then relax." *I want to go home and guard my heart.*

His brows pulled down. "Then tomorrow?"

She started to shake her head—and Axel shoved the door open. She stumbled into Cary; his arms went around her, bringing her even closer, breasts to chest, belly to groin. He groaned, the sound both excited and pained.

"What the hell?" Like a bull, Axel pressed in, forcing them out of his way. His eyes darted from Nora to Cary and back again. One brow arched high when he saw their embrace. "Playing doctor in my office, huh? Can't you rendezvous in your own? It's right next door."

Flustered, almost speechless, Nora shoved away from Cary. "We were just . . . we were . . . talking."

"Yeah, that's what it looked like." Axel's gaze moved over her red face. "Talking."

"Shut up, Axel." Cary caught her arm. "I'll call you tonight."

Because Nora didn't know what else to do, she fashioned a smile and nodded agreement. She'd rather deal with Cary on the phone than in person any day. Over the phone, she'd only hear his mouth, not feel it or taste it. "Fine." She turned to Axel, knew her face was crimson, and brazened it out. "If you're ready to lock up, I'll just go get my purse."

She literally fled the office, aware of both men watching her, aware of her own awkwardness. It had been far, far too long since she'd dealt with an interested male. Never had she dealt with a man like Cary Rupert.

Liza stepped out into the hall, intercepting her escape. "Everything settled?"

Not about to linger for any reason, Nora grabbed her and dragged her in her wake. In the short week that Liza had worked with her, they'd become close. Liza was relaxed and easy to be with, if a little too pushy at times, but she was also very caring and incredible with the patients. "Come on. Time to head home." Nora wanted to be long gone before Axel and Cary made it outside.

Liza laughed. "Running like the hounds of hell were on your heels. Or is it just one sexy hound you're worried about?"

"I'm not worried," she lied. She was terrified.

"You're worried you'll fall in love with him. You told me so."

Nora shook her head. She knew the awful truth: she'd been in love with Cary Rupert for months. Now that he knew why she fought it, what would he do?

She bit her lip. "I'm not going to talk about this anymore. I'm going home for a dip in the pool. The water isn't cold anymore, but at least it's relaxing."

"A cold shower would be better," Liza told her with a grin.

"Maybe," she agreed, accepting Liza's triumphant laugh. But she knew a cold shower wouldn't do the trick, either. She wanted Cary, now more than ever. And the wanting wouldn't go away anytime soon, because Cary wouldn't go away.

He wanted only sex. She wanted it all.

And Nora Chilton was not a woman who settled for half measures. She just had to keep reminding herself of that, especially now that Cary had turned up the heat.

Chapter Two

"So you and Nora have something going on, huh? And you weren't going to tell me?"

Cary turned away from Axel and started out of the office. Damn it, that hadn't gone quite as he'd hoped.

Axel followed along. Like a dog with a meaty bone, he kept chewing. "Never mind that we're friends. Best friends, in case you've forgotten. And Nora works for me. She's my responsibility—"

Cary whipped around. "No way."

Smiling now that he had Cary's attention, Axel said, "Way."

"Don't even think it, Axel. I mean it."

Axel laughed. "What's this? You struck out, but you're afraid I'll hit a home run?" He threw his arm around Cary and dragged him out the door. "Relax, man. I draw the line at fooling around with females in my employ. You know that."

Cary did know it, but lust had helped him to forget. "Yeah, I know." And he added, "Sorry."

"Appreciate the vote of confidence, by the way." They paused beside Axel's new BMW. Axel put on his sunglasses and stared up at the sky. "The glasses didn't throw you off?"

With his mind still buzzing from Nora's nearness,

the feel of her, her taste, Cary was slow to coherency. "What?"

"Her glasses. I mean, even if you overlook the short hair—"

"It's sort of a Halle Berry thing, don't you think?

"—and those shapeless uniforms—"

"Which *you* insist she wear."

"—she still looks . . . I dunno. Studious."

Cary tried that word on for size. "Yeah, studious fits her. She's smart."

"Of course she is. I wouldn't hire a dumb woman."

"No, I mean beyond being a nurse. We've talked about everything from politics to family values, and she always makes sense. Unlike some people I know." He gave Axel a sharp look, so he'd understand whom he meant.

Axel ignored the insult. "She's nothing at all like a bombshell, which since you still appear dumbfounded, I'll point out is the type of woman you usually gravitate to."

Actually, that was the type of woman Axel preferred. Cary just went along for the ride. He grinned at his own sexual pun. Too many times, they'd picked up women together. Not strangers, but friends, acquaintances, sisters . . . Casual sex had lost its appeal a long time ago. Now he wanted more. He wanted Nora. "She's sexy."

Dubious in the extreme, Axel said, "You think?"

"You don't?"

Axel eyed him. "I'm not stupid enough to disagree with a besotted man. If you say it's so, then it must be."

Cary bristled—until he realized that he sure as hell didn't want Axel to start lusting after her, too. Talk about awkward. He slapped his friend on the arm. "Wise man."

"Yeah, so wise that I'm standing here on blacktop, in sweltering heat, trying to figure out how to tell you that you're an idiot."

Sweat trickled down Cary's temple. He swiped his forearm over his brow. "So just spit it out."

"She wants you, you want her. Why are you planning on having dinner with me?"

"She turned me down."

"So?" With typical Axel mentality, he said, "Seduce her."

"You are such a Neanderthal."

"Cajole her. Reason with her. Go to her house and spill your guts." Axel unlocked his car and pulled the driver's door open. Heat rolled out in a suffocating wave. "Get laid—and then maybe you can be worthwhile company again."

Now there was a thought. She'd said she wanted a swim . . . Cary's brain stalled at the image of Nora in a swimsuit with lots of skin showing. Almost to himself, Cary said, "I know where she lives." Her neighborhood wasn't that far from his.

"So what are you waiting for?" Axel gave him a shove. "Go before you start sweating like a pig and gross her out. But if this screws up my office dynamics, I'll kick your ass."

Cary saluted him and headed on his way. He heard Axel muttering about friends who didn't even say good-bye anymore, but he paid little attention to Axel as his thoughts leaped forward. Would Nora let him in? Would she give him a chance to spill his guts?

The idea of seducing her appealed in a big way. Cary got behind the wheel of his SUV and considered his options. By rote, he started the engine and turned the air on full blast before putting the vehicle in drive.

Nora had been pretty pliable in the office, all because of one small kiss. How would she react to him touching her breasts, her belly? What would she do when he sank his fingers into her, making her wetter, making him hotter? He drew a shaky breath. She said she'd been two years without sex—she had to be primed, so it'd be easy . . .

But no, that wasn't fair to do to her. His hands clenched on the steering wheel. Damn it, he didn't just want her carried away for the moment. He wanted her to want him, today and tomorrow and next month. Like Nora, he wanted more than a fling.

He was almost to her home before the air-conditioning finally cooled down the interior. Not that he'd noticed much. The heat inside him put the sultry day to shame.

Parking at the curb, he got out and surveyed her house. Small, neat, a Cape Cod with roses growing everywhere. She had a sprinkler going in the front yard, a summer wreath of flowers on the door. It looked homey. It looked like Nora, like what he wanted with her.

A knock on the front door brought no results. Stymied, Cary thought about it a moment, then remembered her pool. Disregarding formality, he walked around back, his hands in his pockets, his reflective sunglasses shielding his eyes from the low-hanging sun. And there was Nora.

Christ Almighty, she looked good.

Cary drew to a halt and just stared. Like crystals, setting sunlight danced on the water around her. She rested on her back atop a float, her glasses gone, her short hair wet and slicked back—her belly showing.

She was relaxed, limp, drifting in the small, rectangular in-ground pool. One hand rested above her head, the other trailed in the water. Her peach-colored suit was by no means a bikini, but the modest two-piece suited her. It was wet, clinging to her breasts so that the plump shape of her nipples showed. Cary stiffened his thighs, locked his knees. He wanted her in his mouth. He wanted to feast on those nipples and hear her cry out, feel her moving against him.

With an effort, he got a grip on himself and continued his perusal.

The swimsuit's bottom was wide, but still rode beneath her belly button and was cut high on her thighs. He could see the rise of her mound, the tender inside of her thighs.

She wore sunscreen, because she was creamy pale all over, her fair complexion emphasizing her femaleness.

Knowing he couldn't continue to stand there like a voyeur, Cary forced himself forward, moving silently on the lush lawn until he stood at the very edge of the concrete pool.

"Nora."

She jerked so hard she fell off her raft, legs and arms pedaling, sending a splash of water onto Cary's shoes. When her head resurfaced, she sputtered, then squinted toward him, one hand shielding her eyes while she tried to see him without her glasses. "Cary?"

"Yeah." He sounded hoarse, but damn, he was getting hard already just looking at her. Water droplets beaded on her shoulders—and her nipples were no longer soft.

As if she'd only just realized that herself, she crossed her arms over her chest. "My . . . my glasses are up there somewhere."

Cary located them on a lawn chair beneath a towel and knelt down to hand them to her. "Here you go."

She bit her lip, hesitated, and inched forward. Breathless, she said, "Thanks." Maybe hesitant to face him, she slid the glasses on with slow precision. She kept her head bent. "I wasn't expecting you."

"I know."

She swallowed, breathed fast, and finally, with excruciating slowness, raised her face.

Cary pulled off his sunglasses. He wanted her to see his eyes, to know what he felt. "Can I join you?"

Her jaw loosened and her mouth fell open.

"My briefs will look like trunks to your neighbors, if any of them can even see us here."

She looked from one side of her privacy fence to the other. "Neighbors?"

Her confusion charmed him. Gently, he explained,

"There are houses, so there must be people living in them."

She nodded.

Making the decision for her, Cary stood and unbuttoned his shirt. Her big doe eyes widened even more, and a pulse thrummed wildly in her throat. Her fascinated gaze tracked his progress, button to button, the widening of material, until he pulled the shirttails from his slacks and shrugged it off his shoulders. The sun on his bare skin felt good after the long day, and he stretched before putting the shirt on the back of the chair.

"Oh."

She liked his chest? He *loved* hers. Going to the lawn chair, Cary sat down and pulled off his shoes and socks. "Is the water cold?"

She shook her head, still watching him with absorbed attention.

"Pity." He stood, unbuckled his belt, drew down his zipper—and dropped his pants. There wasn't a damn thing he could do about his boner, barely constrained by the snug, black cotton boxers.

Nora stared, drew a broken breath, and licked her lips. Did she know what that small lick did to him?

She turned and swam to the other side of the pool, keeping her back to him.

Cary dove in. The initial force of his entry carried him across the pool so that he surfaced right behind her. She gripped the side of the pool, her toes balanced on a ledge.

Cary mimicked her stance, putting his hands alongside hers, his feet bracketing hers on the ledge. His cock pressed into her firm bottom. If they were naked, he could enter her this way, leaving his hands free to play with her breasts while he thrust deep and slow . . . He turned his face into her neck. "Nora."

As if she'd had the same imagery, she moaned.

Opening his mouth, Cary took a slow love bite of the muscle running from her neck to her shoulder. "I want you." He felt her shiver. "More than you can even begin to guess."

"You . . . you don't want to get married," she whispered.

She was so damn sure of that. And if he told her now, at this particular moment, with an erection prodding her backside, that he wanted marriage and forever after and those kids she'd mentioned earlier, she'd think he was just on the make. She'd think he was making promises just to get laid.

He drew back a little, giving them both some breathing room. But not much, because he couldn't bear the distance between them. "We haven't even been on a real date yet, so how do you know what I want? With you, everything is different."

"You're so determined. But . . . why me?"

He shook his head. "Hell, Nora, that's like asking why I like chocolate ice cream better than vanilla, or why I prefer boxers to briefs, or why I bought an SUV instead of a flashy car."

She turned in his arms. Her glasses were now wet with droplets of water, but her eyes were direct. "And?"

"And what?"

"Why did you make those choices?"

They were both mostly naked. For all intents and purposes, they were alone. It wasn't easy for him to concentrate. "Maybe we should move to your patio for this discussion?"

She nodded—then waited. When Cary just stood there, breathing in the scent of her warmed skin, her wet hair, and the light fragrance that was all woman and hers alone, she cleared her throat. "You need to . . . move, so I can get out."

"Oh. Yeah." He stepped to the side of her, hoisted himself out, then reached in for her. Catching her wrists, he pulled her up and against him. She fit him perfectly, her head at just the right height for his shoulder.

As naturally as if they'd been a couple forever, he put his arm around her waist and walked her around the pool to her towel. She didn't dry off with it. Instead, she wrapped it around herself, hiding her body from him.

Okay, he could deal with that. For right now. He gathered up his clothes and shoes, then reached out a hand, and after a long moment of hesitation, she took it.

Cary led her to the middle of her covered patio. Wet and shaded, he felt cooler on the outside, but no less hot on the inside. He set his clothes and shoes down. They stared at each other. With one finger, he touched her mouth. "Chocolate tastes better to me—just as you taste better."

Her lashes lowered and new color stained her cheeks.

He coasted that same finger down her shoulder to the swell of her breasts, visible above the tightly wrapped towel. "Boxers," he murmured while tugging the towel free of its knot, "are more comfortable." He dropped the towel on the concrete patio. Everything about her, from her hesitation to her sweet little body, turned him on.

"You're saying I'm comfortable?"

"Yeah. Being with you feels right."

She wet her lips.

After a leisurely, heated review of her body, Cary met her gaze, his expression as intent as he could make it so that she'd understand. "Flashy cars don't appeal to me anymore." He caught her waist and drew her close again. "They're just for fun, but these days I'm more interested in the long haul."

Her lips parted, but just before Cary could kiss her, she drew back. Frustration rose up—at himself for rushing her again. Damn it, around her it seemed that his dick wanted to call all the shots, never mind what his brain had to say about it. "I'm sorry."

Shaking her head, Nora said, "I have to explain."

"All right."

She kept her gaze on his chest while visibly working up her nerve. In a voice so small, Cary could barely hear her, she confessed, "I was a virgin when I married."

Her husband must have had one hell of a wedding night. Bending his knees, Cary tried to see her face, but she only tucked her chin in a little more.

"My husband was a virgin, too. What we knew, we learned together."

Cary released her, turned his back on her, and took three deep breaths, then a forth and a fifth. Jealousy raged inside him, though he doubted that was her intent. "I can't miraculously become a virgin, Nora."

Her startled, nervous laugh had him turning back around again with bemused curiosity at her reaction. One hand covered her mouth, but her eyes were still smiling. Cary smiled, too. "Want me to pretend to be?"

Another laugh bubbled out. "No." She swatted at him playfully. "Don't be ridiculous."

"Good." The sound of her laughter filled him up when he hadn't really known he was empty. "I doubt I could have pulled it off anyway."

She swallowed, cleared her throat, and tried to be serious again. Rushing to get it all out, she blurted, "I haven't been with anyone in two years."

"I know." His cock throbbed in renewed interest. Two long years. Damn. Talking about it only made it more real. "I heard you tell Liza that," he reminded her.

"Not even a kiss."

His brain went blank. *Not even* . . .

"Not even . . . holding hands."

"Jesus, Nora, why?" Cary could hardly credit such a thing. "You're beautiful and sexy. I know damn good and well guys have been asking. Hell, *I've* been asking." If she told him she was still in love with her husband, after all this time, he'd howl.

She half turned away from him, giving him her profile. "At first, I didn't want anyone else because I missed my husband too much."

There it was, the one thing he couldn't fight—a dead man. "I can understand that, but it's been *two years.*"

She rubbed her forehead, readjusted her glasses. "I was always really shy with men."

The small voice was back, proving to Cary that this was a difficult topic for her. He moved closer, giving her silent support.

"Dating didn't come easy to me." She flashed him a quick look to see if he understood. "We dated for eighteen months before we married."

Eighteen months of celibate dating? Wow.

"Even after we married, I felt awkward sleeping with my husband." She bit her lip and squeezed her eyes shut. "I don't . . ." She gestured toward him with a hand. "Anything I know about sex I learned with my husband."

Cary was starting to understand. Two virgins fumbling in the dark added up to a lack of confidence in the sack. "And it wasn't all that much that you learned?"

"Exactly." Eyes still closed, she said, "But it wasn't his fault. He loved me and we were both innocent, but I just—"

He stepped behind her, put her hands on her waist. "Did you ever have an orgasm?"

She trembled.

"Nora?"

In a barely there whisper, she said, "No." Then in a rush, "But I loved him, Cary. A lot."

"Shhh. It's all right. I understand." He understood that her husband had been cheated out of a lot of pleasure by dying too young. And Nora had been cheated, too. In a big way.

So what the hell should he do now?

She was a nurse for an OB-GYN. She dealt with pregnant ladies—the result of sex, no two ways about that—every damn day. His brain churned, trying to muddle out the situation. "Do you believe that I care about you, Nora?"

"I don't know."

Well, there was honesty for you. "I do. I wouldn't lie to you." He was caressing her waist without realizing it. Her skin was so silky soft he couldn't wait to feel all of it against him while they made love. "How did your husband die?"

"Massive heart attack. I . . . I woke up one morning and he was . . . he was gone. I didn't hear anything, didn't know he'd had a problem in the night."

Woke up? "He was beside you? In bed?"

She nodded.

Damn. No wonder she hadn't wanted to rush into any other man's bed. Cary turned her, hauled her into his arms, and kissed her. Not a gentle kiss this time, but one of hunger and need and possession. He hurt for her and wished for some way to erase those memories from her mind, even while he sought a way to claim her.

She wasn't really kissing him back, but her hands clutched his shoulders and he could feel her fast breaths. "Give me your tongue."

She parted her lips, shyly did as he ordered—and Cary was lost. He drew her soft pink tongue into his mouth, sucked gently, teased with his own and followed her tongue back into her mouth, licking, tasting. Hot. Damn, she was hot.

The kiss went on and on, sharing, taking, giving. It required all his concentration to keep his hands on her waist and not lift them to her breasts, or drop them to her bottom. It was enough that he could feel her skin, wet from her swim, warm from the summer day.

Slowly, before he pushed too far too fast, he pulled

back. She struggled to get her heavy eyelids lifted, then her gaze locked with his and her tongue flicked out, tasting her lips. "I liked that."

She wasn't helping his self-control, saying things like that. He cupped her face. "You'll like everything I do to you, I swear. We'll be incredible together, Nora."

Her mouth twitched into a small, nervous smile. "Great sex, that's what you're offering?"

"*No.*"

She looked confused. "No?"

Cary groaned. What the hell was he saying? "I mean, yeah, but more than that, okay?"

He wanted her to ask him how much more, but she didn't. With her thoughts clear on her expressive face, she considered everything he said, touched one hot little palm to his chest, and whispered, "Okay."

Such a rush of triumph, expectation, and tenderness rolled through him, it was almost like coming, almost as sweet. But not quite. "Now?" *Please let her mean now.*

Her big brown eyes looked up at him from behind her glasses. She gave a tiny nod, smiled tremulously, and said, "Okay." And then to confirm it, "Now."

Chapter Three

Cary wasn't a gallant man or a guy prone to melodrama. Never in his life had he carried a woman to bed. Hell, he was more likely to race her there, laughing with every step. But now, with Nora, he felt like a cross between Tarzan and a groom on his wedding day. He felt like the Initiator of Virgins and it was such a turn-on, he could barely draw breath.

He lifted her up high against his chest, caught her small sound of exclamation, and kissed her. He could kiss her forever, every day, every hour even. "You won't be sorry, I swear. I'll make this so good for you."

"I know."

When he reached the French doors, she pulled them open and Cary swept inside, a romantic figure to the core. "Which way?"

Appearing a tad overwhelmed, Nora said, "Um, down the hall, last door on the right."

It wasn't easy, but he accomplished a sedate walk rather than a run. He even kissed her twice again without getting carried away. He didn't stop and take her against the wall, or on the floor, as was his basic inclination, given the level of his need.

Her bedroom door stood open, her bed unmade and rumpled. "Wet suits," Cary told her, forcing himself to logic. This was almost like her first time, close enough that he wanted it to be special, so close he was the one trembling like a virgin—with anticipation. Sopping sheets would add nothing to the ambiance for either of them. He stood her on her feet to strip her.

She shied away—but he drew her right back. "I want to see you, Nora. All of you. And I want you to see me."

"You do?"

Trying to curb the drumming of lust, he said, "Of course I do. I've dreamed of seeing you naked."

Heat flared in her cheeks. "But you want me to see you, too?"

See me, touch me, lick me . . . He groaned. "Yeah."

"Oh."

He cleared his throat. "I want you to want me."

"I do."

Thank God. He angled closer, reached behind her, and slowly unhooked her bra top. The cups loosened from her breasts. He untied the string around her neck and the bathing suit top fell between them. Cary pulled it away and dropped it to the carpet. He couldn't breathe. Her breasts were . . . well, they were Nora's breasts, soft and pale, her nipples puckered tight. He bent and drew one into his mouth, sucking gently.

With pleasure as much as embarrassment, Nora gasped. Her hands settled in his hair, tangled there, held him tight. Cary spread his hands wide over her back to keep her close. Her skin was cool in the air-conditioned interior, soft and sleek. He spanned her waist, her hips. Gliding his fingers into her trunks, he pushed them off her rounded bottom, then went to one knee and tugged them the rest of the way down her legs.

Bad move.

He was now eye level with her belly, or more importantly, her soft pubic curls. She was still damp from the swim. Her scent was delicious, making him want so much more, far too soon.

She pressed her thighs tight together and covered herself with her hands.

Hoarse, Cary said, "Step out of your bottoms."

She did, awkwardly, her limbs stiff, her hands still shielding her from his gaze. Seeing her hands there just brought about a ton of sexual fantasies. He should have stood back up at that point, but he couldn't. He cupped her bare, plump bottom, kneaded her for a moment while he argued with himself—and lost.

He leaned forward and kissed her knuckles.

"Cary."

Holding her close, he used his tongue to trace between her fingers, down, back up, flicking just a bit over the middle knuckle of her right hand. He wished she'd part her fingers just a bit, maybe let him . . .

She stumbled back against the mattress.

In a red haze of lust, Cary stood and looked at her. She now had one hand covering her left breast, the other hand over her sex, and he was so hard he could have been lethal. Holding her gaze, he shoved his clinging wet boxers down and off, then kicked them away. He straightened, letting her look her fill.

She nearly went cross-eyed as she stared fixedly at his face.

"Look at me, Nora."

After a few breaths to shore her up, her gaze darted to his erection for a two-second peek. But apparently that didn't suffice, because her attention shot downward again, where it lingered and warmed. Her lips parted.

Hoarse, Cary murmured, "Let me feel you." He removed her glasses and set them on the nightstand, then carried her trembling hands to his shoulders. This time when he pulled her into his arms, there were no barriers. Flesh to flesh, heartbeat to heartbeat. Her nipples rubbed his ribs, her thighs shifted against his. His swollen cock nudged against her silky belly.

He felt cocooned in her softness, her musky female

scent, her timidity and sex appeal. He closed his eyes and pressed his face into her throat, overcome with emotions he'd never dealt with before. He wanted to ravish her. He wanted to absorb her into himself.

He had to keep his head to ensure she enjoyed this. He wanted her to see how wonderful their lovemaking would be. He wanted her to crave more, of him and the pleasure he'd give her.

Taking her mouth with premeditated tenderness, Cary lowered them both to the bed. For long minutes, he just kissed her, sometimes rolling on top of her so she could become accustomed to his weight, sometimes turning so she was atop him, letting her move as she pleased. He kissed her gently, not so gently, deep and slow, wild and wet. But he kept his hands on safe ground—her shoulders, her waist. He held her face, smoothed her hair, teased her nape. And when she was quivering, filling his head with small gasps and making him nuts with the way she writhed against him, he laid her on her back and cupped her breasts.

She arched, firming his hold, giving him more. She was firm, round, and so damn soft. Cary kissed his way down her throat, her chest, until his mouth again closed over one taut nipple.

"Oh God."

Her fingers held his skull, drawing him closer, encouraging him. With leisurely intent, he suckled one nipple while plying the other with his thumb. He shook worse than she did. Restraint, he discovered, was not an easy thing. In fact, it was pure hell. Especially now, because he'd never suffered this level of burning lust before. And here he'd thought he knew all about it. Damn, but it was different with Nora. Hotter and sweeter, so intense. His whole body strained to be closer, to be inside her.

He knew he wouldn't be able to wait much longer, and he needed to know if she was ready. He pressed his hand between their bodies, low on her belly, his fingers splayed. She didn't freeze up on him. In fact, she squirmed, trying to get his fingers where she wanted them. Cary lifted up and looked at her face. Eyes closed, head tilted back, she appeared wanton and ready. Utterly beautiful.

"You'll like this," he told her. With the heel of his palm pressed to the top of her mound, he petted her with his fingertips, slow, easy, gentle. Just stroking.

She moaned and lifted her hips.

With his middle finger, he parted her—and felt her distended clitoris, ripe and ready, so sensitive. She was creamy wet, swollen, very near the edge. Heat raged through him. He locked his jaw, tensed his shoulders against the driving need, and stroked with just one fingertip, teasing, easing her deeper into the moment.

"Cary," she whispered on a thin breath of sound, then her back arched hard and she gave a long, raw moan.

Like a wire pulled too tight, Cary snapped. Two fingers sank deep into her, pulled out, and thrust again, preparing her, widening her. She was so tight, her inner muscles clasping at his fingers, that he knew he'd die when he got inside her.

Before he even knew what he was doing, he was over her, catching her knees, pulling her legs apart. He couldn't breathe, couldn't think—hell, he couldn't even see straight. But he felt her small frantic hands, dragging him down so she could kiss and lick his mouth, her silken thighs wrapping tight around him.

Blindly, he positioned himself and thrust hard.

She bowed beneath him, crying out but clinging to him, adding to the urgency. Cary pressed, retreated, pressed until he was buried deep, as deep as he could go. He rode her hard, no rubber, no soft sex words, just savage, pounding need. Less than a shameful minute later he was coming, so hard and long that he shouted at his release, his head thrown back like a wild man, his hands knotted tight into the sheets beneath her, every muscle straining.

When the spasms finally left him long moments later, he fell heavily onto her, incoherent, damn near unconscious. He thought he might have been breathing, but he wasn't sure. Little sparks of pleasure continued to snap inside him, making him twitchy.

An indeterminable amount of time passed before he became aware of Nora's nose touching his shoulder, her deep inhalations, the restless way she moved beneath him.

Oh shit!

He'd just mauled her.

Ravaged her.

She hadn't come at all, at least not that he'd noticed amid all his shouting and groaning and straining. He had, though. Hell, he'd blown like Mt. Vesuvius after an extended dry spell.

And he hadn't worn a rubber. *Oh shit, oh shit.*

Cary swallowed. *Sit up,* he told himself, but he didn't move. He wasn't sure he could move yet.

And then Nora whispered, "You smell so good," and she nuzzled her nose against his sweaty shoulder again.

With Herculean effort, Cary rolled to the side of her. Or maybe it was more that he flopped like a half-dead fish. Nora didn't follow. She didn't move at all. She just stared at the ceiling—and the damn silence suffocated him.

Cary waited for his heart to slow just a bit more, then he choked down his embarrassment and said, "Yeah, uh, that didn't go quite like I planned."

Silence.

"That's, uh, never happened to me before." *So lame.*

Her big eyes closed, shutting him out. "Sorry."

He did a double take. His brow cocked. "What's that?"

"I'm sorry. I told you I wasn't good at . . ." Her hand moved, fluttered above the bed, then resettled on the mattress. "This stuff."

Oh, hell no. New energy flowed into Cary, enough that he could prop himself up on one elbow. Progress, he thought, as the tingling in his limbs faded. At least his mind was functioning again. He surveyed Nora, and liked what he saw. No, he *loved* what he saw.

Her short hair was still slightly damp, in cute little curls around her face. Her cheeks were rosy. Little tremors coursed through her—the effects of going unfulfilled, no doubt. Her nipples were darkly flushed, still taut. Hmmm. "You're kidding, right?"

Her jaw worked before the words came out. "I can't . . . can't seem to . . ."

Idly, as if he didn't have a care in the world, Cary reached for her breast and toyed with her nipple. Her hands clenched and she moaned. "Nora, listen to me."

"I can't." Her whole body was rigid, stiff. "Not while you're doing that."

Smiling, Cary put his hand on her belly instead. "Better?"

She gave an adamant shake of her head. "No."

He didn't move. "It was my fault, you know. You're wonderful. Sexy as hell. I was going along just fine, prepared to see to you first as any gentlemen would do, then you gave that provoking little moan and I lost it. Kaboom. Control blown all to hell. You should be slapping my face. You should be cursing me. I'm a pig and a lousy lover and I made promises I didn't keep."

Her head turned on the pillow and she stared toward him. Though Cary knew that without her glasses she couldn't see him, her expression of incredulous disbelief was plain to see. "That's nonsense."

He smothered a laugh. "Please tell me you don't think I'm always such a selfish ass."

Her brows came down in a frown. "You were wonderful."

Cary slid his hand a little lower on her belly, until she caught her breath. His fingertips just touched her triangle of hair. "Wonderfully selfish." And in a huskier tone, "I got inside you and you were so tight, so hot and wet, I became an animal."

She bit her lip. "I . . . I liked it."

"Yeah?" He grinned. "Me, too, obviously. But there's a lot more to this whole lovemaking business." When she remained curiously silent, he grew blunt. "You didn't come."

She caught her bottom lip in her teeth. "It, um, felt so good that I wasn't sure."

Damn, she was adorable. "You'll know when it happens, Nora. I promise." She frowned in doubt, which challenged him. "Let me prove it to you."

Sensual interest darkened her eyes as the seconds ticked by. "How?"

God, he loved her. Now and forever, the kind of love that wouldn't ever go away. And he'd just blown it in the sack. The irony was that women he'd merely liked had claimed him an excellent lover, while the woman he wanted most in his life had demolished his finesse, reducing him to a sex-crazed lunatic. He almost groaned again, but instead he sucked it up like a man and set out to make things right.

"Like this." He covered her with his palm and began to gently finger her. She was so hot, and wet. *Very wet.* Which meant he was quickly growing hard again. He would not be a pig this time. Never again. But she moaned, and that small sound tested him. He supposed it was his love for her that made everything with her sharper-edged, so acute that he could barely contain himself.

Because she looked embarrassed he leaned over her and covered her mouth with his own, muffling her sounds of pleasure. At first, he kept the pressure light, the rhythm uneven, letting her orgasm build up again. When her kisses grew bolder, almost desperate, he moved down to her breasts. The dual assault would be sweet, and would help guarantee his odds.

At the same time that he closed his mouth hotly over her nipple, he pressed two fingers deep inside her, stretching her, exacerbating already sensitive nerve endings. Her cries grew more harsh, raw. Using his thumb with devastating effect, Cary stroked her clitoris in small, circular movements that had her groaning and writhing. He kept himself in check with ruthless determination. He could feel the heat pulsing off her, the spiciness of her aroused scent—and she broke.

With a long, ragged moan, her legs stiffened, her hips jerked. He raised up to watch her, seeing the vague understanding in her dark eyes, the rush of heightened color in her face and throat. "Perfect," he whispered, keeping the pleasure steady, ensuring she got everything this time.

By small degrees, she quieted and her legs went lax, naturally sprawling. He wanted to fuck her again; he wanted to hold her to his heart and tell her everything he was feeling. He wanted so much, he honestly didn't know where to start. He should take it easy, play it by ear, wait and see what Nora thought. Yeah, that's what he'd do. He'd be patient for once. He'd keep control.

And he wouldn't make any more boneheaded moves.

Chapter Four

Awareness slowly seeped in on Nora. She felt euphoric. Weak and elated and . . . *satisfied*. Every sense was magnified. She was intensely aware of the cool air on her skin, the rumpled sheets beneath her, the incredible man making a dent in her mattress.

She smiled, so secretly pleased that she had to fight not to laugh out loud. Wow. No wonder everyone did this with such great regularity.

She felt that, at this particular moment in time, new doors had just opened for her. The whole world looked different. She'd never been the type to sleep around, to take a lover. But Cary had just changed all that, and she was so glad.

She turned her head to see him, but without her glasses, he was no more than a blur. As if he'd read her mind, he rolled to his back, did some reaching, and then her glasses were slipped onto her nose. She straightened them and took in his expression, anxious to see if he'd been as affected as she was by the sex.

His warm, mellow gaze filled with tenderness.

Relieved, Nora whispered, "Thank you."

He looked at her mouth.

"For the glasses, and the . . . the . . ."

"Orgasm?" The right side of his mouth kicked up. "Now that was my pleasure."

She matched his grin. "And mine." She pondered how to tell him that she wanted more, that she wanted to do it again, maybe not right this moment, but soon. She put a hand on his chest. "Cary," she said hesitantly.

And he blurted, "Marry me."

Her gaze snapped up and locked onto his. He looked more surprised than she felt. In fact, he appeared floored that those words had come from his mouth. Or had they? "What did you say?"

He actually flushed. Then he scowled. "You heard me."

"I'm not sure I did."

His shoulders bunched. He seemed annoyed with himself, and she could imagine why. Oh God, she'd burdened him with all her leftover dreams for marriage and children, and now he felt obligated.

"I asked if you'd marry me."

Actually, he'd just sort of demanded it, and in fact he still seemed rather combative about the offering. "Cary, you don't need to do that."

His frown sharpened, as did his annoyance. "That?"

"Propose. I mean, I was just thinking that I like it like this."

"This?"

Worse and worse. He'd barely squeezed that word out between his teeth. "Yes, with us as . . . lovers. No commitment, no responsibility." She stroked his chest. "Just pleasure."

"You said you wanted marriage," he accused, and his cheekbones were red, his green eyes incandescent with anger.

"Yes, I know, but . . . not with you."

He bolted upright in the bed. "Not. With. Me?"

Nora wanted to pull out her own tongue. How insulting that had sounded! "What I mean is—"

A distant ringing sounded and they both paused, alert. Working in the medical field, a phone was never ignored.

Cary cursed luridly. "Goddammit, that's my cell phone. I left it on your patio." Buck naked, he clambered out of her bed, out of her bedroom, and quite possibly right out of her life.

Dolt. Idiot. How could she have said such a ridiculous, mean, nasty thing to him? She knew what she meant— that she was happy having him any way she could. That making love with him was a worthwhile trade-off for marriage. That she loved him enough, she'd take what he was comfortable offering—which plainly wasn't marriage.

Stewing in bed wouldn't do her one bit of good. What if he left without even telling her good-bye? That galvanized her into action and Nora was out of the bed in a flash. She was stepping into panties when Cary stomped back in.

He drew up short at the sight of her, with her underwear around her knees, her upper body still bare. His gaze darted here and there, lingering on her breasts and belly.

He was fully dressed, darn it. Well, except for his boxers, which were wadded up and wet on her floor. Drawn back to her senses, Nora tugged her panties up the rest of the way and crossed her arms over her breasts.

As if that broke the spell, Cary gave up his scrutiny of her body. He didn't look at her face. He stayed busy tucking in his shirt, buckling his belt. "I have to go," he said in one of the flattest tones she'd ever heard from him. "One of my patients is having trouble breathing. Probably bronchitis from the sounds of it. But she's older and afraid of most doctors, so I'm going to meet her and her son at the emergency room."

He was such a remarkable, caring man and all she could do was stand there in nothing more than panties, wracking her brain for something to say. "Cary . . ."

He shot her a quick, insincere smile. "We can talk later. Duty calls." He hesitated, then took one long step toward her, put a perfunctory peck on her forehead, and rushed from the room.

Nora sank to the edge of the bed. It was badly mussed, the pillows off on the floor, the sheets trailing over the side. The scent of their lovemaking still lingered in the air, and stupidly, tears prickled her eyes. She was a complete and inexcusable social hazard.

He hadn't promised to call, but he had said they'd talk. Later. Whatever that might mean. She pinned all her hopes on it because if he called, then she could explain.

With nothing left to do, Nora dragged herself into the shower. She still felt weak in the knees, and places she'd barely paid attention to before were now achy.

By eleven o'clock that night, she gave up staring at a silent phone and tried to sleep, but she couldn't put Cary from her mind. She missed him already. She wanted him again. It was almost dawn before she got any rest.

The weekend continued in a heat wave, frazzling her nerves, making her listless. Liza called and wanted to go shopping, but Nora turned her down. She was afraid to leave for fear she'd miss his call. Like a lovesick teenager, she carried the phone with her everywhere, out to the pool, while doing yard work. By Sunday morning, when Cary still hadn't called, she got angry.

How did a man make love to a woman and then just walk away? But she knew it happened all the time, which was one of the reasons she'd avoided affairs. Sex was just sex and these days didn't necessarily imply more.

But this time . . . She covered her face with her hands. He'd asked her to marry him and she'd shot him down. What if that was the only reason he didn't call?

When the phone rang, her heart almost stopped. She stood there through four rings, immobilized by hope before ungluing her feet and racing to snatch it up.

"Hello?"

"Hey, it's Liza. I'm bored. If you don't want to shop, let's do lunch."

Disappointment staggered Nora. "Oh, it's you."

Feigning insult, Liza said, "Gee thanks."

Nora thumped her hand against her forehead. Now she was insulting her friend, too! "I'm sorry. I really am. And yeah, sure, lunch sounds great." She desperately needed a distraction.

"So much enthusiasm." Liza laughed. "I have a better idea. Why don't you tell me who you were hoping to hear from?"

Why not? Maybe Liza could give her some advice. "A hound dog."

"Do tell! A sexy, doctor-type hound dog? Catch me up on what I've missed."

Nora strode to the couch, collapsed onto it, and in practically one breath rattled off her tale of woe.

To her surprise, Liza cackled like a crazed hen.

Bemused by that reaction, Nora explained, "It's really not a humorous story."

"Oh, honey, of course it is. Women don't wait around for men to call anymore. They pick up a phone and do the deed themselves."

The mere thought had Nora wincing. "Oh no. I couldn't."

"Not even to apologize—which you owe him, by the way? If he doesn't want to hear it, or it seems he doesn't care, then you have your answer. It's better than stewing, isn't it?"

Stewing and moping and wallowing in her misery . . . "I suppose." And then, reluctantly, "Maybe after you and I finish lunch—"

"No way. Forget that. I say call him now. Or better yet, just drop in on him. And don't say you can't, because he dropped in on you, right? Turnabout is fair play."

Nora sank lower on the couch. "You really think it'd be all right to do that?"

"I'm betting he'll be thrilled to see you. But hey, nothing ventured, nothing gained."

Nora wished she had Liza's confidence. She drew a long breath for courage, and said, "All right, I'll do it."

"That'a girl. And one more thing."

"Yes?"

"You damn sure better call me later tonight and tell me all the nitty-gritty details!"

"I promise." For the first time since she'd misspoken to Cary, Nora was smiling. She glanced at the clock. It was nearing noon and she hadn't bothered to do more than dress, but now she felt like a woman with a mission. She headed to the bathroom for a cool shower, a touch of makeup, and a dab of perfume.

Within half an hour, she'd donned one of her prettiest sundresses, had her hair and makeup just right, and was on her way to Cary's. He wasn't far from her home, something she considered fortunate given her nervousness. Given any time to reconsider, she was likely to turn back around.

Unlike her, Cary had chosen a condo over a house. She parked in his private drive, and before she could chicken out, she trotted up the walkway and rang his doorbell.

No one answered.

With a feeling of déjà vu, she cautiously, hopefully made her way around back. His was a corner condo, secluded by thick hedges on one side and a privacy fence on the other. There was no pool in his small patch of backyard, but maybe he was grilling. Or just sunning himself.

Nora was several feet away when she recognized Cary's voice barking, "I don't want her, Axel, so shut the hell up."

Nora staggered to a halt while her heart sank into her feet. He didn't want her?

Another voice, not Axel's or Cary's, said calmly, "Keep your voice down. And Axel, leave him alone. Can't you see he's suffering?"

"I am not suffering," Cary growled.

"You're lovesick," that other voice insisted, "but too stubborn to admit it."

"Exactly," Axel said. "But Patti could cure you of that if you'd just give her a chance. If she's anything like her friend, and I think she is, she'll have you moaning with pleasure instead of sorrow. Guaranteed."

Cary said, "Booker, I'm going to break his teeth, I swear, if he mentions Patti again."

Patti? Who the heck was Patti?

"Well, what the hell do you want me to do?" Axel suddenly demanded. "I told you not to screw with my office dynamics. I told you Nora wasn't your type. But do you ever listen to me? No. You even go and propose to her, damn it."

"It was a bonehead move, I admit," Cary said. And then he murmured, more to himself than anyone else, "And I'd promised myself I wasn't going to make any more bonehead moves."

"So now you're sitting here looking like a wolf who got caught in a trap and had to chew his own foot off."

There was a startled moment of silence after that awesomely descriptive analogy, then Booker laughed. "He's not like a self-maimed wolf at all. He's just in love."

In love? With her? Nora hoped so.

"Jesus," Cary complained, "you're both like old women. Can't a man have some peace?"

Booker said, "Not when he's in love."

"I'm going to call her," Axel stated. "I'll ask her just what the hell is wrong with you—no, Cary, I mean it. I can straighten this out—no, let go."

Nora heard a scuffle, a couple of dull thuds, and she hurried around the privacy fence. Axel, shirtless and in shorts, was on his back, gripping a cell phone for dear life while Cary, in shorts and a T-shirt, had him in a head-lock, choking him and struggling to pry the phone loose.

Beside them, arms crossed and smiling as if he didn't have a care in the world, was the man she assumed to be Booker. Nora had never met him, only knew his name because she'd just heard it, but he looked a lot like Axel.

He noticed her and raised a brow. "Can I help you?"

Both Cary and Axel paused in their physical debate to swivel their heads toward her.

"Nora!"

Axel took swift advantage of her presence. "What the hell is wrong—" Cary's hand clamped over his mouth. It wasn't an easy thing, holding Axel down. He was thicker, more muscular than Cary.

She looked at all three men and felt like she'd fallen into the rabbit hole. "Um . . . what are you doing?"

Axel thrashed about, mumbling urgently from be-hind Cary's hand. Cary scowled and pressed a knee into his ribs. "Nothing."

Booker grinned. "Typical male bonding stuff. That's all." He stepped over the fallen men and held out his hand. "I'm Booker, Axel's brother and Cary's friend by association. You're really Nora?"

"Yes." She shook his hand—then found out he wouldn't let go.

"You're here to see Cary?"

"Yes." Nervously, she glanced toward Cary and Axel. They were no longer struggling, but neither were they getting up. She cleared her throat. "I'm sorry to in-trude . . ."

Cary scowled. "You were eavesdropping, weren't you?"

"Yes."

He shoved to his feet, managing to kick Axel twice on his way up. "Say something besides yes, damn it."

Nora lifted her chin. "All right. I did eavesdrop but you did it first. And stop cursing at me. And while you're at it, you look like an idiot rolling around on the ground."

That startled Cary, and he grinned—until he noticed Booker still had her hand. "What the hell are you doing, Booker?" He strode forward. "Turn her loose."

Now that he was free, Axel bounded up. "Why don't you want to marry Cary? Hell, he's a good catch. All the women want him."

Nora blinked while watching Cary's face go blank. His left eye twitched, then he jerked around with a snarl, but Booker caught him before he could reach Axel.

To avoid more physical conflict, Nora rushed to answer. "I don't want him to feel coerced."

"Why would he feel coerced?" Booker asked.

"Because I told him I wanted to get married."

"But not to *me*." Cary looked very aggressive again, making her frown.

"You didn't give me a chance to explain."

"Explain now," Axel suggested. He was busy dusting himself off, so he didn't see Cary reach for him. He got shoved a good two feet and barely stayed upright. "What?" Axel said. "I'm curious, too, you know."

Nora couldn't help it—she laughed. When all three men stared at her, she laughed some more. Misunderstanding, Cary started to turn away, but she caught his arm, pulled him around, and hugged him tight. "I'm sorry. But it's funny, seeing grown men, doctors, grappling like little boys."

Cary stood frozen for only a moment before his arms came around her. With his mouth touching her ear, he whispered, "That's all most men are—little boys at heart."

"I love you."

Cary froze again. He started to push her back so he could see her face, but Nora held on.

Behind them, Axel whispered, "What'd she say?"

And Booker replied, "Shh."

"You love me?"

Nora nodded against his chest. "And I want to marry you, too, if the offer still stands."

"Why'd you tell me no the first time then? Not to belabor the point, but I'd never proposed before. It sort of took it out of me."

"I'm sorry. I didn't want you to feel that you had to marry me just because we . . . you know."

She could hear the grin in his voice when he whispered, "Sex had nothing to do with it. Especially considering I blew it."

"You did not!"

Axel said, "What's that?"

Cary turned to him with a scowl. "Booker, if you want your brother alive and well, you better drag him out of here."

Booker chuckled. "Promise to invite us to the wedding and we'll both go."

"Yeah, sure, whatever."

"I had to leave anyway," Axel announced. "All things considered, Patti's probably out of the question."

Nora flashed him an angry look. "She's *definitely* out."

"That's what I figured. So I better go, uh, let her down easy." He winked, and together he and Booker went through the house. Seconds later, Cary and Nora heard the front door close.

Cary turned back to her, and this time Nora could see the love in his beautiful green eyes. She laughed again and squeezed him tighter. "I've been in love with you for months. Thank you for not giving up on me."

"You were more than worth the chase, Nora." He tilted her back. "Now, about my substandard performance Friday."

"You were wonderful," she insisted yet again.

"Care to give me another shot at proving how wonderful *we* can be? Like . . . right now maybe?"

Her heart started racing at just the suggestion. "Yes."

"I'll wear a rubber this time."

Nora smiled. "I doubt one time will do the deed, but you did say you wanted children."

Cary bent to kiss her, long and slow and deep. "With you, honey, I want everything."

So happy she felt ready to burst, Nora cupped his face and sighed. "With me, you have it."

ONE WILDE
WEEKEND

Janelle Denison

Chapter One

I'm not wearing any panties.

Alex Wilde shifted in his small, cramped seat next to Dana, those wicked words she'd whispered in his ear moments before they'd boarded the plane still echoing through his mind. Leave it to her to play such a seductive game with him, and make him horny as hell in the process—with no immediate relief in sight. They'd been together exclusively for one year and she knew how to get to him. This weekend getaway to Amelia Island in Florida was a celebration of their first date, and he hoped the beginning of their future together.

The lights in the cabin had been dimmed in deference to the passengers watching the in-flight movie playing on the overhead TV screen. Others were engrossed in a book or other reading material, or were catching a bit of shut-eye like the older man occupying the window seat next to Dana.

Resting his head back against his seat, Alex drew in a deep breath in an attempt to relax since they still had a little over two hours left until they touched down in Florida. But instead of the tension easing from his body, his mind raced to the weekend ahead.

No doubt about it, Dana was going to be surprised

when he popped the big question and asked her to marry him.

Surprised. Shocked. Maybe even panic-stricken, Alex thought with an inward grimace. Especially since she had no idea what he had planned.

He thought of the small velvet-textured box he'd been carrying with him for the past two days. Tucked inside was a diamond ring, a symbol of promises and love and a future together—if Dana accepted the piece of jewelry and all it stood for.

Without reservation, he was ready to permanently commit himself to the one woman who finally made his life so full and rich, in so many ways. At age thirty-five, Dana might be four years his senior, but she was sophisticated and sexy and intelligent—she certainly hadn't become a senior account executive for one of Chicago's top imaging firms without having a whole lot of brains behind her incredible beauty. She was warm and genuine and everything he wanted in a lifelong mate.

Ultimately, he was ready to settle down and start a family of his own—with Dana. He wished he could say that she wanted the same, but the truth was, he wasn't altogether certain she was prepared to take that next step in their relationship, or ever would be.

This weekend he'd find out.

Alex couldn't really predict Dana's reaction to his proposal, but he'd learned enough about her to know she was skittish when it came to the subject of love and marriage. And though she'd gradually opened herself up to him on an emotional level over the past few months, she still harbored insecurities and deeper fears that kept her from trusting in what they shared—completely and unconditionally.

This weekend they were going to deal with those issues once and for all. And confronting her fears would either make their relationship stronger than ever, or tear them apart forever.

His senses were given a jolt as he inhaled the exotic scent of the perfume Dana deliberately dabbed on the strongest pulse points on her body—a provocative fragrance that intensified to a warm, sultry scent when she was aroused. Or thinking about sex. With him.

I'm not wearing any panties.

He nearly groaned as the risqué thought dislodged his emotional upheaval and heightened his physical discomfort. There was no escaping the heat and feminine musk radiating off her skin. No escaping the way that familiar, irresistible scent of hers mingled into a darker, alluring fragrance that stimulated his mind, his thoughts, and his libido. It was like a powerful pheromone he couldn't resist, and despite the innocent look on her face as she casually flipped through the women's magazine she'd brought along for the flight, he had no doubt she knew the effect she was having on him. The minx.

Out of the corner of his eye, he watched as she slowly, purposefully uncrossed then recrossed her legs, then released a shivery little sigh—the same exact kind of soft, sensual sound she made when he was buried deep inside her. Her fingers touched the base of her throat and absently slid down the open vee of her silky blouse, until a fastened button impeded her descent. He noticed her breathing had deepened, noticed the heavy rise and fall of her breasts, as well as the erect nipples pressing against her top.

A hot ache settled low, in his belly, along his thighs, and in his groin. She was turned on, unmistakably hot and bothered, and all her touching and sighing and the scent of her was making him hard and crazy with wanting her. It was all he could do to keep from turning toward her, slipping his hand beneath the hem of her skirt, and making her just as wild.

Needing some kind of distraction, he shifted his glance to the open magazine in her lap, and he swallowed hard as he read the title of the article she was reading: "Unpredictable, Spontaneous Sex Acts Designed to Blow His Mind." As if Dana needed any help coming up with innovative ways to keep things exciting in the bedroom, or even out of it!

Sexually, she was more adventurous and uninhibited than any woman he'd ever met before her, her level of desire perfectly matching his own. She was passionate and daring and loved to take risks, except when it came to her emotions. When it came to her feelings and what was in her heart, she guarded those secrets just as fiercely as she clung to her determination to always be in control of her actions, as well as depending on no one but herself.

Those issues were the sticking points in their relationship, areas which she avoided talking about with him in depth. They were issues he was driven to resolve one way or another this weekend.

He nearly jumped out of his skin when he felt Dana's hand on his thigh. She gave him an affectionate, caressing squeeze, one that was underscored with a wealth of sensual possibilities. Unable to believe she'd be *that* brazen in plain sight of so many passengers, his gaze darted to her face to gauge her intent.

Her thick, rich brown hair was tumbled around her shoulders in that naturally tousled style he loved. A mischievous smile curved her mouth, and her sea green eyes glittered with a reckless kind of dare. She wet her lips with her tongue and leaned up close to his side, so that her soft breasts pressed against his arm and her mouth was right up against his ear.

"Care to make us a member of the mile-high club?" she whispered naughtily.

His heart stuttered in his chest, then resumed at a maddening pace. "Are you serious?" he croaked. Stupid question, he realized. Dana was always very careful not to say anything she didn't mean or had no intention of following through on.

"Oh, absolutely," she murmured in a low, husky tone, then nipped playfully at his earlobe. "If you're interested, come and join me in two minutes in the farthest rest room in the back, and tap on the door four times so I know it's you."

With that, she stood and scooted past him on her way to the aisle, giving him a great view of her sweet ass and reminding him once again that she wasn't wearing any panties. That she was most likely wet and ready for him, and getting inside of her was just a matter of shoving her skirt up to her waist and sinking into the giving warmth and softness of her body in one long, easy thrust.

The thought made him shudder, and a rush of heat raised his internal temperature a few extra notches. God, he'd follow her anywhere, and she knew just how weak he was when it came to her, how powerless he was to resist her alluring charms.

Christ, she was killing him. He pulled at the collar of his polo shirt and reached up to adjust the air flow to high, which did little to cool his enthusiastic response to her suggestion.

Like everything else in her life, Dana was certain she was in charge of this little fantasy of hers, that once Alex arrived he'd be hers to do with as she pleased. Normally, he didn't mind her being so assertive—what guy didn't enjoy a woman who was sexy and aggressive and took what she wanted and pleased him in the process? But Alex decided it was time to turn the tables on her. Time to shift the power of control into his hands for a change. Time to coax her into submitting to him, to trust him physically and emotionally, without holding anything back. And he was prepared to use every forbidden desire to do so, if that's what it took to break past those barriers of hers.

He wasn't so arrogant to believe that this one encounter would be the turning point for her, not after a year of letting her hide her true feelings and insecurities behind a tough, self-contained facade and a career that she allowed to consume much of her life. No, this seduction was just the beginning of stripping away her doubts and fears, and would set the tone for the rest of the weekend.

Getting his body back under a semblance of control wasn't easy, but he wasn't about to go anywhere with a hard-on tenting his pants. As soon as he was able, and within her two-minute deadline, he stood and made his way to the back of the plane.

To the woman he was going to make all his.

Chapter Two

Four light taps on the rest room door Dana had designated granted Alex entrance into the small quarters. He slipped inside as inconspicuously as possible, closed and locked the door behind him, and was instantly enveloped in the warm, feminine scent of Dana in the throes of sexual excitement and heated desire. The space was tight and cramped, with less than a foot of space between them to maneuver around in, but they didn't need much room for what he had in mind.

She wrapped her arms around his neck and rubbed her body provocatively along his. "I was beginning to think you were going to leave me to my own resources."

"Not a chance." Grinning, he slid his hands over her short skirt, squeezed her firm bottom in his palms, and angled her hips so that his erection pressed against her mound. "Though I have to admit, this is about the wildest thing I've ever done."

"Me, too," she admitted, her expression glowing with exhilaration as she reached for the front of his pants and started unbuckling his belt with brisk, eager movements. Her lips were inches beneath his and curved into a come-hither smile. "But there's nothing like a bit of risk to heighten the thrill of what's to come, and make things more exciting."

Not to mention that indulging in a hurried, forbidden tryst also meant Dana didn't have to deal with a deeper, more emotional level of intimacy. She expected a quickie, an awesome explosion of passion and lust that ended in a breathtaking rush of pleasure that would leave them both sated. He'd give her body the release and satisfaction it craved, but this time it would be at his pace, and within his terms.

As soon as Dana finally managed to open the front of his trousers, her hands found their way inside his briefs and her cool, slender fingers gripped his fierce erection in a snug hold. She closed the scant distance separating their mouths and kissed him, deep and hot.

He returned the kiss just as hungrily. With her tongue tangling seductively against his, she stroked him from the base of his shaft to the plump head, then glided her thumb across the swollen crown, lubricating him with his own slick moisture that had seeped from the tip.

Shuddering sensation ripped through him. That easily, she cast her bewitching spell over him, making him a slave to anything she wanted or desired.

Still holding on to him, she broke their kiss and scooted her bottom onto the edge of the small sink behind her, her knees rising to settle high around his hips so he was at the perfect angle to drive deep inside of her. The hem of her flirty little skirt slid down her tanned thighs, exposing her soft, pink, glistening flesh to his gaze.

She was inches away from positioning his cock right where he ached to be when he finally found the fortitude to grasp her wrist and hold her at bay.

"Alex?" she breathed, the one word questioning why he'd stopped her.

Figuring his actions would speak louder than words at the moment, he turned her around so she was facing the mirror and braced her hands on the edge of the steel basin. He saw the uncertainty in her reflection, and knew the sudden and unexpected shift in control had thrown her off-kilter.

Holding her gaze in the mirror, he first wedged his shoe between her feet to help widen her stance, then reached around her and began unbuttoning her silky blouse, slowly, leisurely, contradicting her own need for a mad dash toward fulfillment.

"I want you just like this," he murmured, his tone insistent. "I want to take you from behind, watch as you come for me while we're flying up here in the clouds, and let you watch me, too."

"*Yes,*" she whispered, obviously too far gone to realize the implications behind his ploy, or the fact that she was now under his command.

Her breathing quickened as he separated the sides of her top, then pulled down the sheer, lacy cups of her bra. She gasped as her breasts spilled free, full and quivering and tipped with pouting nipples that begged for the touch of his hands.

Not yet, but soon.

He dragged his hands downward, tracing the curve of her waist and hips through her clothing until he came into contact with her bare legs. He skimmed his palms along the satin-soft skin of her inner thighs, letting the hem of her skirt pool around his wrists as he glided higher and higher toward his final destination. Once there, his long fingers delved between her nether lips, finding her hot and wet and ready for him.

She whimpered impatiently, tossed her head back, and pushed her bottom against his groin. "Alex, *please.*"

He found her frustration incredibly sweet, because it didn't happen often during sexual situations. Not when she was the one who normally held the reins of their seduction.

This time, and for the rest of the weekend, he was calling all the shots. "I'm getting there, baby," he promised.

With her hips tilted at just the right angle for him, he slid his rod through her drenched curls from behind, found the entrance to her body, and with a hard, deep thrust, he buried himself to the hilt. Dana's mouth opened in a silent gasp, and though he knew he ought to be just as discreet considering where they were, there was no stopping the primitive male groan that erupted from his chest.

At the moment he didn't care; his only thought was to possess her, completely and thoroughly. So when the time came later on tonight and he upped the emotional stakes between them, hopefully there would be no doubt in her mind as to how he truly felt about her.

As he plunged and withdrew in a building, gyrating rhythm, he swept her hair aside and nuzzled her neck with his lips, his ragged breathing warm and damp against her skin. He used one hand to caress her breasts and lightly pinch her nipples, while his other hand dipped low to where they were joined. His fingers stroked her cleft in that knowing way that never failed to make her come, and it didn't take long for her breath to catch in the back of her throat and for him to feel the clench and pull of her body around his cock that signaled an impending climax. Hers *and* his.

He drove inside her one last time, high and hard, lodging himself as deeply as he could get just as the plane rumbled through an air pocket, causing the carrier to unexpectedly descend, then rise once again. The momentary sense of weightlessness added to the barrage of sensations rippling through him, increasing the intensity of his release. Hers, too, it seemed, as she inhaled a quick breath then moaned softly, her entire body convulsing in a long, continuous orgasm that milked him dry.

He secured an arm around Dana's waist to keep her trembling legs from giving out on her, his gaze drawn to her reflection in the lavatory mirror. She looked utterly debauched. Her face was flushed with passion, a light dew of perspiration had gathered between her bared breasts, and her normally bright green eyes were soft and dark and replete with sexual gratification.

She released a contented sigh. "Thanks for fulfilling that particular fantasy of mine," she murmured, and reached behind her to place her warm palm affectionately on his cheek. "I have to admit that my mind didn't even come close to imagining how amazing the actual reality of doing it 'mile-high' would be."

He chuckled at that and couldn't deny feeling a bit of male satisfaction for giving her such an erotic memory to remember. "So I exceeded your expectations then?"

"Oh, absolutely." A slow, sultry smile eased up the corner of her mouth. "And then some."

He brushed his lips along her jaw to the shell of her ear and felt her shiver against him. "I'm glad you enjoyed yourself, because I have an erotic fantasy of my own I plan to fulfill this weekend."

One that would be satisfying and pleasurable, but would also ultimately test the strength of her trust in him, and their emotional commitment to one another.

Dana sat on the edge of the four-poster bed in the elegant suite Alex had secured for the next two nights at the Ritz-Carlton, which was located on the secluded coast of Amelia Island in northeast Florida. The sliding glass door off the master bedroom was open, giving her a breathtaking view of the ocean and allowing a balmy breeze to drift through the room, as well as the relaxing sounds of waves lapping against the shore.

With Alex waiting for her in the living room while she finished getting ready, she reached for the beige heels she'd set out earlier, along with the strapless, peach-hued dress she was now wearing. Crossing one bare, tanned leg over the other, she slipped a shoe on one foot, then the other, then stood and headed toward the dresser, where she'd laid out her jewelry before she'd taken a shower to freshen up for their late dinner at the resort's restaurant.

As she put on the pair of freshwater pearl earrings Alex had given to her for her birthday a few months ago, her mind drifted back to the unforgettable flight to Florida. More specifically, the naughty tryst she and Alex had indulged in that had made them members of the mile-high club.

She smiled at the recollection, more than a little surprised that he'd actually followed through on her illicit dare. Undoubtedly, Alex was adventurous when it came to sex—whatever she instigated, he was usually quick to follow, reaping the benefits of her provocative ideas—but making love in a plane's rest room with passengers only several feet away went far beyond anything the two of them had ever engaged in . . . with amazing, rapturous results, she thought with a shivery sigh of pleasure that puckered her nipples against the front of her dress.

Picking up the matching pearl necklace, she secured the clasp at the nape of her neck, then reached for the bracelet to put on, too. Another thing that had surprised her about this afternoon's erotic encounter was the way Alex had taken charge of the situation, as if he'd been proving some kind of point. He'd called the shots, the position, had even been in control of her orgasm, and she'd been helpless to do anything but surrender physically to him.

She would have thought that her lustful fantasy turned mind-blowing reality would have set a sensual, seductive tone for the rest of the weekend, yet as soon as they'd arrived at the Ritz-Carlton and checked into their suite, she'd noticed a subtle change in Alex. As they'd perused the resort's numerous amenities, booked a massage for the next day, and spent a few hours soaking up the last of the sun's relaxing rays, her normally easygoing, laid-back boyfriend had grown increasingly quiet and contemplative.

The gradual shift in his mood both worried and unnerved her, because she'd seen this reflective side of him before, and it didn't bode well for her, or them, she knew. The last time had been a few months ago when he'd told her he loved her and she'd done the unthinkable and bolted, as well as avoided the topic every time Alex tried to broach the subject again.

Though she knew deep in her heart that she cared for Alex and loved him to the best of *her* ability, it had taken her weeks to gather the courage to return the sentiment, to speak the words that had the power to make her weak and too susceptible, and could strip her of everything she held dear if she allowed herself to succumb to such a vulnerable emotion. And because following in her mother's footsteps was her greatest fear, it was so much easier to keep her feelings under wraps, as well as maintain an assertive, I'm-in-control edge in any of her relationships.

That motto had worked well with previous men, but Alex had proved time and again that he wasn't at all threatened by her strong-willed nature, and that left her with little protection against just how persuasive Alex could be.

The frantic beating of her heart seemed to roar in her ears, and she drew a deep breath to calm her racing pulse and jittery nerves. She stared at her reflection, silently berating herself for jumping to any conclusions about tonight or what Alex intended. Most likely, his introspective mood was all a figment of her imagination. Or so she hoped.

She smoothed a hand down the front of her dress, and before Alex came looking for her, she headed out to the living room. She found him standing out on the suite's private balcony, his strong, lean body silhouetted by the lights surrounding the resort and the beach beyond, and the summer breeze ruffling his thick black hair. As if sensing that she was behind him, he turned around, his disarming blue eyes taking in her dress in a slow, lazy perusal before returning to her face again.

"You look beautiful," he said, his voice a deep, sexy rumble that felt as intimate as a caress on her bare skin.

She came up to him, slid her arms around his neck, and tipped her face up to his. "You don't look too shabby yourself, Mr. Wilde." Indeed, he looked absolutely gorgeous in a charcoal knit shirt that made his eyes a brighter shade of blue, and black trousers that fit his hips, butt, and thighs to perfection.

She raised up on her toes and touched her lips to his. He returned the kiss, but kept it much tamer than she would have liked. God, she wanted to forget about dinner and whatever had him so preoccupied and spend the evening here in the suite. In their bed. Lost in one another without the outside world or emotional confrontations intruding in any way.

But her wish wasn't to be. Gently, he ended the embrace, took her hand in his, and entwined their fingers. He reached up and brushed long wavy strands of her hair over her shoulder, his sensual touch lingering warmly on her bare skin. "Are you ready to go?"

There was no mistaking the glimmer of hope she saw in his eyes, or the adoring look in his expression, and damn if both didn't make her nervous as hell.

Swallowing hard, she shored up her fortitude and flashed him a dazzling smile. "As ready as I'll ever be."

Alex was obviously a man on a mission, and he wasn't about to let anything distract him from tonight's purpose. And Dana had no choice but to wait and see what was on his mind.

Chapter Three

After eating a sumptuous dinner by candlelight, and with a baked apple tart dish set between them to share, Alex raised his glass of wine to Dana's in a toast. "Here's to our one-year anniversary, marking our first date."

Smiling, she touched the rim of her crystal wineglass to Alex's. "I'll drink to that," she agreed, and took a sip of the Riesling that Alex had ordered to compliment their dessert.

They'd spent the past hour and a half lingering over a delicious meal of lamb, fresh steamed vegetables, and the kind of easy, companionable conversation that came so naturally between herself and Alex. They'd discussed a big-name client she'd taken on at work that could prove to be a coup for her resumé, as well as a leg up to yet another promotion within her imaging firm. They talked about his cousin's new babies, and had a good laugh over his sister Mia's latest run-in with her nemesis, Cameron, as well as tossed out their own predictions on how long the couple would be able to resist the attraction sizzling between them.

All in all, dinner had been enjoyable and relaxing, without anything to spoil their lively exchange or their time together in such a romantic atmosphere.

But now that serious look was back in Alex's gaze, and

as Dana took a bite of the apple tart on the table between them, she suspected that their idyllic dinner was about to come to an end.

Since there was no sense in putting off the inevitable discussion to come, she decided to get it out in the open and be done with it. "What's on your mind, Alex?" she asked softly.

He swallowed the bite of dessert he'd taken and wiped his mouth with his linen napkin, looking more than a little bit sheepish at her accurate assumption. "Am I that obvious?"

She shrugged and set her fork aside. "You don't spend a year with a person without learning to gauge their moods."

"True, and you've become pretty adept at reading mine, it seems." He grinned and took a drink of his wine.

The thing was, unlike herself, Alex was an open book. He never tried to hide his feelings, had never been anything but sincere and truthful with her, about anything and everything. His past. His emotions. His faults and even his strengths. There was little about him she didn't know, or couldn't find out if she wanted to.

She exhaled a breath and swirled the liquid in her wineglass. "So, what's up, Alex?" she prompted once again.

He shifted in his seat, seemingly more anxious than she was feeling at the moment. "There's something I need to know, and I'd like an honest answer." He paused for a moment, met her gaze, and continued. "Have you been happy this past year, being with me?"

"Of course I have," she replied without hesitation, more than a little startled that he'd even have to ask such a question. "I enjoy being with you, and I wouldn't have stayed with you this long if I wasn't happy."

Truth be told, this past year with Alex was the longest she'd ever allowed herself to remain in a relationship with a man. Since she'd started dating in high school, then college, and into the early years of building her career, all her relationships had been short-lived, a few months at the most—by her choice. As soon as things turned serious with a guy, or demanding, or interfered with her career goals, she'd break things off, afraid of becoming too emotionally involved. Afraid of letting her heart overrule her head for fear of finding herself depending on a man like her mother had done for years.

But even though things had gotten serious with Alex, more so than with any man that had come before him, there was something unique about him that drew her in and made her feel safe and secure within their relationship. He accepted that she needed her space at times, seemed to understand her independent personality, and didn't mind her penchant for being in charge during certain situations.

Until lately.

Until now.

She watched as Alex reached into his pocket and withdrew a small black velvet jeweler's box. She tensed, her stomach knotting with a bout of uncertainty as he pushed it toward her.

"What's this?" she asked with an air of nonchalance, more a stall tactic than anything else.

"It's a gift I hope you'll accept. Along with all that it signifies." He nudged the box closer. "Open it and see for yourself."

His expression was so expectant that a fresh wave of anxiety washed over her. With trembling fingers and her heart slamming hard against her ribs, she did as he requested, revealing a stunning, sparkling, solitaire diamond ring.

She gasped, overwhelmed by the size of the stone, along with the unmistakable connotation attached to this particular gift. "Alex . . ." She lifted her gaze back to his, shaking her head in denial and panic. "This is too much."

Too much for her to deal with.

Too much for her to live up to.

Too much emotion, and too many promises she wasn't prepared to commit to.

"It's an engagement ring," he explained, as if she had any doubts about that, which she didn't. "I love you, Dana, and I know you feel the same way about me, too. I want to marry you."

She snapped the box shut, as if making the ring disappear from sight could also make his proposal vanish, as well. But the life-altering words still hung between them, shaking her up like nothing ever had. "I don't know what to say."

He reached across the table and grasped her hand gently in his, his fingers strong and warm against her cool, damp palm. "How about yes?" he suggested with a boyish grin.

She swallowed hard, and needing to regain a semblance of her self-contained composure, she eased her hand from his. "Don't you think all this is too soon?"

Taking her cue that she needed distance and space, he leaned back in his chair, though his compelling gaze never wavered from hers. "We've been dating exclusively for a year now. I don't need any more time to know that you're the woman I want to spend the rest of my life with. I guess the real question here is, am I the guy for you?"

"You know how much I care for you." And yes, loved him, too, more than she believed possible. "But that doesn't mean I'm ready to get married."

"Will you ever be?" he asked gently.

His question was a direct and brutal one for her, and because she didn't have a cut and dried answer for him, she resorted to her biggest defense. "You know how important my career is to me."

"Yes, I do," he acknowledged with a nod of his dark

head. "But you're thirty-five, Dana. Is that all you want out of life?"

He was hitting too close to deep emotional issues, and she bristled in response. "I've worked hard to get where I am."

"And I admire your success and how driven and dedicated you are. I've never made you feel otherwise, and I'm not trying to take that away from you now." His fingers absently strummed along the stem of his wineglass. "But at some point don't you want to get married and have babies and a family of your own? Because that's exactly what I want with you."

She bit her bottom lip, horrified to feel her throat close up with tears. Refusing to let them surface, she resolutely gulped them back. "I don't know that I can give you what you're asking for," she whispered, trying to be as truthful as she could be with him.

Disappointment flickered in his gaze, but was quickly masked by a tougher resolve. "I strongly believe you can give us both that future together, but it has to be what you truly want," he went on determinedly, despite her own doubts. "It's also a matter of you letting me past those emotional barriers of yours, without fearing that I'm going to try and change anything about who or what you are. You need to let go and trust me with your heart and what's inside, and believe that I'll never, ever intentionally hurt you in any way."

That easily, he'd exposed her greatest secrets and fears, proving that he knew her better and deeper than she ever would have believed. God, she felt stripped completely bare, and too damn vulnerable, and it was all she could do to remain seated across from him instead of bolting for the nearest exit.

She'd never seen this assertive side to Alex when it came to her, or them—so firm and uncompromising in what he wanted, and his unwavering attitude sent a shiver down her spine.

She thought once again of their rendezvous in the plane's rest room earlier, and how persistent he'd been with her then. She now realized that the turning point in their relationship, and their weekend together, had started at that moment, with Alex taking charge sexually with her.

Now he was doing the same to her emotions, coaxing her to open up and let him into that soul-deep place that had shaped the woman she'd become.

"As for accepting my proposal, I don't expect an answer right at this moment," he went on when the silence stretched too long between them. "But you need to make a decision before the weekend is over, Dana. You either want to take this next step in our relationship, or you don't see a long-term future with me in your life."

She stiffened against her chair. "So you're issuing me an ultimatum, then?"

He winced at her harsh choice of words and took a moment to form his response. "I'm asking you to make a *choice,* because if you don't want the same things that I do, then maybe it's time we went our separate ways. You know where I stand, so the final decision is yours to make."

With that, he picked up the ring box and slipped it back into his pocket. "I guess I'll just hold on to this for now," he said, then stood and extended his hand toward her. "Come on, sweetheart. It's been a long day, and we'd both benefit from a good night's sleep."

She took his hand, unable to stop the sense of despair taking hold within her. She had no idea what the rest of the weekend would hold, but she hoped and prayed that this moment didn't mark the beginning of the end of her relationship with Alex.

* * *

Alex laced his hands behind his head and stared at the shadows on the ceiling above the four-poster bed he was reclining on, while Dana finished changing in the bathroom before joining him for the night.

They'd both been silent on the walk back to their suite, which was no surprise since he'd given Dana a whole lot to think about and consider. He hated pressuring her for an answer, a choice, and he hated hurting her in any way even more. And there was every possibility that he was going to be the source of a whole lot more emotional pain for her before the weekend came to a close.

Minutes later she came out of the bathroom, wearing a silky black nightie with sheer lace barely covering her breasts. As she walked toward the bed, the short hem slithered across her thighs, making her skin look smooth and creamy and oh-so-tempting. It was a nightgown made for seduction and sinning, no doubt purchased as a special surprise to celebrate their one-year anniversary together.

Alex was more surprised that she'd chosen to wear it, especially after the way their dinner conversation had gone. He'd expected her to be more withdrawn and guarded, and certainly not in the mood to fool around.

As she moved up onto the bed, straddled his waist, and wriggled her bottom against his groin, it became increasingly obvious that's exactly what she wanted. He was wearing a pair of boxer shorts, but he rose to the occasion, growing hard and thick in seconds flat.

He reached up to touch her, but she grabbed his wrists and pinned them to the sides of his head, dominating him. The movement caused her hair to fall over her bare shoulders, her breasts to nearly spill from the bodice of her gown, and brought their faces about a foot apart.

The lamp on the nightstand beside them cast a soft, incandescent light over her, haloing her head and silhouetting her luscious body. It also brought an interesting detail into sharp focus that he might have missed otherwise.

This close, he glimpsed the desperation glimmering in her bright green eyes, and he quickly realized her ploy. She was after a wild, fast, hot tumble that would prove to him, and most likely herself, that she was in control of *them*. And unlike the way she'd surrendered to him that afternoon on the flight to Florida, she was determined to remain on top—literally and figuratively.

As difficult as it was for him to refuse her, they wouldn't be making love tonight, no matter how badly his body ached to drive deep inside of her.

Without much effort, he managed to loosen his hands from hers and slide his arms around her waist. Confusion reflected across her expression as he gently eased her back down to the mattress beside him, then a whimper of frustration escaped her throat when he turned and drew her back up against the front of his body, spoon-fashion.

"Alex?" The one word held a wealth of questions, and emotion.

"Not tonight, Dana," he murmured softly, then switched off the lamp, knowing it was going to be a long, restless night for both of them.

With his arm draped around Dana to hold her close, he felt a sigh of breath shudder out of her chest, much like a sob. He squeezed his eyes shut, her pain and confusion nearly tangible. She thought he was stripping away that control she prided herself on, but he was really just redistributing it so that she'd learn to depend on him every once in a while.

And know that it was okay to do so, without losing anything in the process.

Chapter Four

Reclining on a lounge chair by the resort's lagoon-style pool, and dozing with the warmth of the sun on her skin, Dana frowned as a large shadow loomed over her, blocking the bright, warm sunlight. She waited for the obstruction to pass, but instead felt cold droplets of water splash on her bare belly. Sucking in a shocked gasp of breath, she opened her eyes to find Alex standing above her, drenched from a swim in the pool.

He combed his hair away from his face with his fingers and grinned unapologetically for getting her all wet, his mood playful despite all that still stood unresolved between them. "Hey, gorgeous, would you like to take a walk on the beach before we head back to our suite to clean up for dinner tonight?"

She returned his smile and handed him a towel so he could dry off. "Yeah, I'd like that." She stood and secured her matching sarong around her waist.

Minutes later they were strolling along the shore hand in hand, with the ocean lapping against their feet and their toes sinking into the wet sand. A light, warm breeze blew off the coast, tousling Alex's damp hair around his head and making her wrap swirl against her legs. Their walk was relaxing and serene, and though they were both quiet, there was no tension between them.

Amazingly, the day had begun without the angst in which the previous night had ended, and for that Dana was extremely grateful. They'd slept in until after nine A.M., then ordered breakfast from room service and ate the meal out on their balcony, with a spectacular view of the ocean. At eleven they headed to the spa for their appointment and enjoyed soothing, stress-reducing massages, then opted for a late lunch at the resort's café before going their separate ways for a few hours.

Alex had gone to the golfing range to hit a few buckets of balls, and Dana had taken a book to the pool to relax and read, until she'd fallen asleep. Everything about the day was normal and pleasant and enjoyable, but she knew it was all a temporary reprieve. Alex was giving her time and space to figure things out for herself, which she appreciated, but she was all too aware that the clock was ticking on their time together and she'd eventually have to give him an answer to his proposal.

She'd spent the better part of the morning and afternoon doing a lot of contemplating about her past, her present, and what she wanted in her future. She'd thought she'd had it all figured out—what she wanted out of life and what direction it was heading—but that was before she'd met Alex and he'd added a new, more emotional dimension to her existence.

She still didn't have any concrete answers, just those damnable fears that wouldn't leave her alone. The fear of letting go of all she'd held on to for so long, and trusting in Alex and all he was offering her. The fear of losing him for good if she refused his proposal. And the one fear she'd never expected would make itself known: could she be the kind of woman Alex deserved and needed for the rest of his life?

It was a legitimate concern, and one she had to explore deeper—for herself, and Alex, too. And because there was no better time than the present, she decided to try and find some answers to that question lying heavily on her heart.

She glanced Alex's way and found him already staring at her, his blue-eyed gaze warm and genuine and as real as his feelings for her. He was still holding her hand, the simple connection between them intimate and caring and just what she needed the most right now.

"What's on your mind, sweetheart?" He delivered the same question she'd asked him last night, proving that he knew how to gauge her moods pretty darn well, too.

She smiled and ducked her head. "I think there's too *much* on my mind," she admitted, then looked back up at him and forged ahead with what she needed to know. "Why have you stayed with me for the past year?"

She certainly hadn't made it easy on him, at least not emotionally. It had taken her much longer to admit her feelings to him, and looking back she was shocked that he'd been so patient with her.

Which made her question, and his answer, all the more important.

Alex kicked at the surf foaming at his feet as he mulled over his reply, knowing he couldn't sum up his response in one easy sentence. "Let's see," he mused, and cast her an amusing smile. "There's you being beautiful and sexy and having a great ass, which was the first thing that turned my head."

Her cheeks flushed a pretty shade of red. "Nice to know you're a typical male," she murmured wryly.

"Oh, yeah." He laughed and winked at her. "But you'll be glad to know that I quickly learned that beneath that incredible beauty of yours, and our instantaneous chemistry, you're witty and intelligent and feisty, as well as dedicated and successful and self-assured. It's a combination that intrigued me from the first and kept me coming back for more."

As he extolled all the qualities he admired about her,

he found it ironic that the confidence and independent **attitude** he was initially attracted to was now one of the **main** issues that stood between them and a future together.

He stopped and turned toward her, wanting to make sure he had her full, undivided attention for what he was about to say next. "Then I fell in love with you, *all of you,* good and bad, and that's the first time any woman has ever ensnared me so completely."

With a gentle caress, he brushed back the strands of hair fluttering against her cheek from the breeze and stared deeply into her eyes. "You're amazing, Dana, in so many ways." And he wanted her to realize that for herself. Accept it. Believe it.

"Oh, wow," she breathed.

He'd obviously given her more than she'd bargained for, but considering their relationship was at stake, he wasn't going to hold anything back. And he hoped she'd give him the same in return.

He slid his palms down her sun-kissed arms until he was holding her hands once again. "Now it's my turn for a few questions."

She peered at him cautiously, but didn't shut him out or try to dissuade him. "All right."

He saw her acquiescence as a positive sign. "I want to know why it's so important to you to be so disciplined and in control, of your feelings, your surroundings, and even us."

She glanced away, toward the ocean, but not before he saw the show of guilt pass over her features.

Touching his fingers to her chin, he brought her gaze back to his, refusing to let her withdraw now that they'd come this far. "Tell me why you're afraid of letting anyone get too close, and why you have such a hard time depending on anyone other than yourself, for anything. And I know your reasons go a hell of a lot deeper than being focused on building your career, so don't use that as an excuse to hide behind."

When she didn't answer, he knew he'd hit a sensitive nerve. He squeezed her hand encouragingly and continued. "Make me understand at least that much, Dana." Because all those questions he'd brought up were issues she'd kept private and locked away. And he suspected her explanation was the key to their future.

Now, it was a matter of her trusting him with the truth.

She moved away from him and he let her go. A few steps later she picked up a shell that had washed up on the shore and rubbed her thumb over the smooth surface before glancing over her shoulder at him. "I know I've never told you much about my past, or how I grew up, and that's because it's something I'd rather forget."

"Tell me now, Dana," he urged gently.

She inhaled a slow, deep breath. "Being an only child, and with my parents being divorced by the time I was ten, I didn't have the kind of family life you did, with parents and siblings who were supportive and loving and always there for you, so it makes it easy to depend on them if you need something."

He had to admit that he was very fortunate in that regard. Even though his own mother had died when he was just a boy, and he and his siblings had experienced a few difficult years after that loss, they'd at least had their father and each other to turn to. Apparently, Dana hadn't had anyone to offer her that unconditional love and support when she'd needed it the most.

"Soon after my parents' divorce was finalized, my father married a younger woman, which completely devastated my mother," she went on, and shook her head in annoyance as they started strolling along the beach again. "She was at such a loss without my father, since she'd spent over ten years being completely devoted to him. She'd been a stay-at-home wife, very passive and always trying to please my father, to the point that I was sometimes an afterthought. She'd also depended on him for everything, and once she was on her own she didn't know what to do, or how to support herself."

Her lips flattened into a thin line, her frustration over her mother's inability to stand on her own two feet obvious. "So, instead of getting a job or trying to better herself, she found another man to take care of her, and when that didn't work out, she found another. It became a vicious cycle, and it got to the point that whenever she said she was *in love,* I'd cringe because I knew it was all so superficial and just a matter of having a man around to rely on."

Alex listened quietly, intently, knowing there was more and wanting to hear it all.

With a sigh, she threaded her fingers through her tousled hair before speaking again. "As I grew older, I learned to equate that emotion with being weak and vulnerable and dependent. Mainly, on a man. It's what I saw with my mother on a regular basis and lived with until I graduated from high school, and by that time I swore I'd never put myself in the kind of position my mother had."

So much clicked into place for Alex, especially a greater understanding of Dana's driven, strong-willed personality and why she felt the undeniable need to be so disciplined and in control of everything in her life. Including their relationship.

"You're nothing like your mother," Alex assured her. "And you know me well enough to realize that I'm not anything like the men in her life, or that I'd ever ask you to give up anything for me."

When she made no reply, he pressed his advantage. "Another thing I know with certainty is that what you feel for me isn't anything superficial. And maybe that's what scares you so much, because real love means laying yourself bare and believing that the person you care so deeply about will always be there for you, no matter what, and making that leap takes a bigger amount of trust than walking away with your heart and emotions intact."

She gave him a wavering smile. "You're right," she whispered.

And he hated that he was. "So I guess the biggest issue that remains between us is you trusting in me. In all ways. Physically and emotionally, and with your heart and soul."

And tonight, he planned to put her to the ultimate test.

Chapter Five

Wearing a sexy black cocktail dress, and ready for her evening with Alex, Dana headed out of the suite's bedroom, only to find the living room empty and Alex gone. She frowned, then caught sight of a single long-stemmed red rose on the coffee table, along with a folded piece of stationery with her name on it.

Recognizing Alex's handwriting, she picked up the note and read what he'd written inside: *Meet me down in the hotel bar. Love, Alex.*

Curious, and more than a little intrigued to find out what kind of game Alex was playing, she took the elevator to the main floor, then headed into the hotel bar, named the Lobby Lounge. Once inside, she glanced around, searching for her date.

He was nowhere to be found.

The establishment was spacious, with a large bar, intimate sitting areas, and live musical entertainment. Dana went ahead and chose a vacant table and sat down to wait for Alex to join her.

A waitress came by to take her order; Dana smiled at the young woman and told her that she was waiting for someone, and she'd order a drink when he arrived. With a nod, the waitress moved on to another table.

Ten minutes later the woman returned and placed a drink on the table in front of her. Before Dana could tell her she'd made a mistake, the woman grinned and spoke first.

"The drink is from that good-looking guy at the bar dressed all in black," the waitress told her, and pointed out which man she was referring to.

Dana glanced past the woman, prepared to refuse the drink, until she saw Alex sitting on a barstool. Sure enough, he was dressed in a black shirt and pants, and he looked sexy as hell.

He grinned like a rogue and raised his own glass to her in a silent toast, then downed the rest of the contents.

She stared at him in stunned disbelief, trying to figure out his angle, along with his pretense of being a stranger buying her a drink—which she admittedly found to be an exciting and potentially erotic prospect with Alex.

When Dana took too long to formulate a response, the waitress came to her own conclusions about her silence. "I'm sorry. Did you want me to tell him you refused the drink?"

Dana immediately shook her head. "No, I'll take it," she said, and glanced back at the cocktail Alex had sent her, which didn't look like anything she'd ever had before. "What kind of drink is this?"

Amusement glimmered in the other woman's eyes. "It's called a Screaming Orgasm," she said before heading back to the bar to pick up another drink order.

Dana nearly groaned at that, and gave Alex credit for being so innovative—with the drink and this seductive adventure of his.

Deciding to play along and have fun with the fantasy, Dana raised her glass and acknowledged Alex with a sultry smile. She mouthed the words "thank you" before taking a drink of the creamy, sweet-tasting drink, recognizing the rich, smooth flavors of amaretto, Irish cream, and vodka.

After that initial first sip, she slowly licked her lips and coyly touched her fingers to the swells of her breasts above the low-cut neckline of her dress. Her nipples hardened in response, and she let her lashes fall half-mast, in a way that told Alex just how hot and aroused all this role-playing was making her.

For the next half hour they flirted back and forth from a distance, teasing one another with their eyes and body language, and heightening the desire and anticipation building between them.

Her waitress came by again, blocking Dana's view of Alex.

"That guy is really hot for you," the other woman said with a speculative raise of an eyebrow. "You're a lucky girl. There have been at least three women that have tried to get his attention, but he's not interested in anyone but you." With that, she presented Dana with a sealed envelope. "He asked me to deliver this to you."

"Thank you," Dana murmured.

As soon as the waitress left her table and Dana was alone once again, she opened the envelope and pulled out the contents—a keycard to their suite, and another note, which she unfolded and read.

I want you. In my bed. In my heart. In my future. Come to my room for an evening filled with erotic pleasures and forbidden desires. If you dare.

Dana's heart pounded hard and fast in her chest, seemingly rendering her breathless as she glanced back toward the bar—only to find Alex gone. He'd set the stage for an elaborate seduction, as well as her emotional and physical surrender, but he was leaving the decision to take this provocative fantasy to the next level up to her.

Oh God, could she do this and give Alex what she knew this night would mean to him? She realized she was at a crossroad in her relationship with Alex and had to make a choice that would irrevocably change the course of her life after tonight. She could either trust in Alex with everything she was, or she could end this dare of his right now and end up alone.

Possibly forever.

It was that thought that frightened her most of all. A life without Alex in it.

Their discussion this afternoon filtered through her mind, and she knew this was where she had to make that leap of faith and trust in Alex, to give herself over to him in all ways and hold nothing back. Because there was no doubt in her mind that Alex would be in charge of tonight's seduction, and she'd be *his* willing slave. In all ways.

Minutes later she was standing in front of their suite door, smiling at the DO NOT DISTURB sign Alex had already put out for the housekeeper. Obviously, he planned to keep her very busy—tonight through tomorrow morning.

Without hesitating, she used the key card and stepped inside the adjoining living room. The suite was dark, except for a soft glow of light beckoning her to the bedroom. Setting her purse down, she headed in that direction and found Alex reclining in a chair in the corner of the room, waiting for her to arrive.

His long legs were stretched out in front of him, crossed at the ankles, and his hands were clasped loosely in his lap. A slow, lazy smile eased up the corner of his mouth. "You came." His voice, deep and low, sounded very pleased.

She stopped by the bed, facing him, feeling his hot eyes on her from across the room. "You knew I would."

"There was always the possibility that you'd decided this isn't what you wanted," he said meaningfully. "You and I both know there's nothing safe about tonight, and what I'm asking is a big risk for you."

"And what risk is that?" she asked impetuously. "Sex with a stranger?"

He chuckled. "That, and submitting to *my* wishes and desires." He waved a hand toward the four-poster bed, which had been turned down for the evening.

Her gaze shifted in the direction he'd indicated, taking in the props he'd laid across one of the pillows. A satin blindfold. Cream satin restraints. And a black feather tickler. She shivered at the thought of how he planned to put all those items to good use.

"Are you willing to take tonight as far as I want it to go?" he asked, bringing her attention back to him. "Are you prepared to do as I say and give me whatever I ask for?"

Her pulse quickened, sending a melting warmth swirling toward her quivering belly, and lower, between her thighs. This was it. The culmination of their weekend together. No more hiding from him or her own feelings. She was about to give him complete control and power, over her body, her heart, her emotions. Her very soul.

And she was ready to do so. Without reservation. Without fear.

"I'm yours to command, any way you wish."

A satisfied light burned in his gaze. "Then remember this. No touching unless I say you can. Now take off your shoes, then your dress."

After slipping both of her strappy heels off, she slowly skimmed one shoulder of her dress down and off her arm, then the other, exposing her bare breasts since she hadn't been wearing a bra. Her nipples were already tight and aching, and she hooked her fingers into the rest of the fabric and shimmied it over her hips and let it fall to the floor at her feet, leaving her clad only in a pair of skimpy black panties.

"Very nice," he murmured appreciatively. Standing, he took off his own shirt and tossed it aside as he closed the distance between them, his features bold and masculine and breathtakingly sexy.

She only had a handful of seconds to admire his broad shoulders and well-toned chest before he slid his hand around to the nape of her neck and tipped her face up to his. He slanted his mouth across hers, kissing her with an intensity and primitive hunger that branded and possessed. She whimpered, wanting to touch him all over, and had to force herself to obey his request to keep her hands to herself.

Long minutes later, he slowed the deep kiss, his tongue hot and soft as it lazily chased hers. He gently bit her bottom lip, tugged on it, and suckled it into his mouth until she was moaning and arching toward him in an attempt to rub her breasts against his chest.

He stopped before she could manage to do so. Taking a step back, he grinned wickedly at her. "Sit down on the bed."

She settled herself on the edge of the mattress, and he nudged her feet apart and stepped in between the vee of her spread legs, so that she was eye-level with the thick bulge straining against the fly of his trousers. He unbuckled his belt, opened his pants, and freed his erection. She licked her bottom lip in anticipation.

He rubbed the head of his shaft along that slick moisture and pushed her lips farther apart to gain entrance into her mouth. "Caress my balls and suck my cock."

Ah, finally permission to touch him, and she took full advantage of that small measure of control he'd granted her—all for his own pleasure, of course. But it was her pleasure, as well, because she loved doing this for him. She loved the taste and texture of him. Loved how his body wound tighter and tighter until he gave himself over to the pure, carnal bliss of a shuddering orgasm.

She took his shaft and his testicles in her hands, squeezing gently as she enveloped the length of him in the warm wetness of her mouth. He was huge and hard, and she took him as deep as she could, then began a stroking, sucking rhythm guaranteed to drive him over the edge.

He fisted his hands in her hair and rolled his hips as she increased the pressure, the friction, the tight suction of her mouth around his throbbing cock. His head fell back as he groaned, a raw sound that reverberated in the back of his throat as his climax crested and he came, hard and strong. She took every bit of him, the very essence of what made him male and her opposite.

He stumbled back a step and shook his head as if to clear it. "Christ, I'm supposed to be the one in control here, but damn, you've got such an incredible mouth."

She refined an innocent look. "I only did what I was told."

"I can't argue with that, and you obey orders very well, but don't expect that to happen again." He schooled his expression back into one of dark, unbending authority. "Move up onto the bed and lie on your stomach."

She crawled across the mattress and positioned herself accordingly while Alex stripped out of the rest of his clothes. He came up behind her, straddled her hips, and leaned over to grab one of the satin ties. He secured first one wrist against a headboard rung, then the other, leaving her with plenty of slack so the sashes wouldn't hurt or chafe her skin. Then he slipped the blindfold over her eyes.

Complete darkness consumed her, causing a frisson of panic. She felt the heavy weight of him on her bottom, which kept her pinned to the bed beneath him. She gave a tentative, instinctive tug on her makeshift manacles, and realized she was well and truly at his mercy, and he had complete domination over her.

A shot of apprehension kicked through her at the thought, but she quickly subdued her bout of anxiety. Alex had never tied her up before, but she understood his reasons for doing so now. It was that physical and emotional submission he was after, and her trusting him with both.

And she did. Unconditionally.

Seemingly sensing her moment of distress, he smoothed his hand over her hair in a gentling caress. "Are you okay, sweetheart?"

His voice, so soft and soothing, chased away any last, lingering doubts. She knew with her heart and soul that this man wouldn't hurt her or take anything she didn't willingly give to him. She also knew if he went too far or stepped out of her comfort zone, all she'd have to do was say stop and he would.

"I'm okay," she assured him.

"Good." He leaned over her, kissed her cheek, then moved away. She felt the shift of his body beside her before he issued another order. "Lift your hips for me."

She did, and he pushed two pillows beneath her, raising her bottom a good six inches off the mattress. She didn't know what to expect next, and she gasped as she felt the sweep of a lush feather gliding from her shoulders all the way down her spine, leaving shivery gooseflesh in its wake.

Alex dallied over the curve of her upturned bottom, teasing her with the feather and nothing else, making her squirm and moan and grow impatient for a more intimate kind of touch. He pushed her legs wide apart, making her feel vulnerable and exposed as the cool air in the room rushed over her wet, pulsing sex.

But then those insecurities flew right out of her mind as Alex shamelessly dipped that feather along the crevice of her bottom until he came into contact with her soft, feminine folds of flesh. He swirled the fringed tip in light, gossamer strokes that made her want to weep, the sensation as arousing as the flicker of a silky, questing tongue.

She needed more. More pressure. More friction. And she found herself begging for what she wanted. "Alex, *please.*"

The feather skimmed along the sensitive skin of her inner thighs, then it was gone and Alex was moving over her from behind, settling his groin against her raised bottom so that his erection nudged her opening. He threaded his fingers through the hair at the nape of her neck, tugging gently to pull her head back toward him, while his other hand slid under her and his long fingers delved between her legs.

His breath was hot and ragged against her ear, his body rigid along the length of hers. "I'm going to take you while you're restrained, hard and fast and deep," he said huskily, and instead of his words shocking her, they thrilled her instead. "And I'm going to make you scream when you come."

Her sex softened and tingled and grew damp with anticipation. He took a soft love bite of her shoulder as he pressed in, then with a hard thrust of his hips sank deeper than she believed possible, thanks to the raised position of her hips.

He took her just as he said he would, and she gave herself over to him without inhibition as he surged into her, over and over, his thrusts long and powerful, strong and sleek, and fiercely determined.

She ached. She burned. She rolled her hips sinuously against his, and with his fingers working his special brand of magic on her clitoris, she splintered apart. She tugged on the ties around her wrists and arched against Alex, screaming as she rode the wave of her orgasm with reckless abandon, holding nothing back.

When it was over, she went limp beneath him, and even though she was still blindfolded, that didn't stop her from realizing that Alex hadn't come. He was still rock hard and throbbing inside her, his entire body taut with sexual tension, his thighs quivering against the back of hers. Slowly, gradually, he dragged himself off of her, and she instantly missed his weight, his warmth.

"You didn't come," she said, and waited for him to untie her, or at least remove the shield from her eyes.

"Don't worry, I will." He removed the pillows from beneath her, then gently eased her to her back. Her hands crisscrossed above her head, but there was still plenty of slack left in the silken ties so that there was no pinching or binding. "You took care of me earlier, and we're not done yet."

She groaned as he positioned himself between her spread legs, but instead of wreaking havoc on her body with the feather again, he used his hands and mouth to pleasure her. His fingers touched the base of her throat, then moved lower, gliding over her breasts and delicately plucking at the stiff peaks before he took each nipple into his mouth and suckled greedily, until she was moaning and thrashing and begging him to please, please, please untie her so she could touch him, too.

Ignoring her pleas, he continued to nibble and lick and kiss his way down her stomach, followed by the luxurious sweep of his big, warm hands, all combining to bring her nerve endings back to vibrant life. And when his tongue slid deep into the valley between her thighs and his mouth fastened over her core, she was amazed that she had anything left in her to give him. But she did, and her second orgasm was just as strong and devastating as the first.

She felt him crawl up and over her body, felt the tip of his shaft glide against her sensitive cleft, but before he could drive into her, she clenched her thighs against his hips to hold him at bay.

"Alex, wait."

He immediately stopped.

"Please take the blindfold off and untie me," she implored once again.

This time, he did as she asked, releasing her hands and uncovering her eyes so she could finally see him, touch him. And the first thing she did was frame his face in her hands and stare deeply into his eyes.

He was watching her with a bit of uncertainty, and she was stunned to think that this man had a few insecurities of his own, and most likely feared a rejection from her. His emotions, his feelings and need for her, were so evident in his dark blue eyes that she felt a well of tears rise up in the back of her throat.

God, she was so incredibly lucky to have this man in her life.

She loved him. She trusted him. With her heart, her body, and her very soul. And she didn't want him to have doubts about either. Ever.

She let go of her past, and welcomed her future with open arms. "I love you, Alex Wilde."

It was the first time she'd ever said those words to Alex without being prompted by a declaration from him first, and the relief and joy pouring across his features told her she'd made him a very happy man.

"Oh God, Dana, I love you, too." He lowered his head and kissed her the same moment he joined their bodies.

They both moaned, and Dana wrapped her legs high around his waist as this time around they made love at a slow, deep, gratifying pace. Together. As one. Giving and taking equally, with both of them surrendering physical control in order to embrace the emotional intimacy that would from here on define their relationship.

Chapter Six

Dana awoke the next morning alone, with Alex's side of the bed empty except for the black velvet jeweler's box sitting on the pillow next to hers. An engagement ring. A proposal. A promise of forever.

It was a not so subtle reminder that she had a decision to make, and she knew without a doubt that there was only one choice for her.

She slid out of bed and reached for the hotel-issue robe that Alex had left for her at the end of the mattress, then picked up the ring box and headed out to the adjoining living room.

Alex was sitting at the small dining table, reading the Sunday paper. He was wearing only a pair of boxer shorts, and it appeared he'd ordered in a continental breakfast for the two of them. But she wasn't hungry for food. Not yet, anyway. First, she and Alex had unresolved business to settle between them.

"Good morning," she said, greeting him with a smile.

He set the paper aside, his gaze searching her features, his own expression guarded. Not that she could blame him for being wary, considering she'd yet to give him an answer to his proposal.

" 'Morning," he murmured.

She set the jeweler's box on the table in front of him. "I've made my decision."

He swallowed hard, glanced from the ring box back to her, and gave her a short nod to continue.

"I love you, Alex Wilde," she stated in a clear, steady tone of voice.

A small frown formed on his brows. "But?" he asked cautiously, obviously thinking she was going to qualify that declaration with a dozen reasons why they couldn't be together.

He was wrong. "No buts about it," she said with a shrug of her shoulder. "I love you. And I want to be with you. But I need for us to take things slowly, and I know you're going to have to be patient with me along the way. I'm still scared deep inside, and I'm still learning how to deal with all that. It might take some time for me to become the woman you deserve and need in your life."

Hope shone in his eyes. "You already are," he rushed to assure her.

"I'm getting there." She smiled, unable to believe her heart could feel so full—a feeling that was both scary and wonderful at the same time. "I know I have work to do in certain areas, and it's going to take time, I'm sure. Like being more open with my feelings. Depending on you for certain things without fearing it's going to strip me of my identity or independent nature. And I do trust you, Alex. With everything I am."

She drew a quick breath, and continued before he could issue a response. "But I can't accept the ring."

The slow grin that had been easing up the corner of his mouth quickly fell flat once again. "Why not?"

"It needs to come with a proper proposal," she said, trying not to laugh at his comical expression.

He grabbed the velvet box and dropped to his knees before her, proving as always that he was a man to rise—

or, in this case, kneel—to any occasion. He flipped open the box, took her left hand in his, and gazed up at her adoringly.

"Dana Reed, will you marry me?" he asked, his voice deep and heartfelt. "Will you be my wife, the mother of our children, and my best friend for the rest of my life?"

"Children?" she asked, and bit her bottom lip.

He looked taken aback. "You don't want children?"

"I never thought I'd have kids," she said softly, and trailed her fingers along his strong jawline. "But yes, I do want them, with you."

"So is that a yes?" he asked anxiously.

She was done tormenting him. "Yes," she said, and laughed. "Yes, yes, *yes.*"

"Thank God!" he rejoiced.

He surged to his feet and kissed her soundly on the mouth. Then he quickly slipped the beautiful diamond engagement ring on her left-hand finger, as if fearing she'd change her mind, and claimed her as his. The stone hit a shaft of sunlight, and sparkled as bright as their future together.

"It's beautiful," she said, and kissed him, deeply and intimately.

Within moments, Alex was taking over, guiding her back against the table until her thighs hit the edge. He swept aside their breakfast, lifted her up, set her on the cleared surface, and tugged the lapels of her robe down her arms so that he could feast on her nipples.

She let him have his way with her and sighed in pure, unadulterated pleasure. "I think I could get used to this."

"Used to what?" he mumbled around a mouthful of her breast, even as his hands were sliding up her spread thighs to where she was dewy and hot and already primed for him.

He propped her knees against his hips, and a gasp

hitched in her throat as the hot tip of his shaft pushed into her, filling her to the hilt in one long, smooth stroke. "You being the aggressive, dominant one."

That stopped his steady thrusts. "Oh no you don't," he said on a low growl. "I like you being a tiger in the bedroom."

She reached around him and filled her palms with his muscular butt, pulling him forward as she bucked against him, lodging him deep. She grinned and bit him on the chin. "Then we'll just have to take turns."

He groaned as she clenched her inner muscles around him, beckoning him to finish what he'd started. "Mmmm, I definitely think that could be arranged."

BLUE CRUSH

Erin McCarthy

Chapter One

As the tropical storm waves tossed her like a whale with a beach ball, Sara realized her plan wasn't going to work.

It had seemed so simple at the time. Head down to the beach, walk around in a glam-slam bikini, and attract one of the many surfers taking advantage of the high waves. Show men that she wasn't always Serious Sara, the glasses-wearing pediatrician, but was Sexy Sara, ready for a red-hot affair. Only the surfers hadn't even noticed the new Sara, busy surfing instead, the uncooperative jerks, and she had gotten hot pacing the beach.

A little dip in the water, and the next thing she knew she'd been sucked out twenty feet by vacuum-force winds and her mind wasn't the only thing she'd lost.

Her bikini top was missing, too.

Kyle finished hauling out the "Beach Closed" sign and took one last survey of the water. There were still a dozen surfers in the water, riding the huge storm waves. They'd been warned the water wasn't safe, and had refused to vacate. They were no longer Kyle's responsibility. But he wanted to make sure there was no one else in the water.

This was a hell of a way to end his six-year stint as

head lifeguard of Acadia Inlet Beach. Tropical Storm Bonnie was pummeling the Florida coast, heading their way, and he decided it was a good way to exit. No time for regrets about quitting. His toes curled in the warm sand as he prepared to turn and leave.

That's when he saw something fifty feet out. Just a woman's blond head bobbing in the water, arms and shoulders under the surface. Slumping forward, her position was unnatural, as if she'd lost consciousness. Kyle didn't hesitate but ran for the water, diving in cleanly and moving toward her with smooth strokes, working harder than normal since the water was rough and choppy from the high winds.

As he reached her, Kyle caught a glimpse of startled blue eyes, her head shaking back and forth, and he was relieved she was conscious after all. He said, "Are you all right? Are you hurt?"

Kicking back away from him, her mouth opened in fear. The surf and wind tossed wet hair across her face, and she gave a pitiful gurgle before her head sank beneath a punishing wave.

Treading water, he wrapped his arm around her midsection and hauled her to him, grateful to hear her cough and sputter as she reemerged. "You're okay," he reassured her loudly. "I'm here to help."

She was struggling against him, a common reaction as people panicked. He slid his arm higher around her, trying to get a better grip as she clawed at him and tried to wiggle away.

Then he nearly dropped her and drowned himself. *Holy crap.* She wasn't wearing a bathing suit. He was sliding on the underside of her very smooth, round breasts. Slick, firm breasts. Years of training helped him recover quickly, and he locked his arm around her before they both went under as he rationalized with himself.

It was just wet skin. It was no big deal. It was like an arm, or an ear, or a thigh . . . He gritted his teeth and started swimming back to shore, unwilling to look at her, or admit that he had the sudden deep urge to slip his hand a little higher and cup right over top of her luscious breast.

"Just relax," he said, wondering if he was suggesting that for her or for himself. Certain parts of him were definitely not relaxed.

Maybe it was a good thing this was his last day on the job. He'd seen all kinds of half-naked women parading past his chair every day and it had never affected him.

The woman whimpered in his ear, kicking out, causing his arm to roll over her tight nipple in the water as he almost lost hold of her. Affected? That would be a yes.

"Stop!" she said clearly. "Please . . ."

Kyle dropped his feet to the sandy bottom and bounced lightly in place. The water was up to his shoulders and he caught a splash across his face as the blonde gave another shove at him. Impatient with her hysterical resistance and his unprofessional reaction to her, he just wanted to get her on the shore.

"I'm trying to help you get out of the water," he said, clamping onto her tighter as he trudged forward, hauling her on her back, her breasts breaking the surface like buoys.

Damn. *Bad idea.*

Then she did the most amazing thing. She leaped on him, wrapping her long thin legs around his waist, clamping on and squeezing, her warm breasts colliding with his chest, arms gripping the back of his neck, her dewy, wet mouth very close to his. In less than one second his body responded with an instinctive hard-on that had nowhere to go but out.

It was a futile and desperate wish that she wouldn't notice.

Sara felt *it* at about the same time she noticed something had changed in his green eyes.

Oh. My. God. She had just jumped into his arms, and her breasts were touching him, plastered against him like seaweed. She sucked in her breath, very much aware that a certain part of him was pressing against a certain part of her. His part was big. Hers was wet, and it sure in the heck wasn't from saltwater.

She was surprised her body even knew how to respond, it had been so long since she'd been almost naked with a man, but she shouldn't have underestimated the forces of nature. Or lust. Her red bikini bottoms were tight across her, and the surf rocked her forward. Right onto him, into that big part.

Bump. Bump. Bump.

And neither of them said anything. His chest was hard, muscular, his upper body tanned, and his dark blond hair streaked lighter in spots from the sun. He was holding her with very little effort. Without her glasses, his face was a tiny bit blurry, and it added to the feeling of having fallen into an X-rated mermaid video.

"I lost my bikini top," she said finally, just to distract herself from the very real possibility of having an oceanic orgasm.

"I noticed."

Of course he did. Her nipples were poking him like steel thimbles.

"I don't want to get out of the water, because I'm embarrassed. I'm a modest person." As he could probably tell from the way she was imitating static cling all down the front of him.

His eyes went wide, his voice husky. "I thought you were drowning."

"I kind of figured that. Thanks, but I think I'll just stay in the water until everyone goes home." Not that anything could be more mortifying than what she was going through right that minute, but she didn't think she had it in her to stroll nonchalantly onto the beach like she was on the French Riviera. Sexy Sara had sunk along with the bathing suit top.

He shook his head. "The storm is getting worse. I can't leave you out here." His eyes dropped to her lips.

Which must have been her imagination. She shifted a little, trying to move her chest away from his. Instead, her bottoms caught on his swim trunks and rolled down a little at the waist as she scrambled up on his legs. She froze, swallowing hard. Her . . . *hair* had sprung out of the bottoms like a poodle popping up in a handbag.

His hands had come around her back and he stroked her a little, right above the small of her back, running his fingers on the bumps of her spine. "I'm Kyle, by the way. Head lifeguard."

"Sara." Stupid, sexless Sara.

The thighs she was resting on were very hard, and his leg hair tickled her backside. She promptly forgot what she had been about to say. "I'm sorry, I think I'm having an anxiety attack. I can't think."

"Me either," he said, and once more his eyes dropped down. This time they went lower.

Sara could feel a blush staining her cheeks, heating her skin. Tall, with long legs, she'd been a gangly kid and teenager and hadn't gotten breasts until she was fifteen. When they'd finally arrived, they hadn't been worth the wait.

"There's no one really left on the beach but surfers," he said, wrenching his gaze from her chest. "They won't pay any attention, they're busy. I'll walk first and you can just walk real close behind me until we get to the lifeguard office. Okay?"

Since the other choices were staying in the ocean forever or bursting out of the water in a Bo Derek jog, she figured his way was best. "Okay."

Neither of them moved. He said, "You're going to have to stand up."

Right. Of course. Apparently she'd left her brain along with her glasses on the beach. Still hanging onto his neck, she let her legs unravel from his waist and felt the surf kick her body out a little before she settled her feet on the ground.

Whoa, he was tall. She was five nine, and he was towering over her, his chest and shoulders twice her width. Sara glanced down at the water, expecting it to start boiling from the heat rolling off her. Then it occurred to her that she wasn't fully standing up yet, still bent at the knee.

"Turn around," she said, poking her hand up out of the water and twirling her finger as a directional. Not that he hadn't already felt and seen her breasts, but she wanted to retain an ounce of dignity.

He did, and she immediately reached under the water and fixed her bottoms. That was better. She was five percent dressed now instead of three. Then, with a courage that had gotten her through medical school, she stood up, moving so close to Kyle that her nipples brushed his back. It was meant to protect her from the view of surfers on the beach. It had the side effect of making her want to moan in extended pleasure.

Before she could clamp down on it, one tiny, wispy moan slipped out as heat sliced through her bikini bottoms, and her eyes squeezed shut for a quick view of "what if."

What if she were having sex on the beach with Kyle, the lifeguard? What if she were having sex in the water, right now, with Kyle? Acting completely independent of her brain, her thighs responded with a resounding *Yes, let's do it,* and rocked forward, nudging her mound against his rock-solid butt.

A shudder ripped through her. Have mercy.

* * *

Shit, was Sara trying to torture him?

Her fingers danced across Kyle's back, like she was trying to fool him into thinking that's what had been there the whole time. Hah. He knew a nipple when he felt one, and that had been a nipple. He had the erection to prove it.

"Ready?"

"Ready," came the breathy reply, whispered over his shoulder.

Kyle started walking and wondering. He was not a spontaneous guy, never engaged in one-night stands. He had never even dated a woman he had met at the beach while on duty, though he had done his share of harmless flirting. The reputation of ladies' man came with the job and the blond hair, but he had never lived up to it, and had mildly resented that people assumed he was a beach bum, content to spend his life in a beach chair.

No one really understood the training, hours, and effort that went into being a lifeguard, and he was tired of trying to explain it. After today, he was going to school to become an EMT, ready to move on to the next challenge, the next phase in his life.

But before he did, wouldn't it be fitting if he lived up to the image just once? With the wet and clinging Sara.

He gave a quick adjustment to the front of his trunks before he emerged from the water and decided he was nuts. Sara wanted him to get her out of the water, modesty intact, not take her in the lifeguard office and give her mouth-to-mouth.

Besides, he wasn't a one-night stand kind of guy. It always seemed disrespectful somehow, to use each other like that for pleasure. His brain remembered that even if his body wanted to forget.

Sara pressed closer to him, giving a little sound of distress. Kyle saw that several guys were glancing in their direction, and he reached back and took Sara's hands in his own, threading his fingers through hers and giving her a little squeeze. He thought he felt her relax a little and he walked faster, determined to ditch her before she spotted his hard-on and ran screaming. Or worse, didn't run.

The wind was even more brutal than it had been fifteen minutes ago, and Kyle sensed rain about to drop. The office was right ahead and he led Sara in, turned around, and closed the door. In the cool air-conditioning of the small room, he took a deep breath and tried not to look at her.

It was impossible. Standing in front of him, her hands across her breasts, he was looking at the most gorgeous body he'd ever seen. All long legs, thin hips, and firm, smooth skin, she was bending her narrow shoulders a little, hunching forward, her hair stuck to her like a wet blanket. Her hands covered her nipples, but not the swell of her breasts, not the luscious curve under each, not the flat abdomen that had drops of water rolling down it to a pair of red bikini bottoms.

Bikini bottoms that were low, as low as they could go without giving him a heart attack. Actually, a heart attack was still possible, given the way they fit snug, hugging the contour of her body, the little indentation of her soft folds visible in the wet fabric.

She looked uncomfortable and cold, goose bumps dancing across her wet skin. Yet her cheeks looked flushed, and her breathing was a little ragged, her eyes wide and filled with what he hoped like hell was something resembling the attraction he was feeling.

Either that or it was medical shock.

Which meant he really could do mouth-to-mouth. He never thought he'd be looking forward to CPR.

Sara wanted to speak, but her lips wouldn't move. Kyle was just staring at her, ignoring the drops of water dripping down his face from his wet hair, and she gripped her breasts tighter, like they'd sail off and leap into his mouth if she let go.

"I don't have a T-shirt," he said. "I left it out on my chair. Let me go get it."

"Thanks." Sara glanced around the sparse room. There was nothing but life jackets, flotation noodles, and first aid supplies. She could wrap gauze around her chest, but that would be a last resort, since she didn't think she would be able to wrap it by herself. The image of Kyle, big, large, blond Kyle, rolling thin gauze across her breasts made her want to whimper.

"I left my bag on the beach—it's yellow plaid. I have a towel and a sarong in it." A sarong that was see-through and utterly useless. But with her bag, she could put her glasses back on, drive home topless, and never set foot on this beach again.

Kyle looked thrilled to be able to leave. "I'll go get it. No problem."

Then he bolted, slamming the door behind him.

"Dammit, dammit." Sara dropped her arms and started pacing the room. What a total disaster.

All she had wanted was to leave behind her staid and boring life, where everyone treated her as a doctor and not a woman, and for once, just once, experience what it would be like to have a man look at you and want you. Want you so bad he trembled, his mouth went dry, and he couldn't keep his hands off of you.

It was partly her fault. As a teen and college student, she had dressed herself down, wanting to be taken seriously, and had rebuffed any attempts at flirtation from classmates. Then she had chosen pediatrics as her specialty, and now worked primarily with women. She loved her career, loved children so much she ached to have one of her own. But somewhere along the way she'd forgotten how to be a woman.

This probably had been a lousy plan, trolling around the beach for a surfer to lure into a rip-roaring affair, and her friend Josie had tried to dissuade her. But Josie had a boyfriend, which made her unqualified to give advice to single people, in Sara's opinion. Josie was having sex. Sara was in danger of collecting dust from lack of use.

Now she could either slink home in defeat, or she could turn her plan from a surfer to a lifeguard.

If she had the nerve. She pictured Kyle, remembered the feel of his large chest against her, his hands holding her tightly, and she decided if he gave any encouragement whatsoever she was going to be on him like white on rice.

Sara stuck her hands in her hair, trying to rake the moppy strands back off her face and shoulders. Her nail caught in a tangle, and she was standing like that, arms all the way up, working it loose, when Kyle opened the door, carrying her bag.

His jaw dropped. Then the bag tumbled to his feet.

Mortified, she wanted to run screaming out of the room naked, like a girl in an eighties horror movie. Instead, she forced herself to think rationally. This was just like taking a shower. Wet, hands in hair. Naked. With a complete stranger.

"It's raining," he said to her breasts. "I brought you my shirt, but it's wet. Your bag and towel got hit by a wave and I couldn't find the towel. And there's a tree down on the main road—there's no way for us to leave for the next hour or so. There's a crew out there now clearing it, but it will be awhile."

Sara just stood there and listened to him babbling, thinking this could only be a sign. A sign that maybe the beach was closed, but her plan was a go.

Given the way the last five years of her life had gone, it was possible she might never get another chance to do whatever could happen here with her naked and a gorgeous lifeguard in front of her.

Summoning her inner *Cosmo*, she fought the urge to squirm.

"Can we stay here?" Squeezing the water out of the bottom of her hair, she tossed it back over her shoulder, thrusting her chest out and sucking in her gut.

Kyle made a funny sound, almost like a low growl in the back of his throat. "Yes. We can stay here."

She took a step toward him, holding her hand out for her bag. "That's a relief."

To her horny and humming body.

Chapter Two

If Sara touched him all wet and naked like that, he was going to lose it. In his shorts.

Kyle dodged her arm, forcing his eyes off of her smooth breasts and the way her hips dipped and swayed as she walked toward him.

He should ask her out. That's what he should do. Ask her out, get to know her, show her he wasn't after a quick roll in the sand. *Then* he could have sex with her. Over and over again, burying himself in those narrow thighs, making her call his name . . .

"Kyle."

"Huh?" Damn, she was following him across the room. He wasn't going to be able to hold out if she came within smelling distance of him.

"Can I have my bag? And your shirt to put on?"

Right. He stopped himself from just hurling the bag in her direction and politely handed it to her, staring at a spot on her shoulder so his eyes wouldn't stray. His shirt was draped over the bag and she lifted it over her head, wiggling her shoulders, and he swore he wouldn't look.

God, man, don't do it, don't go over to the dark side . . .

He looked. His white shirt was falling over her breasts, the damp material clinging to her, nipples rosy and clearly visible, as were the dark circles around them.

Little folds of fabric hugged the curvy underside of each breast.

Oh, that was much better. Now she looked like first place in an Acadia Inlet wet T-shirt contest.

"It's kind of big," she said, fisting her hands in the hem, which hovered over her thighs. "But it's drier than I thought."

Then she did what would make a priest rip off his collar and sin. Her hands went under the T-shirt, sending it dangerously high. Kyle had some provocative mental images of what her fingers could be doing under there before they reemerged a second later.

The little red bikini bottoms rolled down her thighs until they landed on the floor with a wet thump, just a minute scrap of material that had only covered the essentials. But at least it had covered them. Now she truly was naked under that shirt. His shirt. Wearing nothing.

"Whew. That's better. Those were so uncomfortable. I hate wet bathing suits."

Now how was he supposed to behave himself when she said things like that?

He wasn't. He said, "Me, too."

"Oh." Her blue eyes went wide. "I bet you're uncomfortable, too. Your trunks are just as wet."

Then she glanced down at them. He knew what she was seeing. Wet trunks, yeah. And a hard-on, which he hoped was impressive. If he was going to be mortified, he at least wanted to put his best face forward.

Sara tilted her head a little, studying him. "I thought the water was supposed to make it shrink." Then she clapped her hand over her mouth, like she hadn't meant to speak out loud.

Noticing how his T-shirt hugged the apex of her thighs, cupping her exactly the way he wanted to, he said without thinking, "Not under the circumstances."

"If they feel really awful—your trunks, I mean—you can take them off."

His heart about stopped.

"I have something you can cover up with."

She rooted around in her damp bag, bending over a little, causing the shirt to ride up in the back. If he just moved a little to the left, he would see flesh where her thighs met her ass. He was on the verge of doing exactly that when she held up a white thing in front of him.

"My sarong."

Her sarong was nothing but white filmy fabric with big red flowers on it. It was see-through. It was a skirt. "I'm not wearing that! That thing wouldn't cover up a dimple."

Sara suddenly grinned. "You've got more than a dimple, don't you?"

Jesus, he was blushing. "Sara!"

The grin was still there, but she tried to sound contrite. "I'm sorry, am I making you uncomfortable?"

Yes. "No. Well, it's just . . ." He took a deep breath and stuck his hands on his hips. "It's just that when I walked in, you were just about naked, and hell, Sara, I wouldn't be human if I didn't react to that."

Taking in those long legs again, he said, "You're gorgeous."

Her cheeks went a little pink and her teeth worked her bottom lip. "Thanks."

He felt the need to elaborate. "Your body is . . ." His jaw worked up and down.

Words failed him.

The ooey-gooey, thigh-warming moment spoiled for Sara. This was not when she wanted to be reminded that she was a blond Olive Oyl. "I know. I look like a boy."

Kyle shook his head, his eyes darkening, voice dropping low. "No boy I've ever seen."

That sounded promising. Sara fished a little. "I'm flat-chested."

There were three feet between them, but Sara could feel the heat rolling off of him, sense the tightness of his muscles, smell the damp sand and water mixed with some kind of light cologne. He gave a soft laugh, shaking his head a little as he boldly dropped his eyes to her breasts.

"Then what am I looking at right now?"

"Uh . . ." She would not cross her arms over her chest like she had for the entire seventh grade. "Mosquito bites?"

His head shook back and forth. "No, ma'am, that is not what I see. I see . . . perfection. They're just right."

His hot gaze locked with hers. "A perfect fit."

Sara hoped she wasn't panting. Or drooling. And she had to know, she had to ask. "For what?"

"My mouth."

Ohmigod. She shouldn't have asked. Wait, yes, she should. This was it, the hint from Kyle that he would be a willing candidate for a fling. Only that was more than a hint, that was a blazing neon sex sign, and if she was smart, which she was, maybe the fling could happen right now.

In the next three minutes, before she spontaneously climaxed on his damp T-shirt.

"I guess we'll never know if it fits unless we try it."

Who the hell said that? Sara was so proud of herself, she wanted to throw her fist up in the air and start singing the theme song from *Moulin Rouge.*

Only Kyle dropped his head into his hands and turned away, pacing back and forth in the small room, muttering to himself. He was either suffering from multiple personality disorder or he was about to tell her no.

"Sara, this isn't a good idea. I mean, I want you. God,

I want you. It's obvious, isn't it?" He flung his hand in the direction of his trunks.

They were damp and showed her quite clearly how he felt about her breasts. In surfing terms, he had a hell of a swell.

Maybe if she approached this intellectually. "Kyle, you said yourself, I'm almost naked. We're adults, we're trapped in this tiny little room together. It's a healthy, normal attraction." She had learned all about hormones in med school, which was probably the last time hers had been quite so active.

Right now same-said hormones were blazing through her body doing the Macarena.

Rubbing the dried sand off her foot with her ankle, she took a step toward him.

He backed up, almost running into the wall. "I don't know you. At all. This isn't right. It wouldn't be fair to you."

Fair? Of course it was fair. She wanted it. Him. Now. Times three.

Kyle said, "What I'd really like to do is get your phone number. I want to go out with you, get to know you. Maybe dinner or something?"

He shrugged, looking miserable and embarrassed, and she couldn't find it in her to be mad at him after all. Kyle was clearly a nice guy who wanted to do the right thing, and despite her body's protest, her brain knew he was probably right.

It was possible she wasn't the one-night stand type anyway. She certainly wasn't skilled at it, having never done it. And who knew how she'd feel about it tomorrow if she slept with a stranger today. "Okay."

He gave a sigh of relief. "Good."

"So sit next to me and we'll talk. Just talk." Sara wanted to hear about him. She had no interest in putting on her glasses, announcing she was a doctor, and sucking all the sexiness out of this encounter. Even if it was just today, for the next hour, she wanted to stay Sexy Sara, with Kyle's eyes filled with longing.

Even if they didn't have sex. Because once they left this room and she became Dr. Davis, any date they went on would be different. Kyle wouldn't treat her like the woman whose bones he wanted to jump. He would keep his distance, she knew, like they all did.

Or maybe she was the one who always kept her distance, hiding behind her white coat and stethoscope.

Kyle wanted to believe that they would just talk. She looked innocent enough. Lowering herself to the floor, she crossed her legs and ankles and pulled his shirt down over her knees. It tented the fabric and kept it from clinging over her. She patted the ground next to her.

The concrete floor was uncomfortable when he sat down, but he drew his knees up to his chest, letting his legs fall open a little, and ran his fingers through his still damp hair. "Do you have a last name, Sara?" That was as good a place as any to start.

"Davis. Exciting, huh?" She smiled at him, looking up under long pale eyelashes. "How about you?"

"Vanderhoff."

Well, this was a thrilling conversation. He shifted, crossing his ankles, wishing he could reach in and give his erection a big old adjustment. He was running out of room in his trunks.

"So how long have you been a lifeguard?"

"Six years."

"Wow. That's dedicated. I've always thought being a lifeguard must be exhausting. You have to be so constantly vigilant. People are relying on you to protect them."

Kyle felt the knot of lust in his gut grow bigger. It just figured. If Sara was sent here to tempt him, she was doing a hell of a job. In all his years as a lifeguard, very few people had understood how challenging his job was, and how seriously he considered that responsibility. Now, here in the lifeguard hut, with a woman with the longest damn legs he'd ever seen, who was naked under his shirt, he was understood.

And he wasn't going to sleep with her? He must be fucking *stupid*.

"Yeah, I love my job, but you get burnout."

"Have you ever rescued anyone?"

He grinned and nudged her arm with his knee. "Besides you?"

Sara laughed. "Besides me. And hey, you rescued me, but not my top."

Which was something he was really grateful for right now, since her nipples were still nudging against the drying shirt, giving him a damn good view.

"There have only been a couple of people who were actually in jeopardy. Lots of jellyfish bites. One guy had a heart attack while swimming. We also had a shark bite just last fall."

"That was my friend's boyfriend," Sara said. "A doctor."

"No kidding? Is he okay?"

"Yes." She wet her lips with the tip of her tongue and shivered. "It's cold in here with the air-conditioning."

"I'm not cold." The total opposite, in fact. Burning. Everywhere. And he couldn't resist. He said, "I'll share my heat with you."

Kyle wrapped his arm around Sara and pulled her snug against his side. She was so thin, her skin clammy cold, but she felt so good. Total woman, her slender fingers curling into his chest as she got comfortable, and her right breast lightly pressed against him. He shouldn't be doing this. But there was no way he could stop himself.

"Mmm. You are warm."

Her breath danced across his bare chest, her cheek boldly resting against his shoulder. "How long before the road is cleared, do you think?"

With a little luck, never. "I'll check in a few minutes. Are you in a hurry?"

"No."

Good. He wasn't in any hurry either. Sara felt delicious in his arms, like sun and sand and a blue sky. Up close like this, he could see the flecks of gold around her pupil, see his desire reflected right back at him there.

Damn, it was just no use.

He murmured, "Sara, I'm going to kiss you. Unless you say no."

Her mouth opened a little, her pale pink lips looking very sweet and moist. "We're dating now, remember? You asked me out to dinner and I'm accepting. And people who date kiss each other."

Who was he to argue with logic like that?

Chapter Three

When Kyle's mouth covered hers, all Sara could think was that Tropical Storm Bonnie was her new best friend.

The pressure was perfect, nothing tentative, but not out of control either, just a firm steady kiss that held his warm lips against hers for a long, long minute.

It was slow, exploratory, gentle, Kyle's hand resting on the side of her cheek, his arm holding her snugly in the crook of his elbow. His mouth came back again and again, his eyes drifting closed as hers did the same.

Her body responded, desire pooling between her thighs and in her breasts, making her lean into Kyle and open her mouth eagerly when his tongue pressed against her. When the tips of their tongues connected, the mood shifted from questing to urgent.

His hand dropped to her breast, caressing her through the thin cotton of the T-shirt, as his other hand slid into her hair, holding her in place while he dove into her mouth. Sara moaned her approval as he brushed across her nipple, giving a light squeeze. She twisted, desperate to get closer to him, turning so she was facing him and gripping his chest with her cool fingers.

He was hard, hot, his muscles tense as she ran her fingers across him. Sara went up on her knees, moving each to either side of Kyle's legs, so that the shirt rode up to the tops of her thighs. Knowing what she wanted, she settled herself against him, the damp of his bathing suit sending goose bumps across her legs. The position had the advantage of nudging his erection securely between her bikiniless thighs, teasing her and thrilling a moan right out of her, loud and unrestrained.

"Oh, Kyle." There was probably a reason she should stop, but Sara couldn't think of it right now. She couldn't think of anything but him, and the way her body was vibrating with pleasure from head to toe.

It only took a little up and down motion and she was caressing herself against the length of him through his trunks, the damp coolness of the wet fabric sending her shuddering as it hit her swollen clitoris.

"Sara." Kyle broke away from her mouth, holding her hair tightly with both hands. "Oh, shit, stop. You're killing me."

"No, it feels good." Sara kept moving, grinding herself against him, mimicking the motion of him inside her with greedy strokes, lost to all rational thought.

His body relaxed as he groaned, then without warning he gave a muttered curse and sat up straighter. Rough and desperate, his hands snaked around to her behind and gripped her, thumbs stroking her skin, moving her harder against him.

Oh yes. She liked that, and held onto his shoulders as he thrust at her.

"It feels better than good." Kyle shoved the T-shirt up and bent his head over her breasts.

Sara leaned back, tilting her head, urging her breasts forward. Kyle's tongue flickered across one nipple, then the other, the airy light motion sending forth a rush of heat and moisture between her thighs. Then his mouth closed over her, sucking her in, covering almost her entire breast with soft wetness, his teeth grazing along her sensitive flesh.

Her hips stilled as she panted, clawing at his shoulders,

the feel of him sucking and tugging suddenly sending her pitching forward into frenzied desire. Just when she thought she couldn't take it anymore, he pulled back.

Then covered her other breast, leaving her left nipple wet and throbbing while he tortured the right. Sara's feet pushed against the floor as she squirmed, his full erection nudging her between the thighs again, the cool damp trunks bumping her hot inner folds.

When he let go, plucking at her nipple lightly with his teeth, she moaned, wanting more. Wanting everything.

Kyle wiped the moisture off his shiny lips and gave her a slow grin. "I told you it would be a perfect fit in my mouth."

"You were right." The shirt gave in to gravity and fell back down, covering her.

Kyle thrust up his hips just a little, studying her. "Should we stop here?"

He nudged her again and she felt it clear down to her toes.

Should they jump into a tank with a thousand hungry piranhas? Was he insane?

"No, I don't want to stop."

Kyle stretched the neck of the shirt and ran his tongue along her shoulder. "What do you do, Sara Davis? I can't figure you out. I want to know more about you."

Sara hesitated. She could tell him she was a doctor. It wasn't a big deal. But being a doctor was her practical self, the glasses-wearing self who invested wisely and never walked in the parking lot at night alone. If she told him, it might not change anything for Kyle, but it would change everything for her.

So she gave him a slow, seductive smile, and with a fluid motion took his T-shirt off over her head and let it drop to the cement floor.

It left her in his lap. Completely naked. "Maybe you'll want to know that I have condoms in my beach bag."

Kyle squeezed his eyes shut and took a deep breath. Hell. She just had to do that, didn't she? Reopening them, he took a good long agonizing look.

What he saw made his cock tighten, pulsing with anticipation. Sara was long and lean, bronzed over every inch and wrapped all around him, arms dangling around his neck, breasts giving a little lift-and-turn display in front of him, her flat stomach descending down to her dark blond curls.

There was nothing between him and those curls, and her soft wetness behind them, but his red swim trunks. He could feel her there, the press of her, smell the tangy hint of her desire, and he wanted to rip off that final barrier and lift her onto his cock until they were both in an agony of pleasure.

Sara was a paradox. She flipped between modest and a confident seductress. The woman who carried condoms in her beach bag didn't match the woman who had climbed onto him in a blind panic when she thought she might have to walk out of the water topless.

He didn't want to be a conquest, another stripe on her beach bag. But despite her eagerness with him, Sara didn't seem like a bed-hopper to him. It was a gut feeling, based on nothing but the way she sometimes looked at him. Needy. Vulnerable. A little shy. Or he could just be seeing what his dick wanted to see.

There had to be an answer, before he went forward. He had to know. Sighing, he kissed her chin.

Sara lifted herself up a little to bring her mouth closer to his. "Kyle, I haven't been with a guy in almost two years. Please don't make me wait any longer."

Relief surged through him. That was all he needed to hear, confirmation of his instincts that she didn't sleep around. "That is a long time, isn't it? What have you been waiting for?"

His thumbs plucked at her nipples, enjoying the taut firmness of them. He wanted to roll them in his mouth again, circle his tongue around them.

"I've been busy working," she whispered, fingers in his hair, urging his head down to her breast. "And men don't ask me out all that often."

That had him snapping his head up, gaze locking with hers. Men didn't ask her out? That was as unbelievable as a *Baywatch* episode. But she looked sincere. There was a little bit of hurt and confusion in her green eyes, and he had to show her how much he truly desired her.

How he wanted her like he'd never wanted another woman. "That's because you probably intimidate them. They know you're too good for them."

She gave a soft laugh. "I don't know what it is. But please, Kyle, don't make me get off your lap and put that shirt back on." Her voice was a pleading whisper. "I'll die of embarrassment."

"There is nothing I want more than to make love to you. Right now. But I want you to be sure, and I want a guarantee that you won't just take off when the road is cleared without leaving a phone number or anything. I don't want that."

"I'll give you my number. I promise."

He had to be satisfied with that or he had to walk away. Sara shifted in his lap, her chest colliding with his, her soft inner thighs bouncing against his cock. Her promise was good enough for him.

"Scoot back so I can get my trunks off."

Sara gave an adorable little murmur of approval and dug her nails into his shorts. "I'll get them."

That worked. Just get them the hell off so he could sink into her.

Sara went back on her knees, tugging at his trunks.

He lifted off the ground, hoping to aid her efforts as he crushed his mouth to hers, sliding his tongue past her thin lips.

The bathing suit was still damp and he could feel Sara struggling to pull it down. He shoved at the waistband, trying to help, her cool fingers setting his teeth on edge as they slipped inside and touched his overheated skin.

"Get on your knees," she said, kissing him back, sucking on his bottom lip.

He did as he was told, no questions asked. Sara's entire hand was in the shorts, fighting her way through the mesh lining to reach him. He was in agony, feeling her, yet not having her exactly where he wanted her. Moving left and right, he tried to maneuver her hand onto his cock.

Sara paused, then started jerking her hand so hard his whole body rocked forward. "My hand's stuck!"

Kyle looked down, and couldn't believe what he was seeing. Sara's hand was wrapped up in the mesh like a dolphin in a tuna net.

"What the hell?" He grabbed the waistband, determined to just rip them off, and yanked.

Unfortunately, Sara tugged in the opposite direction. The twisted mesh caught his testicles like a tourniquet. The room spun like it had when he'd sucked down two shots of Jack Daniels at his brother's wedding.

"Aahh," he managed to say, letting go of his trunks and sinking to the floor, doubled over in shooting pain.

"What's the matter?" Sara finally extracted her hand and gave him a tentative touch on the shoulder.

"My . . ." Hell, he didn't know what to call them. Nuts sounded like he was twelve, balls was a guy word, and testicles was for medical professionals. Gonads? No, that was the worst of all of them.

Settling for gesturing with his hand, he sucked in big breaths and tried to relax. "My . . . got twisted."

"Oh!" Sara's hand went to her mouth. "Well, let me see."

See? What was there to see? His balls weren't a circus sideshow. Through gritted teeth, he said, "I'm fine. I just need a minute."

Sara fixed him with a stare, impatiently pushing her drying hair out of her face. It was heading toward frizzy as it dried, falling into her face in clumps. "I just want to make sure you're all right. You could have suffered a testicular torsion."

That sounded like something he didn't want to know about. He couldn't stop his lip from curling up in horror. Sara reached for the waistband of his trunks.

He jerked away, creating residual stinging in his nuts. Putting his hands on his sides as he forced himself upright, he tried not to wince.

"Fine, we'll do this the hard way."

Sara looked different, like she had shifted into a confidence he didn't understand. Even naked, she commanded a professional respect. It occurred to him maybe she was a nurse.

Then he lost all rational thought when her hand slipped into his shorts and caressed down his shaft, then cupped his testicles, probing gently.

"Does this hurt?"

Holy hell. Eyes closed, he said, "No."

Her nipple was brushing his chest, her hair was across his arm, her breath was hitting him in the gut, and her fingers were on his balls, and yes, dammit, he was in pain. Agonizing pain from wanting her.

Swiftly, Sara took down his trunks.

That didn't help.

Sara eased the trunks past Kyle's knees and discarded them. Mouth dry, she took in his erection, pointing up at her like the hand on a sundial. Obviously the injury hadn't curbed his desire, thank goodness. Leave it to her to just about maim the man she was on the verge of having sex with.

She lowered herself so she could take a good look at his testicles, just to reassure herself they were uninjured. They had felt fine, but she wanted to make sure one hadn't dropped lower than the other.

"What the hell are you doing?" Kyle sounded outraged.

"Everything looks normal," she said, cupping him again for her own pleasure, not for medical examination.

He felt smooth, soft but rigid, and his penis rose above her fingers, temptingly close to her mouth, all hot taut flesh.

"I told you . . ." he said, then trailed off with a groan as she pressed a kiss on the top of his shaft.

"Mmm." He was warm, and tasted salty. She closed her mouth around him, sucking lightly.

"Sara." Kyle's fingers raked her hair back.

"You don't mind, do you?"

"No." His breathing was hard, his answer spit out on a pant.

She liked that. And sucked harder, going a little deeper, enjoying the slide of him in and out of her mouth, the way his hips started to move, thrusting himself into her mouth.

Her hands were still on his testicles and she massaged there. Her knees were on the hard floor, but she didn't notice until Kyle urged her back.

"Here, let me put the shirt down." He reached behind him and snagged the T-shirt, laying it down carefully for her, doubling it over for extra padding.

Sara could see that Kyle didn't even think about his action, and that made it all the more thoughtful. There was just an integrity about him, and she was suddenly very grateful he had found her half dressed in the ocean instead of any other guy.

"Thanks."

It should have broken the mood, should have made her feel awkward, but instead she felt a strange tenderness mingling with her intense desire. So when she bent back over him, she took him in deep, as much as she could handle while he tossed off a curse and dug his fingers into the back of her neck.

When she pulled off him, she sucked the tip hard, arousing herself nearly as much as Kyle. Running her tongue down the length of him, she darted lower and kissed his testicles, smiling at the startled jump he gave.

Fingers on his thighs, brushing back and forth, her mouth hovering over his erection, she said, "Am I making you uncomfortable again?"

He shook his head. "But I want you to sit up. It's my turn now."

She did as she was told, moving her hands to his chest so she didn't topple over from balancing on her knees. "Oh, we're taking turns now?"

"Absolutely."

And to prove his point, Kyle bent over, taking her nipple into his mouth at the same time his finger slid smoothly between her thighs and inside her.

Heat rushed through her, her head lolling back as he started to move slowly, an even, steady in and out. Sara clenched her teeth, squeezed her fingers in Kyle's soft chest hair, and tried not to come.

Since her sexual needs were as neglected as a redheaded stepchild, she was spiraling out of control fast.

Kyle was big, warm, smelling like sweat and ocean water, and he surrounded her with his masculinity, urging her to give up that control and let him make her moan.

Very aware of how naked she was, how bent and spread and laid out before him, she decided it would be a good idea to prolong this as long as possible. Since she wasn't likely to lose her bikini, nearly drown, and be stuck in a hut with a gorgeous lifeguard again anytime soon, she should wring every last drop of pleasure out of it that she could.

And actually a drop of pleasure was an understatement. She was being deluged with the Niagara Falls of pleasure.

Chapter Four

Kyle wanted Sara to come. Now, with no waiting, with nothing but his finger inside her and his tongue on her breast. The look on her face was incredible, and the feel of her tugging on his chest hairs, little sounds of ecstasy jerking out of her, was almost more than he could stand.

The way she had taken his cock into her mouth had been unreal. He wanted to return the favor and finish her off.

Her breasts weren't huge, but they were firm, curvy, just right on her long and lean body, and a golden color like the rest of her. "How do you get tanned everywhere, Sara? Do you sunbathe naked?"

He'd like to invite himself over to watch that.

His finger had stilled and she let out a cry of disappointment.

After sucking in a breath, she said, "It's fake tan lotion. Sunbathing causes skin cancer."

Even better. He could roll on her lotion. "Smart girl."

Rubbing his thumb over her swollen clitoris, he licked around her nipple in a matching circle, teasing her.

Her head was back, eyes half shut, but she closed her hand over his backside. "I noticed you have tan lines."

Great, his ass was probably lily white next to his tanned back. Why couldn't he just keep his mouth shut and enjoy her? He pulled away from her breast. "I bet I look like the Coppertone kid, don't I?"

Sara urged his head back down over her breast, none too gently. She wiggled against his immobile hand. "Hardly. Kids are cute. You're just . . . impressive."

For that, she could have his finger back. Kyle sank into her, using only up to his knuckle, grabbing her ass with his free hand to hold her tight against him. "Is that far enough?"

"No." Her damp hair rubbed back and forth on his shoulder. "Deeper. Please."

He'd be happy to. He went as far as he could before pulling back, then repeated the movement. Again and again, only breaking to massage her clitoris on occasion, feeling the tightness of her inner muscles as she grew closer and closer to a climax.

When he added another finger, Sara arched against him, her body rigid. Her breath came in frantic little pants. "Don't move," she begged. "I don't want to . . . yet."

"Don't want to what?" He waited a heartbeat, then stroked slow and deep, stretching his fingers inside her where she was tight and wet and ready to come.

With a little shake of her head, she tried to move away from him.

He followed her, stalking her, holding her flush against him, moving faster, sliding out one finger to saturate her clitoris with the warm fluid of her desire. "Don't want to what?"

"I don't want to . . ." Sara went still, then jerked in his arms. "Come, oh God."

Oh yeah. Kyle's cock throbbed against her leg as he watched the beauty of her orgasm, the way she shuddered and mewed and clung to him, her eyes lifted up to the ceiling. He kept moving, holding, pleasing her until her inner muscles stopped trembling and she collapsed on his chest, her cheeks flushed and her fore-head dewy from exertion.

She was gorgeous, and nothing was going to make him move until she did. He wanted her so bad that every damn naked inch of him was pulsing and throbbing, but he wasn't going to make one move until she moved first. Sara was so incredible, he wondered for a split second if he was dreaming, then dismissed it. If he were dreaming, he would have already spilled on his sheets.

"Kyle." Sara looked up at him, her chin still pressing into his chest.

"Yeah?" He was a little nervous. She'd told him to stop stroking inside her and he hadn't. It was possible she'd be pissed at him.

"Go get the condoms out of my bag and then lie down. It's my turn."

Whoa. Not only did she not sound angry, she had a bit of bossy in her voice. He liked it.

"Whatever you say." He set her on her feet and searched around the room for her bag.

The room was functional at best, ugly at its worst. Cement and cinder blocks, orange life vests, and a damp moldy smell. Man, this was rough. Sara deserved better, and he felt pangs of guilt. Digging through her bag on the floor, he glanced at her over his shoulder.

Her hands were up in her hair again, in the very pose that had coaxed him into touching her in the first place, only now she didn't even have the tiny bikini bottoms on. She looked hungry. For him. Quickly he found the condoms and dumped the rest of the bag's contents on the floor, intending to spread the bag flat. They'd need everything they could get for protection on this floor.

Of course, there was always standing up.

Kyle opened the heavy steel outside door a couple of inches, the warm wind and rain immediately rushing in.

Privacy didn't concern him. The wind was howling and the beach was probably deserted, so that no one would discover them. And it took the air-conditioned chill out of the room.

He spread Sara's sarong beneath his T-shirt and crushed her bag flat. Then he lay down with Sara still standing over him, the condoms in his hand, and reached for her, curious to see exactly what she planned to do with him.

Sara wasted no time in dropping down as she held his hand. She spread her legs as she tumbled into his lap so that he briefly had a mouthwatering view of satin thighs, blond hair, and the shadows of her backside viewed from between her legs.

Damn. He was paralyzed watching that. Good thing she was coming to get it, because he couldn't move.

Sara ripped the condoms out of his hand, tore one open and rolled it on, her breasts dangling over him, enticing him to move. He reached out and pinched a nipple, and she gave a convulsive squeeze on his cock as she finished with the condom.

She said, "You want these?" and abandoned his cock to cup her breasts.

Yeah, he did want her breasts, her nipples. Hell yeah. But the sight of her with her hands on herself, caressing lightly, with no encouragement from him, was worth holding off for a minute or two.

Or five seconds. Damn, he couldn't hold out any longer, which was pathetic, but he didn't care. "Bring them to me."

Sara leaned over, her hair falling across his chest, and braced one hand on the floor. With the other she reached down between them and stroked his cock before rubbing the length of him back and forth on her clitoris. Her nipple danced in front of his mouth and he reached out and caught it with his lips and sucked hard, enjoying the sweet, salty taste of her.

Then aching so bad he hurt, he grabbed her other breast, squeezed them together, and flicked his tongue across both nipples, growing desperate as she teased his cock between her folds.

He hadn't been prepared for Sara to so confidently take what she wanted, but then again, since the minute he'd grabbed her firm, almost-naked body in the ocean, he'd just been along for the ride, unable to resist her.

She was sluicing him up with her moisture so she could play some more, and she was teasing the shit out of both of them. They panted in perfect accord, and when she went a little too deep in her game, Kyle nudged upward inside her.

Her knees fell out and Sara sank down onto him with a groan. Kyle couldn't breathe. Damn. He abandoned her breasts to lie back and concentrate on not coming.

But she was so tight, narrow, her sex similar to the rest of her slim body in that regard. She was squeezing him with trembling muscles, accepting him more fully as she pushed farther, gripping his chest until her clitoris was pressed against him, pulsing.

Kyle fought not to move, to let her continue to lead, and marveled at how beautiful, how flushed she was. Sara bit her lip and stroked up and down, never really going that high, but letting him fill her more fully each time.

One, two, three strokes, her hands stealing back up to her breasts to cup her nipples, and at the sexy sight of that, Kyle couldn't do it. He couldn't just lie there and take it anymore—he wanted his turn. He had to take her.

In one swift motion, he sat up and turned her so she landed flat on her back, his hand behind her, protecting her bare flesh from the hard floor. Green eyes stared up at him, stunned.

They were still joined, but barely, and he restrained himself for another second, swallowing hard. He said,

"Pretend this is romantic, Sara. Pretend we're lying on the hot sand and the sun is setting behind us."

But she shook her head. "I don't need to pretend. I like it just the way it is. Can't you tell?" She licked her lips. "Make me come again, Kyle. Please."

As if she needed to beg. "Gladly."

Kyle nudged just a little deeper so he wouldn't slip out, drawing a murmur of approval from her. He took the soft flesh of her thigh and crossed her right leg over her left, turning her up onto her side a little, and allowing him a nice view of her rounded cheeks rising in front of him. Not to mention it spread her thighs in a way that gave him a delicious glimpse of her lips, swollen and wet, pink and ready for him, his cock poised in her opening.

Her arms fluttered over her head, her chest rising rapidly. She whispered in excited shock, "This is different."

"This is good. Trust me." Then he thrust hard, forgetting the floor was concrete, forgetting that he hadn't meant for it to go this far, forgetting everything but the way he filled her body, the sensation so pleasurable a sweat broke out all over his body.

This was more than good, it was unreal, and he knew that he could not let her walk away, not after she had done this to him. This shattering, possessive, gut-wrenching feeling of pleasure that ripped through his body and made him thrust harder still.

Sara arched her back as Kyle went deep, the unexpected position giving her heightened sensation. She shouldn't have worried about coming again. It was inevitable with him moving fast, his hands splayed on her thigh and backside, holding on as he pumped hard, and she lay there, taking it.

There was no way to move, no need to move. With each of his movements, he slid fully into her, his torso bumping her clitoris, sending shivers through her. She felt lethargic, blissful, already sated, yet rushing toward another orgasm. Each stroke was a little rougher, a little more out of control, a lot more urgent, and Kyle's eyes locked with hers.

"You're so fucking hot," he said, jaw clenched.

That was the look she had been wanting. The look she had come to the beach to find, a man who wanted her. He had it. That was raw, painful, desperate want, all over Kyle's face, in each of his pushes inside her, and in the fierce way his hands gripped her hip for leverage.

It made her come.

Sara bunched the T-shirt underneath her as she exploded, calling out in a voice so loud they could probably hear her in Georgia. Northern Georgia. With their windows closed.

Which made him come.

Kyle murmured, "Shit, Sara," before his eyes screwed up tight with his own explosion.

She knew the feeling. As his orgasm continued to rip loose, so did hers, and they were both straining and squeezing and moaning together, the sweet smell of their desire between them, and a thin sheen of sweat glistening on Kyle's bronze chest.

This was worth two years of zero action. It was all gone and forgotten in a single instant of screaming satisfaction.

Loosening her death grip on the shirt, Sara fell back, catching her breath, watching Kyle slowly open his eyes and look her over, up and down. He let go of her thigh and buttock, and stroked across her skin gently, making low growls of approval in the back of his throat. His weight was heavy resting against her, but a good heavy. Solid, man heavy.

He made a motion to pull back, and she fluttered a hand out. "No, just stay still for a second."

"Whatever you say, sweet Sara."

His obedience wasn't complete, though. While he kept himself firmly inside her as their breathing settled down, after a minute he moved his hand off her waist and maneuvered it between her thighs. When he stroked her engorged nub, pinching lightly, it hurt just a little but at the same time set her gasping with renewed desire. Kyle ducked his thumb down, sliding it into her alongside his penis, which was only partially erect.

"Oh, what are you doing?" she gasped.

It was obvious what he was doing—he was turning her on all over again. But that she could be spread sideways like this, with both him and his thumb inside her, both shocked and thrilled her.

Kyle brought his thumb, slick from her want, back up to her clitoris and swirled over it, around and around, sliding down between her folds, teasing her, then back up again. Sara whimpered, felt him growing harder inside her, felt the unbelievable sensation of a third orgasm getting ready to rock her.

A third.

Her yearly quota in one afternoon.

He bent over and blew on her nipples, hot forceful breath, and his thumb did those interesting little massage therapist moves. Stroke, stroke, pull.

Oh God.

Kyle couldn't get enough of Sara. Now that his cock was swelling again, he knew he shouldn't push his finger in there, but he couldn't help wanting to. She squirmed, she wiggled around on the floor beneath him, she gave little sighs of approval and tried to lift her leg to spread herself wider.

He couldn't resist that. Didn't want to try. Giving one last swipe over her folds, he slipped into her and slowly thrust both his half-hard cock and finger deep, gritting his teeth at the snug fit, wondering if he had gone too far. He paused to read her reaction.

Sara trembled under him, then lifted off the ground in a shattering orgasm, answering his question in the best possible way. He started moving with languid strokes, watching her cheeks pinken with exertion, her eyes unfocused and dark, her breasts firm little mounds turned invitingly toward him.

"What was that for?" she said after several long seconds. She settled back down, pulling a stray strand of hair out of her mouth.

"I just wanted to watch you come again."

She smiled, lying limp. "Did I look the way you wanted?"

The stuff of fantasies. That's what she looked like. And yes, he wanted.

"Best damn thing I've ever seen."

"Kyle?"

"Hmm?" He slowly withdrew from her, his leg muscles complaining as he eased back.

"I like dating you."

Chapter Five

Sara knew the storm was building outside, probably only getting worse as the afternoon passed, and that she should head home, but she didn't care. She was snuggled up against Kyle's chest, back in his T-shirt to guard against the cold, a nice dull ache between her thighs.

Kyle was quiet, breathing steadily, staring up at the ceiling. She thought he was simply recovering like she was until he said gruffly, "I'm sorry."

That didn't sound promising. She forced herself to say lightly, "For what?"

He threw his arm up and gestured around. "For doing this here . . . like this. You must think I'm a total jerk."

"You didn't do it alone. I had something to do with it, too, you know." Even though her part had mostly involved lying there and exercising her vocal cords.

Kyle kissed the corner of her eye, tickling her. "Yeah, but you deserve more. Better."

So the floor was hard and there a lingering smell like her brother's gym shoes back in high school. It had still made her feel like a woman again. Desired.

"It was impulsive and wild and I wouldn't trade that for anything. Not even for candles and champagne and chocolate truffles. It was incredible." She had no regrets, and she sure didn't want him to have any.

"That's true. It was damn incredible."

Sara wasn't sure what was going to happen when they left this room, and she wasn't going to look too far ahead. Instead she was going to savor the moment while it lasted.

She ran her fingers across his rock-solid abdomen. "Wash-board stomach." Goose bumps rose under her touch. "Are you cold, Kyle? I can give you your shirt back."

"Nah, I'm not cold. Besides, then what would you wear? You can't exactly drive home wearing nothing but bathing suit bottoms." Kyle tugged on the bottom of the T-shirt she was wearing. "You know, there's probably some dolphin out there wearing your bikini top, thinking she's hot stuff."

Sara laughed. "Well, I hope she gets good use out of it, it cost eighty bucks."

"Eighty bucks? For a piece of nylon smaller than my thumb?" He pushed her gently into a sitting position and reached for his trunks. "These cost nine ninety-nine."

Sara watched him slip his bathing suit back on and remove her beach bag from behind them. He handed it to her, and she took it with a sigh.

"It's time to go, isn't it?"

"Yeah, I think so." He cupped her cheek with his hand and studied her, caressing his thumb along her bottom lip. "Remember, you said you like dating me. So this isn't over here."

That's what she had said, but she had also been nearly comatose from fabulous sex. She wasn't responsible for what she said under the influence of orgasms.

Sara wasn't sure she wanted to ruin this day, this moment, by seeing Kyle again. What if they went out on a real date and it was awful, or boring, or they had sex again and it was bad? Like yawning, off-rhythm, gee-is-he-done-yet sex? She really didn't want to learn the art of faking a climax.

Trust her to stumble across the only man in Acadia Inlet who didn't just want a roll in the sand with a beach bunny.

"Sara?" Kyle dug into her hair and shook her just a little. "I'm not leaving until I get your number. And I'm going to take you out on a date, then I'm going to make love to you in my bed all night long, with soft sheets and music. You want that, don't you?"

Lord, but he was a nice guy.

She nodded as he brushed across her nipple. No, she'd be lying if she said she didn't want to do this again. And again. She'd take the risk of it turning out bad because she wanted to see if this could go anywhere with Kyle. And truthfully, she didn't believe for one second that sex with Kyle would ever be anything less than phenomenal.

It was fear holding her back, plain and simple, fear that he would lose interest in the real Sara. But she owed it to herself and Kyle to take the chance.

"I'll give you my business card." Sara reached over to where Kyle had neatly piled everything from her bag. She found her wallet and pulled out a card, fingering it a moment before giving it to Kyle.

She bit her lip nervously as he took it, surprise on his face.

So long Sexy Sara.

Kyle didn't know what he expected to see on the thick ivory business card Sara handed to him.

He certainly didn't expect it to read: Premier Pediatrics, Sara Davis, MD.

"You're a *doctor?*" he blurted out in disbelief. He had made wild love on the concrete floor with a *pediatrician?*

"Yes." Sara watched him, straightening her shoulders, like she'd expected his shock.

He'd thought she might be a nurse, but hell, a doctor? He immediately felt like a giant jackass. Sara must be smart, a hell of a lot smarter than him in order to be a doctor. What was she doing screwing him in the lifeguard hut?

His thoughts were so scattered that he said nothing. Sara turned and crawled across the floor on her knees and retrieved her bottoms. The flash of golden thigh brought him back to his senses.

"Wow," he said to her backside. "I'm impressed."

She sat down, and drew the briefs on over her feet, grimacing at their dampness. When she drew them up past her knees, Kyle went hard. He could see her cheeks pressing into the ground and a flash of dark blond curls before the suit covered them.

"Not what you expected, huh?" Sara stood up and went over to her bag, pulling it off the ground and rummaging around putting things back in it.

"Actually I thought you might be a nurse."

"Really? Why?" She looked genuinely surprised.

"When I . . . twisted things." He winced just at the memory. "You didn't panic. You were calm, you took charge."

"Oh." She pulled some rubbery looking tieback out of her bag and twisted her hair up into a big pile and secured it. Then she popped black-framed glasses on her face.

Kyle stared at her, stunned. Glasses? She wore glasses?

"That's better," she said with a sigh. "I was starting to get a headache without my glasses on."

Despite the fact that she was still wearing his T-shirt with no bra and those little red bottoms, she looked completely different. Serious eyes blinked at him behind those glasses. He had no trouble picturing her wearing a skirt and a white doctor's coat.

"I guess we should see if that tree has been cleared."

Kyle just stared at her, speechless. How could one

woman be so sexy and so smart all rolled up in one package? And how could he ever hope to hold her interest? Hell, she must have a dozen guys dying to go out with her every single week. Why would she want him, a lifeguard who was probably responsible for a layer of skin being sloughed off her back from doing it on the fucking floor?

He had forced her to give him her number. She clearly hadn't wanted to. Apparently all she'd wanted was exactly what they'd done. Sex with a stranger.

"Kyle, are you okay?" He didn't look so good to Sara. He looked gray beneath his tan.

"Fine," he said curtly, and bent over to scoop up her sarong. "Here's your skirt thing."

Sara felt her cheeks burn. The air between them had changed the second he had read that business card. Gone was the relaxed protectiveness from Kyle. In its place was remoteness.

She took the sarong from his white-knuckled fingers and stuffed it in her bag. Her sandals were tumbling around in the bottom of the bag, covered in sand and a little damp, but not too bad. She pulled them out and stepped into them, hopping on one foot at a time for balance.

Kyle reached out and held her steady.

And when those warm strong hands held her securely, Sara knew she had made a mistake. She should have listened to Kyle and resisted temptation. She should have gone out on a date with this amazing guy and gotten to know him first.

Because while he was an incredible lover, she could see that he would be an even better boyfriend. Thoughtful. Gentle. Loyal.

And he would never be hers.

Which made her want to kick out her feet, throw back her head, and wail like her little patients did when they got a needle stuck in their leg.

Chapter Six

Sara pulled into the parking lot of her apartment building and breathed a sigh of relief. She only lived a couple of miles from the beach, but it had been a rough
drive. The wind was treacherous, tossing her car back
and forth, and the rain had fallen in torrents, making
visibility difficult.

Kyle had insisted on following her in his SUV, to
make sure she got home all right, and she had to admit,
she was grateful. Just knowing he was behind her helped
her stay calm. Now she threw open the door, stuck her
beach bag over her head, and ran toward him. He was
already getting out of the truck.

"What are you doing?" she yelled, waving him back
into his truck. There was no reason they should both
get soaked.

"I'm walking you in." There was a stubborn set to his
jaw that she was starting to recognize.

"The door's right there. You can watch me go in. I'll
be fine." She had to shout to be heard over the wind,
and rain was sluicing down her legs in icy rivulets.

He shook his head and took her by the elbow, starting toward the door. It wasn't worth it to protest anymore.
Besides, she couldn't see anything through her glasses,

since they were covered in raindrops and a misty fog from the cooling temperature.

Her apartment was on the first floor, and a minute later they were dripping on the beige ceramic tile in her foyer. Sara shivered, removing her glasses. "Yuck. Let me get some towels and I'll start some coffee. It's freezing."

The storm had knocked the temperature down into the low seventies, and Sara reached over behind Kyle's back and turned off her air-conditioning. He didn't say anything, just stood there and dripped.

It was making her uncomfortable. She wanted him to say something, didn't want to leave it like this between them. So she tried to joke, sticking her hands on her hips. "Why is it that when I'm with you I always wind up wet?"

Kyle's lips pressed together, and his eyes went dark right as she realized there could be a different interpretation to that statement. Clearly the one he was making. Her hand clamped over her mouth.

Kyle let go with a grin, enjoying the pink that stained Sara's cheeks. It reminded him of the Sara who had lain beneath him an hour ago, not the efficient Sara who had waved him off in the parking lot. As if he'd just leave her to fend for herself in this kind of weather.

He said, "The rain, sweetie, that's why you're wet. Or did you mean something else?"

"Well." She licked her lips. Her nipples were hard, plastered against the once again soaked T-shirt.

Holding his breath, he waited. In the truck on the ride over, he had decided that whatever Sara wanted to share with him would have to be enough. If she wanted sex and nothing else, he'd find a way to deal with it and hope eventually she'd want more. He just had to keep seeing her, however she wanted, because he had it bad for her.

"I am wet in that other way, too," she said in a whisper.

Hot damn. Kyle clenched his fists and forced himself not to attack her in a fit of lust, no matter how sexy she was. His cock went hard, straining against his swim trunks.

"Oh yeah? Why is that?"

Sara fisted her hands in her shirt and drew it up a little as she rolled on her heels nervously. "I think it's because when two people are dating, they like each other. And they . . . want each other."

This was good. Kyle took a step toward Sara, shaking his head a little to get a water drop off his eyelash. "I want you. Do you want me?"

Her eyes squeezed shut briefly before she said, "Yes."

His heart was racing, but he held himself very still, hanging on to control. "Are we dating then, Sara?"

Hands twisting the T-shirt convulsively, she said, "I wear my glasses all the time."

That statement caught him off guard. Frowning, he said in confusion, "So?"

"I work, I come home . . . I'm very boring, Kyle." A long finger reached up and flicked a rolling raindrop off her cheek.

He bent forward and sucked the droplet off her finger, running his tongue down over her knuckle and back to the tip. Sara gasped.

"I don't find you the least bit boring. And I can't wait to get to know everything about you." He hovered over her finger, wanting to see if she'd pull it out of his reach.

She didn't.

"That is, if you're interested in dating *me.*" Instead of holding his breath or begging, he reached under her shirt and put his hand on her waist. Then he drew her still-wet finger back into his mouth and sucked hard. Give her something to think about before she answered.

"Oh, I am interested." Her hips rocked toward him,

bumping him in the thigh. "And I'm going to have so much fun telling my friends I'm seeing a lifeguard. They'll never believe me."

Kyle took hold of her tiny backside and helped her grind against him, their wet clothes sticking and tugging, frustrating him. "Well, I'm sorry to tell you this, but today was my last day as a lifeguard. I'm going back to school to become an EMT."

Her head snapped up and she laughed, a deep throaty sound that made his testicles tighten. And not from a torsion.

"Hmm, maybe we have more in common than I would have thought." Nails scraped across his back. "You know, I was never the smartest in med school, by any stretch of the imagination, but I worked hard. Good luck with your classes."

He nuzzled her neck, licking along her wet skin, feeling her shiver beneath him. "You can help me study."

Stepping back, he struggled with her wet shirt, yanking and pulling it up, causing a lot of jiggling of her breasts, thighs, and belly. When the shirt finally landed on the floor in a sopping wet heap, he was fighting for breath, deep want for Sara snaking into every inch of his body and making him nuts.

"Of course I can help you study," she said, standing in front of him, firm and golden, damp, with goose bumps on her breasts, nipples a deep pink. "Toxicology?"

That quirky little grin she gave made him growl. He reached for her. "I was thinking more along the lines of anatomy and physiology."

"Oh," Sara said, striving for innocence, but knowing she sounded more eager than anything else. "If you want, we can get started with all the major muscles. In a warm shower."

Kyle's hand on her behind squeezed harder. "I think I'm going to like dating a smart woman. You have such good ideas."

Sara certainly anticipated a great deal of her own pleasure in dating a large, blond, courageous, and caring ex-lifeguard. "I have other ideas, too."

Involving a very thorough examination of his muscular body.

He groaned, then kissed her forehead, then her nose, then her chin, brushing past her lips. "You're so beautiful, and I'm really damn grateful for unreliable bikini straps."

Sara laughed, knowing she'd gotten way more than she'd ever expected when she'd stuck her sandaled foot on that beach.

"Now, let's get in that shower," Kyle said, tilting his head toward the hall. "And I'll touch and you teach."

Feeling Sexy Sara rejuvenating within her, she warned, "It could take hours."

His green eyes darkened. "I'm very dedicated."

Then he kissed her, and Sara forgot that she ever knew a thing.

MY THIEF

MaryJanice
Davidson

*For Ethan Ellenberg, who fearlessly bats for me,
and for MT, who fearlessly reads rough drafts.*

Chapter One

John strode out of the elevator, shifting his suit bag from one shoulder to the other to dig out his key card. He related to Richard Gere's character in *Pretty Woman* . . . he missed keys. Not that he ever watched girly movies like that. Well, hardly ever.

He stopped outside this week's home-away-from-home, Room 666 . . . hmm, not *too* disturbing. Not that he ever watched cheesy horror movies like *The Omen*. Well, hardly ever.

As he slipped his key card into the slot, the door was thrown open and an arm snaked out and dragged him inside.

He dropped his suit bag, ready to rumble, then realized the arm was attached to a woman. A stunning, red-headed, blue-eyed woman with prodigious freckles.

"Strip," she ordered.

He thought that over. Naw. He must have misunderstood. She'd probably said something like, "You're in the wrong room, dicklick," and in his shock he'd misheard her, which was perfectly understandable because—

"Dude! My lips are moving, can't you see 'em? I said strip."

"What?"

"Strip. Undress. Take. Off. Your. Clothes." He noticed

with surprise bordering on alarm that her own clothes were flying off her as she spoke. "Do I have to write it on my forehead?"

As more and more creamy skin was exposed, alarm changed to something else. And speaking of something else, she certainly was. Her hair was shoulder-length and curly, bouncing around with a life of its own. The shades were drawn and the lights were out, and her glorious hair was the brightest thing in the room. It looked like coals banked for the night. Her limbs were long and slender, and she had the cutest little belly, which rounded out slightly above the darker red thatch between her—

"Jeez, all right, I'll help you," she said, clearly annoyed at his slothfulness. "Don't take this the wrong way, but did you take a special bus to high school? A *short* bus?"

"What?"

"Never mind." Then her hands were on him, pulling his jacket off, loosening his tie with nimble fingers, tugging his shirt.

"All right, all right," he said mildly, but he didn't feel mild. She was stunning. It wasn't so much her looks, which were very fine. He had never met a woman who possessed more natural charisma in his entire life. She fairly vibrated with life. And impatience.

Clearly pleased to see he was finally getting with the program, she bounded over to the bed, yanked the covers back—he was treated to a flash of a creamy white bottom—and then was as snug in his bed as a redheaded bug.

Nude, he followed her, sliding between the sheets and wondering exactly what the hell to do now. "They really take this hospitality suite thing seriously," he said.

Then he said, "Mmmff!" because she had grabbed him by the ears and was kissing his socks off. If he had still been wearing any. Which he certainly wasn't.

His arms slipped around her, drawing her closer, relishing the silky skin of her back. Her breasts flattened against his chest and his hands slid lower, caressing the fine globes of her butt. Her tongue snaked inside his mouth and he nearly groaned.

Bam! Bam! Bam!

"Oh, here we go," she mumbled into his mouth.

"That's the spirit," he mumbled back.

Bam! Bam! Bam!

"Go away!" they shouted in unison.

"Hotel security! Open up in there!"

Chapter Two

She pulled back from his embrace and peered into his eyes. John waited for a breathless declaration of love. "Hmmm, that's not quite right," she said, then reached out and mussed his hair.

"Stop that," he protested. "It took me hours to get it just right. Also, why is hotel security after you?"

She didn't answer. Just stood up, bent over, mussed her own hair, flung her head back, grinned at his gasp of appreciation, then grabbed the comforter and slung it over her shoulders.

She marched to the door and opened it. *"Whaaat?"* she whined. "Can't you see we're busy?"

Two men peered past her, and John at once realized what they thought they were seeing: a barely clad redhead, an unclad John, lights out, shades drawn, and an air of musk and impatience pervading the room.

The smaller man, dressed in a blue suit, shirt, and tie that made him look embalmed, rubbed his hands together. John could hear the rasping sound all the way across the room. "Sorry—so sorry—there's been—that is to say—"

The taller man shouldered him aside. "I'm Ron Wilde, hotel detective. This is the hotel manager, Ken."

"Pleased—very pleased—"

"Someone cracked one of the safety deposit boxes downstairs. You haven't seen anything unusual, have you?"

"She's a natural redhead," John volunteered. "I'm not quite sure if that's what one would consider unusual, but—"

"You hush," the redhead said, but she was smirking. "Gentlemen, if you *don't mind . . .*"

"Terribly sorry—never meant to disturb—" The rasping was coming faster. If Kenny boy didn't get some lotion on those hands, he was going up in flames from pure friction.

" 'Bye," Red said pointedly, starting to swing the door shut. The detective stuck his foot out, and the door stopped.

He fished around in his jacket—dark brown, which almost exactly matched his hair and eyes—and finally extracted a card. He handed it to Red with a leer. "If you need anything *else,* just give me a buzz."

John bristled. The punk was coming on to his would-be fake girlfriend! He thought about grabbing the suit by the lapels and tossing him into the tub, or possibly out the window, but then Red slammed the door and they were alone again.

She flung off the comforter like a titian-haired Wonder Woman and, he noticed with total dismay, began dressing as rapidly as she had undressed.

She slid into her jeans, shrugged into her T-shirt ("Come Along Quietly"), then stepped into her sandals. She dug into her pocket, pulled out a rubber band, and efficiently tamed her vibrant hair into a ponytail. As an afterthought, she kicked the comforter in the general direction of the bed.

"Thanks tons, doll," she said, sketching a salute. "It's been great working with you."

Three steps to the door, and she was gone.

Gone?

Not fucking likely.

Chapter Three

John bounded out of the bed and caught up with her just as she was stepping into the stairwell. "Wait!" he said, and she turned around in surprise. Then her gaze dropped to his groin and she grinned. "I don't even know your name."

"So?"

"Where are you going?"

"MYOB, pal."

"I don't know that club."

"Very funny. Seriously, thanks for helping me out and all, but I have to run. And dude . . . you need to get dressed. Not that *I* mind. But still. Public hotel and all that."

"It's too bad," he said regretfully. He leaned casually against the doorframe. Then jerked upright—the metal frame was *cold.* "You could have stayed in my room as long as you liked. Now, of course, I'll have to call the house detective and let him know you're on your way down."

She glared at him, her eyes slits of laser blue. "Blackmailer."

"Actually, I'm an accountant."

"Yech! Even worse."

"Oh, come on," he coaxed. "Whatever's going on, it's

obviously too hot for you to leave right now. Why not come back to the room for a while? Frankly, I'm dying to hear all about it."

"Why?" she asked suspiciously.

"Because I'm an accountant in town for a convention. What *else* am I going to do?"

"Good point." She nibbled on her lower lip, which instantly made him want to do the same thing. "Well . . . I s'pose you're right. I mean, it'll be tough getting out of here for a while. And you did help me out . . . and kept your mouth shut when Frick and Frack came knocking."

He snorted at Frick and Frack, then shrugged modestly.

"All right," she decided. He was so relieved he nearly toppled down the stairwell. "I'll come back. For a while. But you *really* have to put some clothes on."

"Why?" he asked, escorting her back to lucky Room 666. "You've seen it before."

"Yeah, but . . . do you, like, work out every day or what? I've seen bodybuilders in worse shape. Seriously. Clothes. First thing."

They stopped outside his room and he smacked himself on the forehead. "Dammit! I was in such a rush to get you, I forgot the keycard."

She smirked at him and ran his card through the slot. "Grabbed it from your pants on the way out," she said.

"You keep your hands out of my pants."

"Oh, like you really minded five minutes ago."

"Irrelevant."

"Besides, I didn't know if it'd come in handy later."

"You are an unregenerate pickpocket."

"Whatever you say, pal. But your wing-wang isn't wagging out in the hallway anymore, thanks to me."

He'd have liked to strike up a strenuous argument to refute this point, save for the annoying fact that she was right. "That's not going to be your pet name for it, is it? Wing-wang?"

"We'll see," she said mysteriously, and practically shoved him inside.

Chapter Four

"Mmm nnn'd eeel eeeeg," she said with her mouth full.

"What?"

She chewed and swallowed. "I *said*, I didn't steal anything."

"That's nice. Back up." She was still dressed, and gorging herself on room-service chicken, gravy, mashed potatoes, broccoli, and chocolate milk. Sadly, she had not instantly disrobed after room service had come and gone.

He was wearing the standard-issue lux-hotel white terrycloth robe, sitting on the bed and watching her. He was hungry, but not for food. "What is your name?"

"Oh. Didn't I tell you? Sorry." She stuck out a hand, shiny with chicken grease. He shook it gingerly. "Robin Filkins."

"And the girl named 'Robin' didn't steal anything."

"Har-har. And nope. How can you steal your own property?"

"Lots of ways. Why don't you start at the beginning?"

"How about, not?"

"Why don't you want to tell me? An unburdened conscience is a light one."

"Who talks like that? And to answer your question, because it's none of your business?" she guessed.

"You involved me," he explained patiently. "You made me your alibi. At the least, you owe me an explanation." He eyed the gorgeous mounds under her T-shirt. "Or, barring that—"

"Simmer down, El Horno. I'll cough up the scoop."

"Only if you promise to stop mixing your metaphors. And to never call me that again."

"Hey, a bird in the hand is worth a pig in a poke." She laughed and a few red curls escaped her ponytail and bounced around her face. "Besides, don't get uppity with me. You never told me your name, either."

"It's not like you gave me time for civilized conversation."

"I didn't hear any complaints, pal." She smirked.

She was really quite something—shameless, funny, blunt. He itched to touch the curls framing her face, to see if they felt as silky soft as they looked. "Point taken. It's John Crusher."

"Seriously?"

"Sounds like a professional wrestler, doesn't it?"

She gnawed on a chicken leg. "I bet all the other accounting weenies are terrified of you."

"Actually, I'm a freelancer with my own business, and rarely run into other accounting weenies. So, you were going to explain your curious yet refreshing actions of the last hour . . . ?"

"I was? Oh, right. I was. In a nutshell: cracked my uncle's safety deposit box. Got my property back. Took off. Cracked the first door I found on the highest floor. Jumped your bones—temporarily. The end."

"Why my room?"

"Cracked the hotel reservation system *first*—you weren't supposed to check in until tonight, Early Boy."

"You're quite right," he said, surprised. "I caught an earlier flight."

"Yeah, and thanks for nothing. I go to all that trouble to lift a universal housekeeping card, and *you* show up early. I just about dropped my panties when I heard your key card rattling in the slot!"

"If memory serves, you *did* drop your—"

"Yeah, yeah. Anyway, figured I'd hang out here for a couple hours until the heat was off, then slip out the back. This was, of course, totally foiled when you showed up. Although I must give you snaps for your cooperation."

"Cooperation," he said dryly, "is my middle name. And you're welcome to stay here as long as you like. We can be—"

"Mr. and Mrs. Crusher?" she teased.

"Something like that. But I do insist on knowing exactly what you st—uh, got back."

"Why?"

"Overreaching curiosity. I'm taking a survey. Pick a reason." He frowned. "It wasn't a gun or something, was it? Because if that's the case, I'll toss you right out on your pretty behind."

"Hey, I do have *some* scruples, pal. And no, it wasn't a gun. It was—"

"Open up in there!"

They both jerked around at the sound. "Never a dull moment around here," he said, starting to recover from his heart attack. "What now?"

Chapter Five

Robin grabbed Studboy's arm just as he reached for the doorknob. And nearly dropped his arm in surprise—solid as a rock. It was like grabbing a two-by-four. The guy probably bench-pressed small automobiles to stay in shape. "You know, just because they tell you to open up, doesn't actually mean you *have to open the door.* Ever watch any movies?"

"I'm a slave to direct commands." But he took a moment and peeked through the peephole, at least. "Hmm. The manager's back, but the detective isn't with him. I don't recognize the gentleman who is."

She started to get a nasty suspicion. "Move over. Let me see." She peeked. As if he knew he was being watched, the taller man waggled his fingers at the door in a cheerful wave.

Dammit! It was that crook, that conniver, that blight on society, Uncle Rich.

Enraged, she jerked the door open. "Cheat!" she hollered as the manager cowered away from her. "This is a total cheat! Game over!"

"Fine, thanks, and how've you been?" Uncle Rich shot his cuffs—he was impeccably dressed, as usual—and smiled at her. "Besides, I'm here to concede. This round's yours."

"Oh." That was an entirely different story. "Ha! I mean, thanks for coming up."

"I don't understand," the manager said. "You're saying she has your property—"

"It's *my* property," Robin interrupted.

"—but it's no longer a problem?"

"Oh, it is, but for now, we're calling a truce. It's a long, dull story and I'm sure you have many duties to attend to." Rich shook the guy's hand and Robin saw the fifty-dollar bill disappear. Masterful! Every time she tried that, the bill either stuck to her sleeve or fluttered to the floor. "Thanks for your help."

With that, he stepped into John's room and shut the door in the manager's bewildered face.

"Nice robe," he said politely to Studboy.

"Nice scam," Studboy said back, just as politely.

When Rich poked her, Robin remembered herself. "Oh, right. Uncle Rich, this is St—uh, John Crusher. John, this is my uncle, Rich Calque."

"Robin and Rich. Hmm. Well, it's nice to meet you."

"How did you get past all the employees to crack the right safe deposit box?" Rich burst out. She nearly chortled as he continued. "And how'd you know which one was the right one? And how'd you avoid—" He eyed John in his robe. "Never mind, I figured that one out on my own."

"Uncle Rich, you know I can't divulge gory details. That'd be cheating."

"And I'm sure you two paragons of morality have a horror of cheating," John said dryly.

"You hush up. Uncle Rich, you know the rules: we get it however we can, whenever we can. Drawn out confessions aren't part of the game."

"Listen here, young lady, I taught you everything you know—"

"And my dad taught me the rest. And one of the things he drummed into me was that thieves are like magicians . . ."

". . . you never tell them how you did it," Rich finished. "She's quoting my own brother at me! Niece, who do you think taught *him?*"

"I'm confused," John said. "But then, I've been that way since I checked in."

Rich wandered over to the chair in the corner, glanced over his pleats, and sat down. Robin knew he meant to look vague and well-to-do. That was about half right. "Oh, it's this silly little game my niece and I have been playing for . . . uh . . ."

"Ten years."

"Right. She steals from me, I steal from her. It's the only way we could agree on who got to keep it."

"Keep *what?*"

"This," Robin said, handing the small blue velvet bag to John.

"Really, Robin, you're getting too good at this," Rich complained while John gingerly felt the bag. Robin almost laughed; John looked like he was expecting anything—a mousetrap, a rattlesnake. "I'd barely moved the thing to this hotel and you snatched it away."

"Cry me a river, old man."

"This bag," John announced, "is empty."

"Yeah, that's right, it's—*what?*"

"Of course"—Uncle Rich coughed—"I know a few tricks myself."

For a minute Robin thought she'd popped a blood vessel—everything was red—but then realized the only thing that had broken was her ponytail holder, and her hair was in her face. Then she leaped for Rich and actually managed to get her hands around his neck before Studboy pulled her off.

"You miserable, crooked, lying, shifty—"

"Darling niece!" He brushed himself off. "You nearly mussed my shirt. This thing was over two hundred bucks at Harrod's."

"—two-faced, lying, slippery, tricky, sneaky—"

"And," he added smugly, "you're a sore loser."

"—lying . . . lying . . ." She was winding down; there wasn't another thing to say! She was sure there were several more odious adjectives to describe her father's older brother, but damned if she could think of any. "You'll pay, old man. Through the nose."

Uncle Rich rested his index finger along said elegantly pointed nose. "No doubt. But not this minute." His eyebrows arched. "Dinner?"

"I'd rather eat my own puke."

"Rain check, then."

"I think it's time you bid a fond *adieu,*" John said. "You've upset my guest."

"Damn right! But it's no good, he won't leave until he's ready—whoa."

Studboy—rats, she was really going to have to stop calling him that—had somehow gotten Rich into a vise-like grip and was propelling him across the room. They were the same height, but Rich's toes were practically skimming the ground.

"The suit, watch the *suit,*" Rich yelped.

John yanked the door open and paused in the midst of tossing her uncle out like a drunk in a bar. "I suppose searching him's no good."

"Don't you dare! I'm extremely ticklish."

Robin shook her head. "It's long gone from here. But thanks for the offer."

"You have a nice day now," John said, and gave her uncle a firm shove into the hallway. "Good-bye."

He shut the door, then shot the deadbolt for good measure.

"That was impressive," she commented.

"You should see me during an internal audit."

"I'm sure. Dammit!" Robin threw herself facedown on the king-sized bed. "Now I have to steal it back. How, *how* could he have gotten it back so *fast*? It took me six days to figure out a plan, and he got it back in six minutes. How?" Then she rolled over and glared at John. "Unless you're in on it?"

"Don't go all annoying and paranoid on me now. More so, I mean," he amended. "I never laid eyes on your uncle before twenty minutes ago. And we both know exactly when I laid eyes, so to speak, on *you.*"

She glared at him for another long moment, then stopped. He was right; it was too absurd. Uncle Rich was slippery, that was all. She ought to know. He'd practically raised her. Or she'd raised him—sometimes it was hard to remember.

"Well, now I've got to get it back. I've got to!"

"The family honor is at stake?" he guessed.

"No, *mine.*" She slapped her fist into her palm. "He's not getting away with this. Again, I mean. I'll get him back. I'll get *it* back. Then we'll see who has the last laugh and the bird in the hand! Ho ho! Vengeance will be mine, *mine!* D'you mind if I stay here for a day or two?"

He blinked at the abrupt tone change. "Consider this your base of operations. But only if you stop mixing metaphors. I'm begging you."

She rolled over and looked up at him. The robe came to his knees, revealing splendidly muscled calves sprinkled with dark hair. Loosely belted, it gave tantalizing glimpses of his broad, lightly furred chest and masculine throat. He was staring down at her with eyes the color of Godiva milk chocolate. His dark brown hair stood up in thick spikes, well mussed from all that had already transpired, and stubble bloomed along his jaw. Yum. And again, yum. Snuggling between the sheets had definitely been the high point of her month—even more fun than snatching from Uncle Rich! And *that* was saying something.

"—plan of action?"

"What? Sorry. Man, you are *sooo* good-looking. How come you're not married?"

"All my girlfriends have been strictly law-abiding. Tiresome, don't you know. And thank you. You're something of a knockout yourself. Not to mention direct. It's disconcerting, yet refreshing. If you don't mind a personal question—"

"Fire away. We're a little beyond secret-keeping, I think."

"—what happened to your folks?"

"My mom left right after I was born. Uncle Rich always said having a red-haired baby freaked her out. He was only kidding, though," she added at the appalled look on John's face. "And Dad was in and out of jail most of my childhood. He died when I was in high school. Uncle Rich raised me. I love that slimy, slippery, crooked son of a bitch," she sighed. "He's my only family, the rat bastard."

"There, there," he said, sitting beside her on the bed and patting her knee. Then, "That's it. There, there. That's all I've got."

She sniffed and gave him a friendly shove, but he held on and they both toppled back on the bed. She stroked the stubbly skin on his jaw and said, without looking at him, "Thanks for helping me."

"Thanks for being . . . different."

"That's, like, the lamest compliment ever."

"Thanks for not stealing my wallet? Yet?"

"A little better," she said grudgingly.

Chapter Six

"Have you ever thought about opening safes and, uh, what's the word you use . . . ?"

"Cracking."

"Right. Ever thought about doing that for the police? They need those services all the time. Did you ever see *The Italian Job*? You could do stuff like that."

She was lying on top of him, her elbows propped up on his chest, her chin resting on her fists. Her knees were on his thighs, her feet in the air, waving gently back and forth. She peered down at him with those blue, blue eyes and said, "I can't say the idea ever crossed my mind. Also, I saw the original. The remake sucked."

"It did not. Mark Wahlburg is the finest actor of his generation. And anyway, what do you do when you're not chasing your uncle across the country to steal what he just stole from you?"

"Nothing. This is what I do. Well, sometimes I enter marathons."

"How, uh, completely unfulfilling. Not the marathon part. How do you live?"

"My dad left me a trust."

"Out of ill-gotten gains, I'll bet."

"That, and his Army pension."

"Your dad was in the—never mind, one stunner at a

time. So this is it? You're like a female Leonardo di Caprio in *Catch Me if You Can?*"

"Sometimes Uncle Rich is Leo," she pointed out.

"And this is what you do, and this is what Rich does."

"Yes."

"College?"

"Why? I could crack the school's computer and award myself a BA anytime I want."

He put a forearm across his eyes. "So, were you born without a conscience, or did it drain away slowly and gradually?"

She poked him in the ribs. "Let's just say I had an eventful adolescence and leave it at that."

"Followed by an eventful adulthood. The mind reels."

"Norman Rockwell, we weren't," she said cheerfully. "That's all right. I've got the most interesting life of anyone I know. That's always been good enough for me."

"'Interesting' being your euphemism for 'larcenous.' "

She smiled. "Well, yeah."

"So, what's your plan? How are you going to get it—whatever it is—back from Rich?"

"I don't know," she said. "But I'll tell you what helps me think. A good wrestle in the sheets."

"What a coincidence," he said, cupping the curve of her skull in his hands. "That helps me think, too." Then he pulled her down for a long kiss.

"Mmmm," she said when he broke the kiss to nibble on her chin. "I've been thinking about *that* since I jumped into your bed a few hours ago."

"What a coincidence," he said again.

"Besides, we owe it to ourselves to get it out of the way." While she talked, she was tugging at the belt of his robe. "The sex part, I mean. Then we'll be able to think."

"I totally agree."

"Okay, then."

He pulled at her shirt, tugged at her jeans, and in a few minutes they were rolling around in his bed, tickling and wrestling. Her limbs were sleekly muscled, and there was that charming belly again, gently curving above the fiery thatch between her legs. It was a true relief to be with a woman who wasn't skin and bones—Robin had substance. In more ways than one.

He felt her fingers close around his throbbing length and nearly groaned aloud. He should have known she'd have a nimble grip, given what she did for a living, but this went beyond nimble—it was more like heaven on earth. Her thumb stroked his now slippery tip, and her other hand cuddled his balls, gently testing their weight.

He buried his face in her cleavage, trailed kisses across her breasts, and sucked on her impudent pink nipples. He felt her gasp beneath him, felt her small tongue dart into the cup of his ear, heard her whisper, "Harder."

He bit, very lightly, and sucked harder, and gloried in the feast her body was providing—she was all candy-studded cream, all roses and pale skin. And her hair—once again it was the brightest thing in the room, and he could see strands of copper mixed with all the auburn.

He felt her heels press into his back, drawing him closer, felt her mouth open beneath his like a flower, and oh, he was an instant away from burying himself inside her, an instant from the exquisite—

"Wait," he managed.

"It's all right," she said, almost gasped. "I'm on the Pill. And I'm going to assume you're not riddled with disease."

He nearly snorted. "Hardly. I—is it—it's not too soon, is it? I don't want to hurt—"

She was pressing him closer and wriggling beneath him to good effect; he grabbed the corner of the pillow in an effort to hang on to the bare shreds of his control. Had he thought she was like a force of nature? He hadn't known the half of it.

"You're sweet," she said, "but I've been ready for ages. Since the minute you walked in the room, frankly."

"Thank God." He parted her with his fingers, relishing the feel of her slick folds, then entered her with one thrust.

She threw her head back and groaned at the ceiling. "Oh, jeez, that's *really* good. Don't stop."

"As if I could," he panted. Her arms were around his neck in a stranglehold and he didn't mind at all. Being inside her was like being inside a dream—the best dream of his life. "Oh, that's nice. That's . . ."

She pumped back at him, levering her hips to meet his thrusts, and he buried his face in the soft fire of her hair and tried to think about baseball. Unix. Zero-based budgetry. Anything but how close he was.

"Harder," she husked, and he obliged, and the headboard slammed against the wall, keeping their beat. "Oh, jeez, that's—that's going to do it . . ."

He felt her tighten around him, actually felt her get warmer for a moment, and then she was writhing beneath him, her eyes looking straight through him as she found what she needed. That was enough for him, as well; he felt himself tip dizzily over the edge, and came so hard the room went dark around the edges for a moment.

"Wow."

"That's it, huh?"

"Well, that's one for the diary, anyway."

He laughed, and brushed her sweaty curls out of her face. "Terrific. I can see the entry now. 'Dear diary, today I broke into a room that wasn't mine—after committing grand theft—and seduced a stranger.' "

"Uh-uh, pal. You seduced *me.*"

"What?"

"Well, you did! It's your own fault, being so cute and all."

"Well," he said modestly, "that's true."

She bopped him lightly in the ribs. "Conceited creep."

"That's also true."

She yawned against his neck, and he cuddled her closer for a moment. Then he asked, "Well, now that we have, as you so quaintly put it, the sex thing out of the way—"

"Um, I dunno, there might be some remnants . . ."

"—do you have any ideas?"

"Actually," she admitted, "I was thinking it'd be nice to do the sex thing again. That's about as far as I got."

He snorted. "I'm thirty-eight, sunshine. I'll need a few minutes at least."

"Ancient! God, you're practically decrepit."

"Oh, that's nice. How old are you?"

"Twenty-six."

"Great. On top of everything else today—including missing my conference—I've robbed the cradle."

"Good. Serves you right. I should be stealing something right this minute, but instead I'm obsessing over your dick."

"Progress."

"Sure," she said, and laughed.

Chapter Seven

John left, at Robin's insistence. She wanted a nap, and to regroup. He should use the opportunity to "catch a seminar, or whatever it is you were going to do this weekend." Funny how being kicked out of his own room didn't bother him. If she wanted to rest, it was completely fine with him. She'd earned it.

But what did "regroup" mean, and how many laws would be fractured while she did it?

He strolled through the lobby, wondering exactly how a citizen's arrest was performed, and if the participants had to be naked, when he spotted a small placard propped outside a conference room. THE CHICAGO MARRIOTT WELCOMES THE NSA!

Ah, the NSA . . . the National Society of Accountants. His herd. Was that right? What did one call a group of accountants? A herd? A calculus? An audit?

He sidled closer; they hadn't shut the doors to the conference room yet and he could hear the keynote speaker. There were at least a hundred suits in the room—literal suits; from where he was standing, they were a sea of black and gray shoulders.

It was funny—he should be one of the suits. He certainly had the wardrobe for it. There was plenty of time; he hadn't missed much. And he'd paid over six hundred dollars of his own money to attend. It was one of the disads of owning his own company—stuff like this came right out of his pocket. The six hundred big ones didn't even count the hotel room he was sharing with Robin.

Ah . . . Robin. It was all her fault. It was tough to get excited about ASO management roundtables and earning sixteen hours of CPE credit when he'd just rolled around in the sheets with a charming, larcenous redhead. A woman utterly unlike anyone he'd ever met. A woman he'd known less than a day, and yet, couldn't get out of his head. Always before, he'd bedded them and been done with them, but Robin was different. He was beginning to appreciate just how different—

"Mr. Crusher."

He nearly walked into a pillar. There was the dreaded Uncle Rich, looking like a benign southern gentleman. Tan suit, closely trimmed salt-and-pepper beard, dark hair shot with skeins of pure white. Blue eyes—Robin's eyes.

"You look like you're waiting for someone," John observed.

"Not at all." Rich shoved a chair out with his foot. "Why don't you sit down in this handy chair, talk a bit with an old man?"

"You're almost as terrifying," he said, taking the proffered seat, "as your niece."

"Oh, stop it," Rich said modestly. "She's *much* scarier than I am. You're missing your conference."

John looked over Rich's head to the conference room doors, which were now swinging shut. Odd, to be on *this* side of the doors. Odder, he didn't mind. "Yes, I—I was just thinking that."

"Well, they'll have another one next year."

"Yup."

"A charming young lady, my niece."

"I'll go along with that."

"But lonely."

"It's not fatal. You don't die from it."

Rich's eyes actually twinkled—twinkled! The man was able to do something with his face, with his laughing blue eyes, which made him look lovable and roguish. It was uncanny. Suddenly John had to fight the urge to hand over his wallet. "Ah, you know a bit about that condition yourself. It's no wonder you found each other."

"Uh . . . she sort of found me. And by 'found,' I mean—"

"I'm familiar with her *modus operendi.*"

"How do you do that thing with your eyes?" he asked, unable to resist. "You must have zero trouble bilking people out of millions."

"John, I'm hurt!" The hell of it was, the guy *sounded* hurt. *Looked* hurt. "I've been waiting down here for some time hoping to have a nice chat with you."

"Spinning your web like a spider waiting for a big fat bug . . ." he prompted.

"Oh, now you've been listening to my niece's side of things," Rich said reproachfully.

"How did you get it back so quickly? And what is *it?*"

Rich waved the questions away. "Something that belonged to my brother. He died without a will, and there were some . . . problems . . . with property disbursement. So I decided to keep the item in question until Robin came of age. She disagreed, and stole it. I stole it back. And so on. And so on. And now I look around, and ten years have gone by."

"That's some screwed-up family you've got there," John said, not unkindly.

"You're right, and wishing things were different doesn't help. But sometimes . . . sometimes new players come to the game. And things can change."

"I'm not a player," John said, astonished. "I'm an accountant."

"And thus, the crookedest of us all."

"I'd like to be able to kick your ass for that," he admitted, "except a glance at the headlines will prove your point, and so I'm just going to sit here and sulk for a few minutes and pretend things like Enron didn't wreck my industry's credibility."

"As you wish. Would you like a drink while you sulk?"

The question was so solicitous, John laughed in spite of himself. "Yeah. Let's see, what's ridiculously expensive . . . ? I'll have a shot of Dewar's over ice."

"Ice in your glass . . . barbarian." Rich grumbled, but waved the concierge over, and in another couple of minutes, John was sipping Dewar's. Neat.

"Control freak SOB," he mumbled into his glass.

"But isn't it much nicer without ice water diluting the taste?"

"It's like drinking room-temperature piss," John said politely. "But thank you anyway."

"Arrogant pup." Rich coughed into his fist.

"I heard that. You're about as subtle as a brick to the temporal lobe."

"Getting back to Robin—"

"Oh, were we?"

"—do you have any idea how often she's hooked up with a gentleman during our country-wide jaunts?"

"We haven't had much time for get-acquainted chitchat."

Rich put his thumb and index finger together, forming an *O*. "Zero times. Cracking has been her life—to my sorrow."

"What? According to her, you raised her after her father—"

"Yes, and I did a damned poor job of it," Rich snapped. "Brought her up to be a no-good thief like me, like her old man—what the *hell* was I thinking? That I didn't know how else to do it," he said to his lap, answering his own question. Then he looked back up at John. There was no friendly twinkle in those blue eyes now. "So here we are, an old man and a woman in her prime, and she thinks this is *normal*. And so it is, for her. But she also stole you, and that's interesting, isn't it?"

"Stole me?" He had to grin; the mental image was just too delicious. Still, it wasn't an entirely inappropriate observation. "Is that what she did?"

"The question is, what next?"

"Uh . . . she's going to steal it back. Whatever it is. And then . . ."

Rich waved that away impatiently. "And then, and then . . . too right, and then another ten years have gone by. No, it's enough. I've made too many mistakes. But there might be enough time. It's the one thing you can't steal, you know."

"No, I didn't know, and this is the oddest conversation I've ever had. And that's saying something, because I've also chatted with your niece. Which is why I'm not in there," he said, jerking his head toward the closed conference room doors. "It's quite a bit more interesting out *here*."

"That's telling, you know."

"So you're—what? Putting an end to it? This life? Why now? Why this time?"

Rich gave him a look. "Well, now there's you, isn't there?"

"What does *that* have to—"

Rich stood, and John rose, as well. "It's been enlightening," he said, and to John's surprise, the older man stepped forward and hugged him.

"Uh . . ." John extricated himself. "I guess we're going to have the 'personal space' discussion now . . ."

"No need," Rich said cheerfully, and walked away.

With my drink in his hand, John noticed about six seconds too late.

Damn! How did he *do* that?

Chapter Eight

Robin sat up as soon as he walked into the room, and bounced excitedly on the bed when she saw him. He couldn't help it; just seeing her made him smile.

"Finally!"

"I've been gone less than half an hour," he pointed out.

"Tell me about it. It's *soooooo* boring in here without you."

"You kicked me out, remember?" He grinned. "Now stop it, I'm getting misty. Even more alarming, I ran into your uncle downstairs."

"Check your wallet," she said immediately. "Do you have all your credit cards? Missing any cash? Limbs? Organs?"

"No, it wasn't like that. And I checked in the elevator—nothing's missing. We had—actually, we had a very *weird* talk, but it was nice. Interesting, anyway. He seems fond of you."

She shrugged and toyed with the sash of her robe.

"And he seems like he has regrets. With, ah, with regard to your childhood."

Her eyebrows arched, reddish gold feelers against her pale skin. "Yeah, he gets like that once in a while."

" 'Like that'?"

"You know, the whole 'woe is me, shouldn't have raised her to be a crook, bad, bad' thing. But he's never told a stranger about it." She stared at him thoughtfully. "That's kind of weird."

"It's a weekend for change, it seems," he said cheerfully. "Also, he walked off with my drink."

"A true bastard," she said, then ruined her scowl by giggling.

"Well, he is. So, in an awkward yet endearing attempt to change the subject, are you wearing anything under my robe?"

"There's only one way to find out," she said primly, then rolled over, lithe as a cat, and crawled toward him. "Let's get that suit coat off—jeez, how many layers are you wearing? Are you aware that it's ninety degrees outside? Are these *wool* pants?"

"It's fifty in the hotel lobby," he retorted. "Don't pull—I have no intention of spending the evening sewing buttons back on." He shrugged out of the jacket and tossed it carelessly over a nearby chair. "Now where—"

They both heard the tiny *clink* at the same time, and looked. The chair was in the kitchenette part of the suite, resting on tile, and the *clink* had been the sound of a small gold ring hitting the floor.

"What the hell . . . ?" Robin bounded off the bed and crossed the floor in half a second. "That's *it!* And you've got it!"

"What, *it* it? As in, the it you've been stealing? *That's* it?" He stared. "But . . . it's so small. It's just a gold band. You probably couldn't get fifty dollars for it in a pawnshop. And you've been stealing it back and forth for a decade?"

She scooped the ring off the floor and locked it in her small fist. Her eyes were narrowed, furious. She was pale with rage. "It's my father's wedding band. And *you* . . . "

John remembered the hug, remembered thinking it

was an odd move for a man like Rich to make. Not so odd if you wanted to plant something . . . "Wait, Robin, it's not what you—"

The ring, within her fist, looped toward his face. There was a bright flash, and then there wasn't anything.

Chapter Nine

"You crooked, slippery, sneaky, willful, stubborn *bastard!*"

"And my niece will be joining me," Rich told the waiter without missing a beat. "Could you bring her a strawberry daiquiri, please? Nice robe," he added as she sat down across from him.

"You think you're so smart," she said bitterly. "Pulling a new guy into this. Getting him to trick me. Giving him *my father's ring.*"

Rich rubbed his temples. "Please don't shout. I was up rather late last night entertaining in my suite, and the bourbon flowed like wine. And what are you talking about, getting him to trick you?"

"Don't play games, Richard. Not now. I . . . I really liked him and you had to go ahead and ruin it."

"Oh, Robin. What did you do?"

"Left cross," she admitted.

He slapped his forehead. Then he leaned across the table and slapped her forehead.

"Ow!"

"Serves you right, and if I were younger, you'd get worse. Where's your brain, Niece? Of *course* John Crusher isn't involved. What use is a goody-goody accountant to me? I've got all the crooked ones I need on the payroll."

"Well, then how—"

"Use your head. I slipped him your dad's ring when he was still trying to decide if I was making a pass at him."

"But that means—"

"You just made a humongous ass of yourself."

She sniffed, and when the waiter brought her drink, took a gulp. "I think *humongous* is a bit harsh," she muttered, then chomped on her strawberry garnish.

"Robin, Robin . . . you're screwing up all my perfectly laid plans. As usual. Do you know how long I had to sit in that freezing lobby until your boytoy wandered by? And then you go and leap to the wrong conclusion and coldcock him—in his own hotel room!"

"I thought he was on your side," she whined. "I thought he'd used me. And you, you rotten old puppet master, the last thing I need is for you to be interfering in my life, pulling strings—"

"Well, someone's got to pull your head out of your ass," he snapped back. "This all started because you didn't want to leave your father's ring in my keeping. In other words, ten years of silliness because you couldn't trust the one man in your life. Now there's a new one, and you don't trust him, either."

"Wllalleavenyway," she muttered.

"What was that?"

"I said, well, you all leave anyway." She glared at him defiantly, then dropped her eyes.

He sat back in his chair and studied her, with that keen regard she both loved and hated because it missed nothing. "Ah," he said after a long moment. "So that's how it is."

"That's how it is."

"Your father didn't *leave*, darling."

"Well, he's not here having drinks, is he?" she bitched.

"He went out kicking and screaming, and you damned well know it. He was still walking around when doctors

were sure the cancer would have him in the ground by
your tenth birthday."

She rubbed her forehead, forcing the thoughts—

*Ah, there's my Robin-bird, how's my best girl? I have to see
my P.O. and then we can go to the playground, won't that be
nice? And see, look what I found! Isn't it pretty? Just right for
my Robin-bird's neck.*

—away.

"All this time," Rich was muttering. "I had no idea. I
thought it was your nature, you're so like your father, I
thought you didn't want to settle down, I never
dreamed—"

"It doesn't matter now," she said dully.

"Everything can be fixed," her uncle corrected firmly.
"There's still time. You can make amends. You can . . .
start a whole new life. One where you're not chasing me
all over the country, and vice versa."

That was ridiculous. That was too good to be true.
Start a new life? Live like a normal person? Like Mrs.
John Crusher? What had her uncle been smoking?

"Is that . . . is that why you gave John the ring?"

"No, I thought he should accessorize more. Of *course*
that's why I gave him the ring."

"Don't bite my head off, old man, I'm in no mood,"
she snarled back. "We were doing just fine before you
stuck your fingers in and started to interfere."

"Ha. And again I say, ha."

"So I'm supposed to believe that you gave the ring to
John, that you're not going to try to steal it back?"

He yawned.

"Seriously?"

"Ten years, Robin, for the love of God! I'm tired, do
you understand *tired?* John can have it. Or you can take
it from him. Or you can take it from him and then give
it to him. Or you can flush it down the toilet. I'm tired,
and this has gone on far too long. Here's your escape

hatch, Robin. Take it, if you love me. And even if you don't."

"Of course I love you," she said absently. "I just fantasize about strangling you sometimes. Also, I'm having a little trouble keeping up. You have to admit, this is a big—sudden!—one-eighty."

"Worry about it later. For now, get some ice, get a washcloth, and minister to your man. Assuming he'll still talk to you."

"I—"

"Too late."

She turned; John was staggering toward her, and right on his heels was Ken, the embalmed-looking hotel manager.

Chapter Ten

"Hi, honey," she said weakly as he staggered up to the table.

"You—you—"

"Care for a drink?" Rich asked. "You look like you could use one. Or five."

"Mr. Crusher, are you sure you don't require an ambulance? I didn't mean to intrude, but you practically fell out of the elevator. Pardon me for saying so," Ken-the-manager stammered, "but you don't look well." Rasp-rasp, as he rubbed his hands together.

Robin tried not to shudder. *Cripes, hasn't the guy heard of hand lotion? He sounds like a snake getting ready to molt. Or whatever snakes do.*

John grasped the back of her chair to steady himself. "I'm fine. Go away. Robin, you—you—"

"Treacherous idiot?" Rich supplied helpfully.

"*You* stay out of this. And don't hug me ever again. Come on, Robin. Back to our room. Gotta figure this out."

Her eyes widened. "Really? You want me to come up?"

"Errr . . . Mr. Crusher . . . I thought you were in a single for the week," the manager ventured.

"I, uh . . ."

"Better check your reservations computer," Robin said sweetly. "Mr. and Mrs. Crusher, big as life."

"Oh. Beg pardon. Well, if you don't want an ambulance . . . and everything's under control . . ."

"You could talk to the chef," Rich suggested politely. "The endive's a bit wilted."

Looking relieved to have a task at last, Ken immediately departed.

"Mr. and Mrs. Crusher? When," John muttered as the manager scuttled away, "did you do *that?*"

"Some things will never be told. Come on, let's get you back upstairs. I think you better lie down."

"I think you'd better sling an arm across my shoulders. Unless you've noticed the room is spinning, too—it's not just me?"

"Uh . . . sorry. It's just you." She stood and stepped to his side, and put her arm around his waist. "Come on, poor thing. We'll have you prone in five minutes."

"Spare me the sordid details," Rich said. "And bring me a waiter. My Perrier is flat."

"I bet you say that to all the girls." Startling them both, she bent and pressed a kiss to the top of his head. "Now buzz off. Leave us alone. No more puppet mastering."

"I do have a life outside of you, Robin," he said dryly. "Not much of one, granted . . ."

"I can't believe you did that."

"I'm so, so sorry. I thought you were working for Uncle Rich. I thought . . . I thought what we did—what we had—was a put-on. That you were putting me on. And . . . I lost my temper."

"Lost your temper? You unleashed the hounds of hell—on my face!" He touched the knot rising on his forehead and winced. "Christ, I've been in bar fights that weren't this bad."

"Oh, come on. It's not that big a deal. Okay, the whole felony assault thing, that's not so great, but does it really still hurt?"

"Have you noticed this third eye growing on my forehead?" he growled. "Yes, it still hurts!"

"Oh, come here." She had him lie down beside her, and cuddled him in her arms. He sulked in her embrace for a long moment, then fished around in his pocket.

"I noticed it, that time. You're not quite as good as your uncle. Now *there's* a guy who knows how to hug while slipping stolen merchandise onto a fella. Here's your ring back."

"No, it's for you," she said quietly. "You keep it."

He reared up and stared at her. "Are you shitting me? And am I actually yelling when my head hurts this bad?"

"John—"

"You and your uncle have been stealing this back and forth forever, then you punched me when *he* gave it to me, and now *you're* giving it to me?"

He's right, it sounds ridiculous. "I'm—I guess we're both tired of the game," she said slowly. "It was fun at first—fun for years—but there's got to be more to it than . . . than all this. And I . . . I want you to have it."

He softened. She could tell he didn't want to, that he was trying hard to hold on to his righteous anger, but it just wasn't in him. *Oh, jeez, I'm crazy about this guy, I really am.*

"I can't, Robin. It was your father's. It's all you've got left of him, I bet."

She refused to close her fingers over it, and the ring dropped to the bedspread.

"Now you're just being stubborn."

"It runs in my family," she agreed.

"Well. I suppose I could keep it. You know, hang on to it for you and Rich. For a while."

"A long while."

"That's kind of what I was thinking. A long while. Because if it took you guys ten years to decide what to do with it, I should be prepared to hang on to it for at least that long, don't you think?"

"Possibly longer," she said seriously.

"Right. Uh. Do you know what this means?"

"Uh-huh. I stole you. And I'm keeping you."

"Oh. Okay. That's what I thought it meant," he said, sounding supremely satisfied. He slipped the ring onto his third finger and pulled her down for a long kiss. She could feel the gold against her cheek as he cupped her face, cool at first, then quickly warmed by their skin.

When he broke the kiss they were both breathing hard, and she had trouble looking away from the gleam on his hand. "Explaining you to my family is going to be fun," he said cheerfully.

That got her attention. "Oh, God . . . you have parents?"

"And siblings. And aunts and uncles. All of whom are strictly law-abiding. Yep, no two ways about it, it's going to be a hell of a Thanksgiving."

She groaned and buried her face in the pillows while he laughed and laughed.

HOT AND BOTHERED

Kayla Perrin

Chapter One

She was back.

Trey Arnold spotted her out of the corner of one eye the moment she entered the bar. His hands froze on the bottles of liquor he held, causing at least an extra ounce each of vodka and Kahlua to spill into the ice-filled tumbler. The beautiful Cuban woman before him hadn't asked for a double shot, but that was what she'd have now—courtesy of the woman who had just walked through the door.

In all the years Trey had been serving drinks at Castaways, he hadn't once lost his rhythm. Until now.

No, that wasn't entirely true. There had been one other time. The first time he had poured a drink for *her.*

"Hey, sugar. You trying to get me drunk?"

The soft voice with the distinctive Spanish lilt drew his attention. Trey grinned absentmindedly at Adriana's comment, then placed her drink on a napkin and slid it across the counter to her. "A double shot for the price of a regular. I'd say that's a good deal."

She arched an eyebrow. "So you *are* trying to get me drunk."

"Just trying to keep you happy," Trey countered. "That'll be four dollars."

But as he spoke, his eyes wandered. Wandered to Jenna.

She looked just the way he remembered her, from her luscious caramel skin to those full, pouty lips. Even her hair hadn't changed. Her short black tresses looked like they had been finger-combed, creating an unkempt appearance that was entirely sexy.

"Here you go."

With effort, Trey looked away from Jenna and met the Cuban beauty's eyes. This was Adriana's third time here in as many days. Her bashful smiles and lingering looks told him she was attracted to him. They had chatted briefly yesterday, which was how he knew her name. He also knew that she had been born and raised in Cuba, but was now living in Miami. She liked to get to Key West at least a few times a year, but this was the first time she had discovered Castaways.

If there was one thing Trey knew about tourists, they were a different breed altogether. At home, they might be model citizens. Kindergarten teachers, demure secretaries, cops. But on vacation, getting drunk and stupid was par for the course. They left their inhibitions at the door and looked for a good time wherever one was to be had.

He didn't have to be a rocket scientist to know that Adriana wanted to have a good time with him. He'd also bet this bar that she had a husband back home, if the pale rim on her ring finger was any indication.

Adriana's lips curled in seductive invitation as she slid a five across the bar, along with a slip of paper. With deliberate slowness, she got off the bar stool, then cast Trey a simmering look before walking away.

Trey glanced at the note. *I'm here till Friday, staying at the Best Western. Room 1202. Call me.*

Trey crumpled the paper and dumped it in the nearby trash bin. He was flattered, sure, and had this been a few years ago, before he'd met Jenna, he would have been tempted to lose himself in a night of mindless sex with a gorgeous woman like Adriana. But he had come a long way since the lonely days after Irene had left him and he'd thrown himself into his work.

Besides, he was a married man now. The kind of married man who believed in the sacredness of his vows, no matter what Jenna might believe.

"I'll have a draft," a guy said, squeezing his way between two bar patrons. "Whatever's light."

"Sure thing." Trey reached behind him for a draft glass, then whirled around in one fluid motion, trying to get back into his flow. But as his hand curled around the draft beer's tap, his stomach clenched.

Where was Jenna?

He pulled the tap, his eyes searching the dimly lit, well-populated room. Only once the glass was full of beer did he spot her again. At the far right of the room, she was standing at a high, round table with a girlfriend.

Not just any friend, Trey realized. Ruby.

Ah, Ruby. He couldn't help smiling. So Jenna had come with reinforcements.

Trey watched Jenna and Ruby settle onto bar stools at the table as he handed the man his change. Ruby swayed her body to the calypso beat. Jenna, on the other hand, looked like she was facing a firing squad.

That firing squad being him.

She didn't want to be here, didn't want to see him, but he had given her no choice. And if Jenna was the way he remembered, a fireball of passion, he knew she had to be pissed.

But he'd be damned if he was simply going to stand by and let her walk out of his life forever, so he had done what he'd had to do to get her back here.

Here, where it all began.

She may have traveled over fifteen hundred miles to get a divorce, but by the time he was through with her, he'd make sure she knew that she was still his wife—in every sense of the word.

Two years, three weeks, and four days after she had fled Key West, Jenna Maxwell was back. Back in the place where it had all begun, after a whirlwind courtship and spur of the moment marriage two and a half years ago.

This was the last place in the world she wanted to be. But, like someone about to go under the knife to remove a tumor, this was a necessary evil.

Still, she would have done almost anything to avoid this trip, avoid a reunion with her estranged husband, Trey—including give up chocolate for a year. But Trey had forced her hand, making her come here to deal with him in person before she could move on with her life.

"Earth to Jenna."

"Huh? Oh, we're here."

"We sure are." Ruby, Jenna's longtime best friend, reached across the front seat of their rented sports car and squeezed her hand. "How're you feeling?"

"Like I'm about to be disemboweled."

Ruby threw her head back and laughed. "It's not *that* bad. At least the weather's great."

That was the only plus about this trip. Jenna and Ruby had left behind four feet of snow and thirteen-degrees-before-the-windchill weather up north. Getting to sunny Florida at a time like this would top anyone's To Do list. If only the occasion were a pleasant one.

"Are you getting cold feet?" Ruby asked.

"Of course not," Jenna replied quickly. Too quickly. But the truth was, she was dreading seeing Trey.

The last time she had seen him was that awful January morning two years earlier. They'd had an explosive argument, said all kinds of hurtful things to each other, and Jenna had known that their marriage was over.

Devastated, she had thrown her things into her car and left hastily—left without even thinking of signing any type of official separation document. It was that legal glitch that had her coming back here now, to get Trey's signature on separation papers her lawyer had drawn up. Because although they'd physically been separated for two years, barring adultery or cruelty or some other "cause" for a divorce, the state of New York wouldn't grant her one without an official separation of at least one year.

She hadn't even considered the legal ramifications of simply up and leaving him, but at the time she had been utterly distraught over the death of her marriage, which had been incredibly short-lived. In her grief, she had simply wanted to run away, avoid the unbearable tension between them, while in her heart a smidgeon of hope still burned that she and Trey would work things out.

Trey knew her cell number, as well as her parents' number back in Buffalo. And he had to have known she would head back to work at the WBLK radio station as a receptionist. But he had never called. The only thing he'd done was ship her bookshelf and novels back to her—as per her last parting instruction.

It was all water under the bridge. She had learned a valuable lesson, and was ready to move on with her life. This time, when Jenna left Key West, she would be officially one step closer to her freedom—freedom from a foolish mistake that was holding her back. It had been her New Year's resolution, to get the ball rolling on her divorce before she turned thirty in May. God knew she was practically over the hill, and if she wanted to settle down and have a family, she had to do everything in her power to make that happen.

Thankfully, this would be the last time she had to see Trey. Once he signed the separation agreement, effectively letting her go, she doubted he'd be stubborn enough to get on a plane and head to Buffalo to sign the final divorce papers, rather than see a notary here. Then she could finally get on with her life, search for Mr. Right without the dark cloud of her failed marriage hanging over her head.

"Ready to head inside?"

Jenna slipped off her sunglasses and stuffed them in the *V* of her cotton shirt. The sun was already setting, so she hardly needed them, but she'd kept them on in an attempt to avoid seeing this place with clear eyes. "I may as well get this over with."

Ruby closed the sunroof and got out of the car. Jenna followed her, her stomach fluttering as she did.

"If he's not here, do you want to swing by the house?"

"Oh, he'll be here," Jenna said confidently. This bustling bar and eatery was Trey's baby, his life. She knew he would be inside, doing his thing. He made an art form out of serving drinks.

She had appreciated his commitment to the bar in the beginning, until she'd realized that he preferred spending time here as opposed to spending time with her.

Ruby pulled open the heavy wood door, then stood back, allowing Jenna to enter first. Jenna hesitated. But after a moment, she took a deep breath and stepped across the threshold.

Her eyes did a quick sweep of the place, yet avoiding the one spot she knew she'd find Trey. An energetic calypso beat pulsed through the bar. The place was crowded, filled nearly to capacity with lively tourists. For a Tuesday evening, this was amazing. Things had certainly picked up in the two years she had been gone. Trey must be pleased.

Trey. Even thinking his name made her body quiver. Anticipation mixed with the anxiety she was already feeling. She would be lying if she said she didn't fear looking his way because she was afraid of how she'd react.

The first time she had seen him, her body short-circuited from sensual overload. There was no reason to expect that seeing him now would be any different.

He was that kind of man. Sinfully sexy, impossible to regard and not feel even a twinge of lust. It didn't matter that they didn't have a future. Her body would react to him in a purely carnal way.

But she couldn't ignore looking his way forever. So, swallowing a deep breath, and knowing exactly where she would find him, her gaze went to the bar.

Though she expected him there, her heart rammed in her chest at the first mouthwatering sight of him. The black shirt he wore was unbuttoned as far as the eye could see, giving her a delicious view of his smooth, hard chest. His well-muscled arms looked amazingly strong. She could only see a shadow of dark hair over his head; he must have shaved it. The low-cropped look worked very well for him.

No doubt about it, the man was an Adonis. From his perfectly sculpted biceps to his flawless, golden brown skin, he looked good enough to sink her teeth into.

Jenna was certain that the woman with the long black hair and hourglass figure thought so, too. She seemed mesmerized as she watched Trey pour liquor into a glass with pizzazz.

And for a moment, Jenna was mesmerized, too. Mesmerized by Trey's smooth and utterly sexy movements. But the magic fizzled when she saw the stunning woman at the bar give Trey an over-the-shoulder look that screamed *I want you in my bed.*

That Trey glanced at a slip of paper a moment later only served to reinforce the point of why Jenna was here: to cut ties with her hottie heartbreaker and move on with her life. Clearly, the woman had given Trey her information. How many others had done so in the two years she'd been gone? And how many had he bedded, the way he had her? Flirty tourists were a dime a dozen here. Surely many of them had solicited sex from her husband in her absence.

Her husband. Was he ever truly hers? Considering how little she really knew about him, she doubted it. Regret lodged in her throat at what could have been but never was. So much hope; so much disappointment.

"Are we heading to the bar?" Ruby asked.

Ruby's voice rescued Jenna from her trip down Miserable Memory Lane. "Not yet," she replied. "Let's find a table."

Gripping her small clutch purse, Jenna took tentative steps toward a rear table that was surprisingly free. Once, this bar had felt like home. Now, she felt entirely out of place.

"I like this music. Don't you like this music?"

Jenna scowled lightly. As if they were here for entertainment! But leave it to Ruby to have a good time, despite the circumstance. Of course, Ruby was always on the hunt for her Mr. Right, and according to her the best way to find him was to put out positive energy. Short shorts and a cut-off T-shirt didn't hurt, either—which was what the dark-skinned diva had decided to change into at the hotel. Left alone, Ruby would be getting laid by Mr. Wrong by the end of the night.

Jenna eased her body onto one of the high stools, saying, "I think I need a drink."

Ruby gave her forearm a gentle squeeze. "You don't need booze to get through this. You just have to tell him what you want."

Easy for you to say, Jenna almost blurted, but somehow managed not to. Ruby had been with her two and a half years ago when she'd met and fallen for Trey. In fact, Ruby had met him first, then dragged Jenna to the bar to introduce them. She'd had some "psychic vibe" that Jenna and Trey were soul mates in search of each other, and at the time Jenna had been so smitten she'd believed that bullshit. And even though time had proven that concept clearly untrue, Ruby, ever the romantic, still thought Jenna and Trey were right for each other.

She had given Jenna an earful of the "your soul mate comes along once in a lifetime" speech on the plane, which had surprised Jenna, considering that Ruby had offered to accompany her on this trip for moral support. Jenna would have gotten more support from her father—although he would have given her an entirely different type of speech.

"I know I don't *need* booze," Jenna said in response to Ruby's comment, "but I could use a drink nonetheless."

"You're right. It's been a long day. I'll take a rum and Coke while you're at it."

Jenna gaped at Ruby. "*I'm* not going up there."

"Right, of course. You're not ready." She hopped off her chair. "I'll go. What can I get for you?"

"A piña colada. No, wait. Make that a scotch on the rocks."

"Uh-oh."

"I need it, Ruby."

Ruby's shoulders rose and fell in a nonchalant shrug. She dug money out of her wallet, then she weaved her way through the crowd. As Jenna watched her friend, she wrung her fingers together. Her anxiety was in stark contrast to Ruby's bubbly mood, evidenced by Ruby's flirtatious smiles as she moved toward the bar.

It was amazing how two years could change things. Jenna had been flirtatious and fun her first time here, not uptight and on edge. Of course, she'd been on a *real* vacation, her first one in ages—one that had become that much more exciting after she'd met and instantly fallen for Trey.

"You can deny it all you want, but that man's your soul mate," Ruby had told her on the plane.

Soul mate, her butt. Ruby was too romantic for her own good.

Trey was no more her soul mate than he was her husband in any real sense of the word. Marrying him at the end of her month-long vacation had been the dumbest thing she had ever done, and by the end of this trip, she would be well on her way to rectifying that mistake.

Chapter Two

"Ruby." Trey greeted her in a cheery voice, as if her sudden appearance in his bar wasn't a surprise. "Long time no see."

She grinned as she rested her elbows on the counter. "So, you remember me."

"Remember you? How could I forget you?" Trey popped the lid off a beer and passed it to a customer, then scooped up the coins the man had left for him.

"You're looking good, Trey."

"Hey, I try." Trey's gaze wandered over Ruby's dark, round face. Her eyes held a hint of mischief. "And you're looking . . . quite happy."

"You expect a frown?"

"No, I guess not. I always figured you the type to smile when bringing bad news."

"Bad news?" Ruby *tsk*ed, shaking her head. "Now why would you say that?"

"If you've got an envelope behind your back, you can toss it in the trash."

Ruby lifted both hands. "No envelope. Only cash."

"Good." Not that Ruby's answer meant she and Jenna had come here for a sun-filled vacation. Trey knew better. He had received the couriered package from her lawyer containing the proposed separation agreement.

She didn't want any of his assets and assumed he didn't want any of hers. All he had to do was sign the document before a notary and send it back to her lawyer.

Simple.

But there was nothing simple about this situation. First and foremost, he loved his wife. Even though they hadn't been in touch in two years, the last thing he wanted was a divorce. The separation papers had been a big wake-up call that he had to make a move or lose her forever. And the best way to win her back was to get her down here so that he could deal with her in person. So instead of signing the agreement she wanted him to, he had written a note on it: *If you want out of this marriage, you'll have to come here and tell me to my face.*

"I tried to talk her out of it, by the way," Ruby said. "I know she still loves you."

"You think so?"

"Oh, she denies it, but I know she does. She talks this crap about how she has to move on with her life, but she's never once said that she stopped loving you. And I swear, she's been wound up and tense ever since she returned to Buffalo. Barely cracks a smile anymore." Ruby scowled as she shook her head. "When she was here with you, she was happy. Carefree. A person doesn't need a degree to figure out that she still wants you."

"She wants a divorce."

Ruby waved a hand dismissively. "It's a cry for help. Even if she doesn't know it. And as for you, I'm sure you just needed a nudge, right?"

The registered package containing the separation agreement had been a huge nudge. "True, dat."

"I'm never wrong when I know two people should be together. And I knew right from the start that you and Jenna were meant to be. I can't say I'm happy that you've sat on your ass for two years instead of trying to win her back." Ruby paused as she gave him a pointed look. "But since you didn't want to sign the separation papers, I have to assume you still want this marriage."

"I do."

She smiled. "That's what I wanted to hear."

"Good. Then you won't mind helping me out."

"That's why I came on this trip with Jenna, although she thinks otherwise."

"What is she planning?"

"Not to drug you and force you to sign the separation agreement." Ruby smiled sweetly. "But she does want you to do it. Figures you'll do it here and not make a fuss about it."

Trey shook his head. "I need to get her alone."

"I agree. You two need to talk. And . . . whatever else suits your fancy."

Not to drug you and force you to sign the separation agreement. As Trey replayed Ruby's words, an idea took shape in his mind. "Are you getting my wife a drink?"

Ruby nodded. "She wants scotch on the rocks."

Trey shook his head. "Naw, I've got something else for her." He reached for a bottle of gin, chuckling softly as he did. "Tell her it's the special of the day."

"Oh, wait. Trey, what are you up to?" Ruby fought to control her smirk. "Gin?" When Trey nodded, Ruby said, "You know her allergy to gin knocks her out like a felled tree."

"That's what I'm counting on." Jenna was allergic to the juniper berries gin was made from. Trey knew the gin wouldn't hurt her, but it would knock her out and buy him time to get her to his place. "Will you help me?"

"She'll have my ass on a platter—"

"Not if you hightail it out of town."

"Ooh, shit."

"*After* you help me get her to my place."

Ruby moaned. "You want me to head back to Buffalo? Do you know how miserable it is there right now?"

"I don't care if you head to Orlando. As long as you're not anywhere Jenna can find you."

"And here I was, hoping you had some gorgeous friend to set me up with." Ruby frowned. "Unfortunately, I'm only a good matchmaker when it comes to other people."

"No offense, Ruby, but I'll be too busy trying to mend things with my wife to set you up with anyone. Maybe next time." Trey filled the blender with ice and fruit. "Will you help me?"

"You may as well plan my funeral now."

Trey chuckled as the blender whirred. There was enough strawberry and lime to mask the taste of gin. But even if Jenna did detect a hint of gin, given the look of distress on her face, it would probably be after she'd chugged a good portion of the drink—at which point it would be too late.

Moments later, he poured the thick, alcoholic smoothie into a tall glass, garnishing it with a morsel of lime spiked with a miniature umbrella. Then he poured one for Ruby.

"They're on me," he said, passing Ruby the drinks.

Ruby sipped the drink through the straw. "Mmm. This is delicious. You might have to make me a few more of these before I leave Florida."

"No offense, Ruby, but after tonight I hope I don't see you again."

"Hey!" She feigned a hurt tone.

"Is the rental car in your name?"

"Yeah."

"Excellent." No loose ends to tie up on that front. "Then once Jenna's in my care, take off. It's the only way we'll have time to work things out for ourselves."

Ruby's expression finally grew serious. "I hope this works, Trey."

"Yeah, I hope it does, too."

*   *   *

Jenna was in a warm, vanilla-scented bubble bath, surrounded by vanilla-scented candles. Resting her head against the tub's wall, she raised a leg, watching the thick bubbles stick to her skin. A satisfied breath oozed out of her. How long had it been since she'd taken a bath like this, luxuriated in such a simple delight?

Not in . . . forever.

Her eyes flew open. As the sweet fragrance of vanilla hit her full force, she bolted upright.

She wasn't in a tub. She was in a bed.

Trey's bed. She knew it even before she saw the telltale four posters and mosquito netting surrounding her.

Panic curled around her stomach like groping tentacles and squeezed hard. Darting her eyes around the candlelit room, her mind scrambled to make sense of the situation. The last thing she remembered, she had been at Castaways with Ruby. So how had she ended up *here?*

Breathing in slowly, she surveyed the room. The dim lighting came from a row of fat candles lining the windowsill. No doubt, they were also the source of the delicate vanilla scent.

This place looked like . . . like a scene of seduction.

The realization was jarring, but it made her body thrum with sexual awareness nonetheless. There was no escaping the erotic memories this room held for her. She and Trey had made love countless times in this very bed, something she had hardly been able to forget at home in Buffalo, much less right here where the magic of their union had happened.

"Oh, no," she told herself sternly. "You will *not* do this." She pushed aside the netting and scrambled off the bed. She headed straight for the candles on the windowsill and blew them out. Many of the times Jenna and Trey had made love, they'd done so to the ambience of romantic music and candlelight. The last thing Jenna wanted was a visual reminder of that now.

Enshrouded in darkness, she turned around. A sliver of light slid under the bedroom door. Surprisingly, the place was quiet. Surely if Ruby was here, her outgoing friend would be filling this place with laughter. So where was she? And how, if the woman was her friend, had she let Trey snatch her from Castaways?

Jenna's bare feet made no sound on the hardwood floor as she crossed the room. She swung the bedroom door open, prepared to give Trey a piece of her mind—and drew up short.

There were more candles, these ones mixed with a sprinkling of rose petals. Both created a path leading from the bedroom to the sliding patio doors. And was she wrong, or did she detect the scent of her absolute favorite dish—chicken marsala? Surely after two years, Trey wouldn't remember that detail about her. But maybe that was yet another surprise in what was turning out to be a very surprising evening.

Jenna wasn't stupid. She knew what this was about. Trey was laying it on thick in an attempt to get her to forget about moving on with her life. Why, exactly, she had absolutely no clue. But she'd be damned if she was going to stay here and let him play out whatever he had planned.

Placing her hands akimbo, Jenna strode to the patio doors. Peering through the glass, she saw Trey trying to light yet another candle on the table. The breeze off the ocean blew it out, but he tried one more time. When the flame flickered and died once again, he dropped the matchbox onto the table.

And then he saw her.

Whirling around, a smile lifted his lips. Jenna swallowed, unprepared for the mix of emotions that swirled inside her. There was anger and nervousness, both of which made sense, but the overwhelming desire to reach out and touch him shocked her to her core.

Surely the reaction was carnal. A completely normal female reaction to one hunk of a man. How could Jenna *not* react to Trey's perfect butt, clad in a pair of well-worn, faded jeans? Or to those arms? They looked even more solid and muscular than she remembered. Trey had set up his spare bedroom as a home gym, and given his perfectly sculpted body, he was putting it to good use.

Trey slid open the screen door and slipped into the house. "I was just about to check on you."

Jenna stopped her pleasure gazing and looked up at him incredulously. "What am I doing here?"

"Oh." He dragged a hand over the back of his neck. "Wouldn't you know it, you passed out at the bar. Must have been jet lag. I figured I'd bring you—"

"Jet lag, my ass. I saw you and Ruby chatting for quite some time. Then she brought me a drink—not the one that I requested, but one that you made for me. You put gin in it, didn't you? The only time I ever conk out is when I have gin."

Trey's sexy lips curled in a guilty grin. "Darling—"

"Don't *darling* me. You did this on purpose!"

Trey slowly raised a hand. "All right. I confess. I did do it on purpose."

Jenna glared at him. "How long was I out for?"

"Close to three hours."

"Three hours!" Jenna sounded outraged, although the three-hour blackout was about average. Before she'd discovered her allergy to gin, the few other times in her life she'd had the liquor, she had lost anywhere from three to five hours of time.

"Well, thanks to you, I have a killer headache." It was more like a dull throb. "Why would you do something this crazy?"

"Because I wanted to get you alone."

Trey's words gave her pause. Clearly, he wasn't going to make this easy for her. "I came down here to divorce you, not to get cozy with you."

"I know why you came," Trey said simply.

The deep timbre of his voice unnerved her. Needing to look away from him, she gestured toward the candles. "And what are you trying to do? Set the house on fire?"

"It's never caught fire the other times."

The other times. An image of Trey grinding her while she braced the candlelit kitchen counter zapped into her mind. She and Trey had gotten hot and bothered more times than Jenna could count, and those memories were indelibly etched in her brain.

In her heart.

The feel of Trey's finger on her face caught her off guard. Jenna looked up to see that his large, sexy body loomed over hers. When had he gotten this close to her? She drew in a shaky breath, inhaling the incredibly intoxicating scent she had committed to memory. The spicy aftershave he wore had always made her think of sex, and this time was no exception.

So did the scent of vanilla, which was why Jenna had never bought anything vanilla-flavored after leaving Trey. One whiff of the stuff and it was a throwback to the intimate times they had shared.

Intimate times followed by an emotional shutdown on Trey's part. He got close, then pushed her away. He would be incredibly romantic, then push her away. And every time, Jenna had felt the tear in her heart growing larger.

Trey's inability to open up to her emotionally was why their marriage had ultimately failed. They'd shared an instant and fierce attraction, one that had thrilled and fulfilled her beyond her wildest dreams. But his emotional aloofness had hurt her more than she could bear. With each day, it had become increasingly obvious that her marriage to Trey had been a horrible mistake.

But what had she really known about him when she'd said "I do" other than that they were fantastic in bed?

That thought returning her to sanity, she demanded, "Where the hell is Ruby?"

"Out on the town, I think."

"The bitch," Jenna muttered. Talk about a fairweather friend. Ruby was supposed to be on *her* side, yet she had given her over to the enemy without a second thought. Jenna would have her head on a platter the moment she saw her.

But what was she going to do about right now? She was alone. With Trey. Two and two added up to four as surely as the two of them alone added up to undeniable chemistry.

Jenna turned and walked toward the glass coffee table. She should leave. Call a cab, track down Ruby, and get the papers—

"Jenna."

Trey's voice was as rich as dark chocolate, and just as tempting. And ooh, she was tempted. But what was he offering? For her to stay and enjoy one last night of wild sex with him, or stay and be his wife till death do them part?

Jenna mentally chastised herself for her last thought. Trey wasn't interested in marriage. He had made that clear two years ago. Maybe his ego had been hurt when she'd sent him the separation papers, but he would get over that, just as he had gotten over the excitement of being in love with her.

That bitter reality sobering her, Jenna faced him.

"I know," Trey said before she could open her mouth. "You're thinking you want to leave."

"No." Jenna wagged a finger at him. "Don't you do that. Don't you presume to know what I'm thinking. Not after two years."

"All right," Trey conceded. "Then why don't you have a seat outside? Dinner's ready and warming in the oven."

"You want me to have dinner with you?"

"I made your favorite."

Jenna was speechless as Trey walked past her. She didn't move as she heard utensils clinking in the kitchen. Didn't move even as Trey strode past her again, heading onto the screened-in patio.

Finally, her brain kicked into action. She followed Trey onto the patio, saying, "You can hold me captive all you want, but this isn't going to work."

He made a show of straightening the silverware. "What's not going to work?"

"You know what I'm talking about. I didn't come down here to have dinner with you."

"You traveled fifteen hundred miles only to turn around and leave?"

"You know damn well why I came here."

Trey turned his back to the table and faced her. "We need to talk, Jenna. And I'd much rather we do so over dinner and wine."

"Like I'd trust another drink you gave me."

"Touché. Well, I'll have a glass, if you don't mind."

Jenna watched Trey reach for the bottle of chardonnay—also her favorite—and fill one of the wineglasses. A glass of wine right now would be wonderful. But if she had one, she'd be playing right into Trey's hands.

She said, "I still want a divorce."

"We're going to talk about that, sweetheart. Right after we eat dinner."

Sweetheart?

Trey pulled out a chair. "Please, sit."

"Tell me why you're doing this."

"Because I'd like to think that after all we once meant to each other, we're not enemies. I don't know what tomorrow holds, but right now I'd like to spend an amicable night with my wife." He paused, then added, "Is that so wrong?"

Score one for Trey. Jenna couldn't deny his sentiment. They *had* fallen in love. They *had* shared some incredible times together, many of them right here in his house. The thought that she would come down here and end up in an ugly fight with him had given her far too much stress, so she should be glad that Trey was being pleasant.

"All right, Trey. I'll have dinner with you."

His smile warmed her insides like a shot of bourbon. This man was dangerous to her heart. He always had been.

So she added, "But as soon as we're done, we're going to talk about why I came down here. We're going to talk about our divorce."

Chapter Three

Jenna spiked the last morsel of chicken on her plate, stuffed it in her mouth, then sat back in her chair and sighed with contentment. The chicken marsala and Portobello mushrooms had been absolutely scrumptious.

Trey stood and reached for the bottle of wine. "You sure you don't want any?"

"Oh, why not?" Her head's dull ache had dissipated once she'd put some food in her belly. Besides, her mouth had practically watered as she'd watched Trey drink two glasses. What was she accomplishing by not indulging? A good wine to cap off an excellent meal—there was nothing wrong with that.

Trey filled her glass, then poured the remnants of the bottle into his. As he sat back down, his eyes held hers. His fingers fiddled with the glass's stem, and Jenna thought he might make some sort of corny toast. But he didn't.

She sipped the wine, savoring the flavor on her tongue. "Thank you for dinner."

"Wasn't that better than acting like enemies?"

"Mmm-hmm," Jenna answered truthfully. She hadn't felt as awkward as she'd imagined she would, sitting and dining with him. But that didn't change the reality of their situation.

She sipped more wine. Braced herself. "Now, about the separation papers—"

"Eh eh eh." Trey pushed his plastic chair back and got to his feet. "I have something else for you."

"Oh, Trey. I honestly couldn't eat another bite."

"Sit tight," he told her.

Jenna watched Trey disappear inside the house, wondering what on earth he was up to now. Her stomach fluttered with that thought. She tried to take her mind off the matter by listening to the sound of the waves crashing against the shore, but that only made her remember the times she and Trey had scurried across the sand buck naked in the middle of the night to have a dip in the ocean beneath a moonlit sky.

For God's sake, stop thinking about it! Jenna lifted her wineglass and took another sip—more like a gulp, really. Everything about this night reminded her of her first night as Trey Arnold's wife. They had dined at this very table, enjoying this exact same meal of chicken marsala and wild rice. But instead of wine, they'd had champagne to celebrate their new union. The memory was completely unnerving, considering she wanted to end the marriage.

Just as Trey's friendliness was a bit unnerving. She had expected anger, and ego, but she'd gotten neither. The calm before the storm? For a guy who hadn't once called her after she'd left, she couldn't understand why he'd want to prolong anything between them now.

Jenna stopped thinking when Trey returned carrying two small CorningWare bowls. He placed them on the table, and Jenna could see that one bowl contained strawberries while the other held melted chocolate.

The very treat they'd enjoyed just before feasting on each other on their wedding night.

Jenna's heart pounded like it was about to explode. How could she have been so blind? Of course everything had reminded her of her wedding night—Trey had set this all up.

Should she be touched that he remembered, or slap him silly for resorting to this type of emotional torture? He had to know she didn't want to take this trip down memory lane. Not to a night that had been filled with so much promise—promise that had turned to wrenching heartbreak.

Jenna hastily pushed her chair back and stood. "If you don't want to talk tonight, then let's set up a time tomorrow. All you have to do is sign on the dotted line and I'll be on my way."

"Where are you going?"

In her haste to move away from him, Jenna's foot hit the chair's leg. She lost her balance, tumbling backward. Trey reached for her, easily securing an arm around her waist, pulling her fully to her feet.

God, but he smelled wonderful. And there was something about being in his arms that felt so right. Her nipples hardened as they pressed against his solid chest, and the lustful thought that there were too many clothes between them passed through her mind.

Trey didn't let her go. Instead, he closed his eyes, leaned forward, and pressed his nose against her hair. He inhaled deeply, causing a shiver of delight to tickle Jenna's forehead.

Jenna closed her eyes and curled her fingers around Trey's biceps. Oh, how she could lose herself in this man. It would be so easy. It would be so . . .

Wrong.

Opening her eyes, Jenna squirmed to escape Trey's arms. He didn't fight her; he let her go. But suddenly she felt cold where a moment ago she had been warm.

Why was this so hard? "Trey, I think you've gotten the wrong idea."

He reached for her, took her arm in his hand. Turning it palm up, he ran the pad of his thumb back and forth over the inside of her wrist. "I know why you're here."

His touch was electric. Distracting. "No, I don't think you do."

"You say you want to end our marriage."

"Yes. Yes, that's right. So why . . . why are you touching me . . . like this?"

"You don't like it? You used to."

Of course she liked it! But she could hardly think with the sexual sensations raging within her. She should have been more prepared for this. Thought of some way to protect herself from these feelings. Sex was the one area where she and Trey were always on.

"If you don't like that, then maybe you'll like this." Trey released her arm and reached behind him. From the bowl on the table, he lifted a fat strawberry. He dipped it in chocolate, then brought the piece of fruit to her mouth.

"Open," he said softly.

Without even a token protest, Jenna parted her lips. Trey put the strawberry into her mouth, skimmed it over her tongue. She sank her teeth into it, and a burst of delicious flavors filled her mouth, damn near making her weak in the knees. Her absolute favorite food was chocolate, seconded by strawberry. The combination was deliciously sinful.

"That wasn't so bad, was it?"

Jenna chewed, swallowed. "I see you remember what I like."

"I remember a lot of things. *Everything.*"

Trey's voice dropped several octaves, resonating with pure lust. It hadn't been so long that Jenna no longer recognized the sexual signals between them.

He wanted her. In his bed.

Jenna couldn't allow that to happen. "This is wrong, Trey. Completely off course."

"Because you want a divorce?"

"Y-yes."

Trey ate the last morsel of the strawberry, watching Jenna as he did. The fire in her eyes spoke the exact opposite of what she said. It was why he'd known that he had to see her, to gauge for himself if there was still anything between them.

And there was.

"What if I don't want one?" he asked.

Jenna's breath oozed out of her in a rush. "Please—don't make this any harder than it has to be."

"You want me to make it easy for you to leave me?"

"You and I both know that we don't have a marriage. Not a real one, anyway."

And that was something Trey wanted to change. He and Jenna hadn't had a real marriage because he had been a different person when they'd said their vows, one who'd been afraid to show her how he felt. But if she gave him tonight, that's exactly what he was going to do—show her what was in his heart.

"I understand why you might think that," Trey said. "That's why we need to talk, sweetheart."

"Trey—"

"Shh." He placed a finger over her lips to silence her. "I let you walk away two years ago. Didn't fight for what I wanted. I don't plan to make the same mistake twice."

Jenna could hardly believe her ears. How could he now say that he wanted her when he'd so easily let her leave? This had to be about ego, about the chase that guys loved so much. She couldn't give him the power to hurt her again. "It's too late."

Trey paused before saying, "If that's true, then spending one night with me won't change that."

Jenna's heart went berserk. "Spend the night?"

"It's already late. Ruby's out having fun. You may as well stay here with me."

"You can't be serious."

"We'll talk—talk about everything. And in the morning, if you still want to walk away, I'll let you go. But this time you'll know exactly what you're walking away from. You'll know exactly what's in my heart." Trey shrugged. "If it's not what you want, then at least this time we'll have said a proper good-bye."

"This is about sex." She was crazy, but the thought excited her.

"I'm not going to lie. I want you. Hell, you know I can't be in the same room with you and not want you."

His words made her body throb. There was a part of her—a very big part—that wanted Trey, too. Hell, more than a part. Wanting Trey had been as second nature as breathing.

Trey dipped another strawberry in chocolate. But this time, when Jenna opened her mouth for it, he didn't give it to her. He stroked it across her bottom lip.

A groan rumbled deep in Trey's chest, and the next moment he was lowering his head to hers. He flicked his tongue out and ran it across her lower lip, slowly lapping up the chocolate.

Jenna stood motionless, not even daring to breathe. Trey had done the exact same thing on their wedding night, not only licking the chocolate from her mouth, but from other parts of her body, as well. Now, all of her senses were alive and screaming for more intimate contact. But Trey didn't kiss her, only left her longing.

"You want more?" he asked.

"More . . . strawberry?" Jenna managed lamely.

"Uh-huh," Trey said, a gleam in his eyes.

Not trusting her voice, Jenna nodded.

Trey didn't coat this one in gooey chocolate. Jenna soon found out why. Because this time Trey touched the strawberry against her skin, right at the apex of the V in her shirt. Slowly, he trailed the fruit upward, over the mound of one breast, along the column of her neck, and finally bringing it to her mouth. The touch of the fruit was as erotic as his hand, leaving a path of delicious sensations in its wake.

"Is there someone else?" he asked.

"What?" Jenna asked, then realized the meaning of Trey's question.

"Is there another man in your life? Is that why you want to leave me?"

The hint of vulnerability in Trey's tone surprised her almost as much as his question did. "That's what you think this is about?"

"Isn't it?"

"No." Jenna met Trey's gaze, then glanced away. The intense look in his eyes was unsettling. "This isn't about another man."

"No one's waiting for you back in Buffalo?"

She should tell him yes, make it that much easier for him to let her go. But she found herself saying, "No. There hasn't been anyone since you."

His lips curled in a satisfied smile. "I've waited for you, too. Waited for my wife."

His lips came down on hers then—hard—as if he wanted to brand her with his own special blend of heat and passion. He claimed her mouth with deep sweeps of his tongue while his hands roamed over her back like they belonged there.

"God, I want you," he rasped.

Jenna moaned into his mouth as her arms crept around his neck.

"If you're going to leave me, at least give me tonight." Trey's hands gripped her butt. "Give me this."

Trey moved his mouth to her ear. "One last night, Jenna. One last night together before you move on with your life."

Chapter Four

It wasn't a demand. It was an urgent plea. One that had Jenna's body tingling with an age-old desire.

And when Trey's hot tongue flicked over her ear, Jenna cried out. His grip tightened around her as her knees buckled, preventing her from collapsing into a quivering heap on the floor.

"I know, sweetheart. I know how much you love it when I do that." He dipped his tongue into her ear. "When I do this." He pulled on the lobe with his teeth.

"Oh, Trey. Don't stop. Please, *don't stop.*"

"Tell me you want me."

"I want you."

Trey slipped a hand between Jenna's legs and covered her mound through her shorts. "You don't know how much I've missed this. So many nights I've dreamed about touching you again. Fantasized about tasting you."

White-hot heat shot through Jenna like an electrical current. She tightened her hands around Trey's neck and opened her mouth wide to accept his tongue. His tongue tangling with hers, he urged her body backward until she was pressed against the glass door.

Lord, this wasn't enough. She wanted more of him. All of him.

Slipping her hands under his shirt, Jenna flattened

her palms against his chest. The feel of his solid pecs made her want to sink her teeth into his flesh.

Trey gyrated his groin against her, and Jenna felt his erection hard and hot against her lower belly. She reached for it, stroking the length of him through his jeans.

"Oh, man." A groan escaped Trey's throat, and in a flash he spun Jenna around to face the large glass door. He splayed his hands over her ass, then traced the seam of her shorts with a finger until he reached the center of her. He flicked his finger back and forth in a steady motion, creating more and more heat, until Jenna slammed her hands against the glass and cried out from the pleasure.

Trey kissed the back of her neck. The feathery touch made a shiver of desire dance down Jenna's spine. "Two long years." He rubbed his rock-hard erection against her and Jenna moved her hips with his. "I want you, Jenna. Right here. Right now."

Trey reached around to her front and undid her shorts, then dragged them over the swell of her hips. When they hit the concrete floor, Jenna kicked them aside.

"A red G-string." A raw, sexual growl rumbled in Trey's chest when he saw Jenna's perfect ass. "You know how much I love red." He squeezed her buttocks, kneading the soft flesh with his hands. He wanted to rip off the scrap of underwear and enter her with a powerful thrust, the way he knew she liked. But the moment he was nestled inside her, he knew he would climax. That's how hot he was for her after two long years.

And the last thing he wanted to do was disappoint her. He would tease her without mercy, make her come with his fingers and his tongue. And when he was through, she would have no doubt that he would always be the man for her.

"Sweetheart, I have waited so long to do this."

Letting out a low moan, Trey slipped his fingers beneath the string at the back of her underwear and ran them along her body until he reached her fleshy folds. His cock throbbed when he felt her creamy essence. She was wet for him, the way she always had been. He slipped a finger inside her, pushing it deep. Jenna's soft mewls stoked his passion for her, and he withdrew his finger, only to thrust it deep inside her again.

"Oh God, Trey. It feels *so* good."

Trey inserted a second finger. Jenna moaned long and hard as he rotated them both inside her. Her splayed fingers extended and contracted against the glass, her attempt to grip something futile. Trey kept up the pressure, knowing he was bringing her to the edge. Just a few more strokes . . .

As her inner walls started to tighten around his fingers, he pulled them out and whirled her around.

She looked up at him in confusion.

"I want you to come, Jenna. But not yet. Not here."

Her gaze flitted around the patio, saying she understood. They had made love with the ocean as a backdrop before, but Trey didn't want a quickie. He wanted both of them naked, and he wanted the comfort of his bed for what he had in mind for her.

He took her hand and led her into the house. As they followed the path of candles and rose petals to the bedroom, Trey took off his shirt. Jenna pulled hers over her head and tossed it onto the sofa. Trey hung his on the doorknob to the bedroom before they both entered.

The moment they crossed the threshold, they came together in a wild embrace. Trey's tongue delved into Jenna's sweet, hot mouth. God, he would never tire of her. No other woman had ever turned him on with such raw sexual passion as Jenna did.

He needed her naked. It had been too damn long. Kissing her deeply, Trey searched for the snap on her bra. He found it at the front and popped it open. The moment Jenna's large breasts were free, Trey covered them with his hands.

"You're so beautiful," he whispered.

He tweaked her nipples into hard peaks while planting feathery kisses on the soft mounds of her breasts. Jenna arched her head back, yearning for him to take her nipple in his mouth. She needed this. Needed it like she'd never needed anything before. But Trey touched every other part of her breasts with his lips and tongue, leaving her nipples aching with want.

"Trey . . ."

"I know what you want."

"Then give it to me!"

Trey chuckled softly, and Jenna thought she would die from his exquisite brand of torture. He ran his tongue around the circle of one areola, then the other. Then he squeezed her breasts together, bringing her nipples closer. His warm breath fanned her, making her nipples pull into even firmer peaks.

"Please, baby," Jenna begged.

And then his tongue was all over, swishing back and forth from one nipple to the other, laving, biting, suckling like a man starved.

"Oh, God," Jenna moaned. She was seconds away from an explosive orgasm. "Touch me," she said. Her pent-up lust needed finally to be unleashed.

She reached for her vagina but Trey pulled her hand away. She whimpered her displeasure. "Please, Trey. I can't take it anymore."

"I know, sweetheart." Trey abruptly dropped to his knees. He pressed his face against her center and drew in a long breath. "Have you dreamed about this, Jenna? Remembered me touching you here?"

He stroked his finger across her distended nub. "Hell, yes," Jenna panted.

Pushing aside her panties, he flicked his tongue slowly over the nub. Jenna's body jerked from the first intimate contact. Trey fastened his fingers to her butt, holding her in place. "You're still as sweet as I remember." He suckled her softly and Jenna whimpered. "Open your legs, darling. I want more of you."

Jenna clutched Trey's shoulders as she spread her legs wider. The bedroom door was open, allowing light in from the living room. That fraction of light enabled her to see Trey's head at her center, and she thrilled in the erotic delight of watching him love her this way.

Trey eased a finger inside her. "You are *so* wet."

He slipped another finger inside, then swirled his tongue around her clitoris, creating deliciously hot friction. Jenna closed her eyes and clung to him, gripped his broad shoulders for dear life.

"It's okay, sweetheart. Let go."

Jenna's head rocked from side to side. "Oh, baby . . ."

With two fingers deep inside her, Trey took her clitoris completely in his mouth and suckled her.

And then, with the force of a volcanic eruption, Jenna exploded. The sweetest of orgasms started at her center and overflowed to every part of her being. She screamed Trey's name, held onto him as her climax continued to rock her. He suckled her harder, and Jenna thought she would die from the pleasure.

"Trey . . . oh, God . . ." Jenna's scream turned to a sob and her body went boneless.

Trey gathered her in his arms. Holding her tight, he kissed her deeply. She didn't realize that she'd been crying until he wiped tears from her eyes.

"It's okay, sweetheart."

But was it? Jenna had allowed him to open the door on their relationship, allowed him back into her heart.

Given him the power to devastate her again.

"What are you thinking?" he asked her.

"Nothing," Jenna lied.

"I know you're afraid, but you don't need to be. I swear to you on my life—"

Jenna covered Trey's mouth with a finger. She didn't want to think about anything other than the here and now.

"Kiss me," she told him.

Trey kissed her gently, and some of Jenna's fears ebbed away. No matter what happened tomorrow, she would treasure tonight. She loved this man deeply and always would. And she knew in her heart that she would never find with another man the kind of connection she shared with Trey.

Why did that thought make her want to cry?

"Maybe I should just hold you," Trey said.

"What?" Jenna asked, surprised.

"I want to make love to you, but we don't have to rush. We have all night." He kissed the palm of her hand. "I know you have some reservations."

"I'm ready," Jenna said, but to her own ears she sounded sad.

"I want you to know that this is about more than sex. It's about what I feel for you in my heart."

Jenna drew in a deep breath and closed her eyes. Maybe Trey was right. She was suddenly wistful and nostalgic, and if they made love right now, she'd bawl like a baby.

Trey pulled her to a standing position. "Come, Jenna. Let's lie down."

Two hours later, Jenna coaxed Trey awake with a lingering kiss.

His eyes popped open. "Hey, you."

"I'm hot and bothered and I need some of your lovin'," Jenna said in a feigned southern accent. She'd had all she could take of their lying naked together.

"Is that right?"

"Mmm-hmm."

Smiling brazenly, Jenna got to her knees beside Trey. She reached for his penis and stroked him until he was hard. His body was magnificent, his erection massive. From the top of his head to the tips of his toes, he was complete centerfold material. Everything about him was perfect.

"How do you want it?" Trey asked her.

"I want to ride you," she answered shamelessly.

Jenna straddled her legs over Trey's body. He reached for her, fingering her folds.

"You're already wet."

"For you, always." She leaned forward and planted her lips on his. As her tongue twisted with his, she reached for his erection, wrapping her fingers around his hard, hot length. She moved her hand up and down his shaft, delighting in his gutteral groans that said she had power to tease and torture him the same way he had her.

He moaned his displeasure when she eased her body backward. "What are you doing?"

"This," Jenna replied. As she stroked him, she flicked her tongue over the tip of his shaft. Trey's loud groans were her sweet reward.

Their short reprieve had rejuvenated her, and now she was ready to love like never before. This was going to be a night of carnal satisfaction and no regrets. No more emotions to ruin the mood.

"Oh, sweetheart. Don't make me come. I'm not through with you yet."

He reached for her and pulled her up. "Sit on me."

Jenna moved her body backward. So long she'd had to fantasize about her memory of making love to Trey. Finally she was going to experience it again.

And enjoy every damned minute of it.

Staring into his eyes, Jenna positioned herself over

him. She braced her hands on his stomach as he guided their bodies together. When the thick head of his penis entered her, she gasped in pleasure.

"You okay?" Trey asked.

"Mmmm."

Trey gently eased himself farther inside her. Quick, shallow breaths escaped her with each inch he moved. His shaft was large and hot and filled her completely.

The same way he filled her heart.

There was no denying it, no matter how much she wished she could concentrate on the physical.

Trey placed his hands on her hips and gyrated slowly. But Jenna wanted more. "Faster," she told him.

"Oh, baby." Trey's grip tightened on her hips as he picked up speed. Jenna rode him, matching his movements. She arched her back, taking in more of him, needing more of him. The pressure building, their pace quickened to wild and frenzied, until Jenna was riding Trey as if he were an untamed stallion.

Her head grew light as her orgasm took root. "Oh, God. Trey!"

Trey pulled her head down and kissed her as she came. Kissed her as his own moans grew louder, more intense.

"I love you," he rasped.

And then he let go, toppling with Jenna into the abyss.

Chapter Five

Jenna awoke with a sense of panic—and knew she had to get out of there.

Oh, the scene was perfect. Her back was snug against Trey's front, his arm secured around her waist. Their embrace was cozy. Intimate. It spoke of a comfort level many lovers only hoped to achieve.

And that's what scared her to death. That to all appearances, they *looked* the loving couple. They had acted on their fierce attraction for each other, ending up in bed as they had so many times before. But had anything between them really changed?

As much as Jenna simply wanted to pick up where they'd left off, go back to him and trust that he'd always love her, she couldn't do that. Yes, Trey had told her that he loved her last night, but was love enough to ignore the issues that had driven them apart?

The biggest issue had been honesty. Trey hadn't exactly lied about his past—he just hadn't disclosed it. And that last morning, when Jenna had point-blank asked him about what she'd learned, he'd become enraged. He had kept a vital part of his history secret from her, yet he'd been angry with *her.* How could Jenna spend the rest of her life with a man who didn't let her into his heart?

Sure, last night had been beyond incredible. And what a way to end her two-year drought! But she and Trey had fallen into the old routine of going to bed in hopes of solving all the problems between them. That was something she just couldn't do anymore.

Very carefully, Jenna slipped Trey's arm off her body. She was relieved when he didn't stir. Then she eased her body to the edge of the bed and sat up, aware that there was a hole in her heart bigger than the state of Florida.

She had made up her mind to go, but she couldn't quite bring herself to stand up. Not yet. Sighing softly, she stole a glance of him over her shoulder. Regret slammed her in the gut like a sledgehammer. Maybe it was the peaceful look on Trey's beautiful face, but it was hard to believe that she would be walking away from him forever.

It was the very reason she hadn't wanted to see him again. She'd simply wanted his signature on the separation papers because it would have been easier that way.

At least with him sleeping, it would be easier to slip out of here now. Then she'd find Ruby and get the separation papers, and meet up with Trey later at Castaways. Ruby would have a lot of explaining to do when she got back to their hotel, but Jenna would worry about that later.

She inched herself to a standing position. Still, Trey didn't stir. A part of her wanted to climb back into bed and wake him up with hot kisses. But the other part, the part that was afraid he'd revert to his morning-after emotionless shell, told her she couldn't risk her heart.

Her eyes lingered on his sleeping form. The bed sheet was strewn over a part of his hip, but other than that she could see all of his naked body. There was no doubt about it—Trey was the picture-perfect man of any woman's fantasies.

But one who had never fully given her his heart.

Jenna gathered her bra and thong from the floor, wondering where her shorts were. Then she remembered the strawberries and chocolate and Trey's skillful fingers. A hot flush stung her cheeks.

She had been wanton. Insatiable. Greedy with a lust that was shocking in its intensity. She and Trey had reacquainted their bodies by making love in every conceivable position until the early hours of the morning.

Her lust was satisfied, but her heart was sad. Staying here for another hour or a day would only be delaying the inevitable. She had come here with one purpose—to end a marriage that never should have been.

Her bra and panties in hand, Jenna crept across the hardwood floor.

"Jenna."

Trey's deep, raspy voice stopped her dead in her tracks. And though she'd just been trying to sneak out on him, she felt an odd sense of relief that he was now awake.

Turning, she did her best to look casual. "You're awake."

"Where are you going?"

"Um . . . I'm just . . ."

"Are you leaving me?"

The touch of sadness in his voice sent a jolt of pain straight to her heart. "I need some time, Trey," she admitted. "Time to think."

"Time so you can run."

"That's not what I said."

"But it's what you'll do, Jenna. The moment you get a chance. Because we haven't resolved anything."

Jenna didn't say a word as Trey climbed out of bed and approached her. "We still need to talk," he told her. "Believe it or not, that's what I wanted to do most last night. We just got . . . carried away."

"That's our problem. We always get carried away and forget the important issues."

Trey reached for her hand and linked their fingers. "Do you remember the day you left me?"

Meaning, did she remember their argument. How could she forget it? "Yes."

"That day, we started off in this bed full of happiness and hope—until things turned ugly. I wish I could go back in history and change all the happened, but I can't. So the best thing I can do is backtrack to before the argument." He paused. "And finally answer your question."

Trey's words left Jenna in shock. That question had been the catalyst for their breakup. He had outright refused to answer it then, at a time when the truth had been vitally important to her. Did he honestly think that responding to it now would change things between them?

A million times, Jenna had played out that morning in her mind, wondering if she had been unfair. Insensitive. Ambushed him, as he'd said. She always came up with the same conclusion. She could understand how the question might have been a surprise, but asking him about his past should not have led to an explosive argument. Not if he had nothing to hide, and certainly not if he loved her as deeply as he had claimed.

Even now, Jenna felt a sting of pain in her gut as she remembered how Trey had shut down. She had been in the throes of passion one minute, the pit of despair the next.

Reliving the day their marriage ended wasn't something she wanted to do. So she stepped away from him and said, "I gave you the chance to answer that question two years ago. You didn't want to. Maybe it's best that we not bother with it now."

"I wasn't ready then."

"And now you are?" Jenna asked, a hint of incredulity lacing her tone.

"Yes."

This was a trick. A ploy to get her into bed again. God only knew why, but clearly Trey wasn't ready to let her go.

Maybe it was their sexual chemistry that he couldn't walk away from. Neither of them could deny that the passion between them was explosive. But Jenna wanted more out of a marriage than just hot sex. Even mind-altering, toe-curling, spicy hot sex.

"Why don't I make some breakfast. We can talk while we eat."

"Don't you have to go to work?"

"Nope. I took the day off to spend it with you."

Trey never took a day off. He'd acted as if Castaways would fall apart if he wasn't there personally. "Then who's running the restaurant?"

"Someone new. A guy you don't know. A guy I trust completely."

"Wow, that's a shock."

"I told you, Jenna. Things are different now."

Trey kissed Jenna's cheek before slipping into his white boxers. Then he strolled out the door, leaving her to ponder his words.

She hugged her torso for a good ten seconds before putting on her panties and bra. She found her shirt in the living room and pulled it over her head. Bright sunlight spilled into the house, lifting her spirits a little. The clear blue sky and vast ocean always helped improve her mood.

While Trey opened and closed cupboards in the kitchen, Jenna headed toward the patio. The terrace table still held their dirty plates, the bowl of strawberries, and the now hard chocolate. If this had been any other morning-after-great-sex with her husband, Jenna would blush like a schoolgirl as she helped to clean up. But today, all she felt were mixed emotions.

Stepping outside, she inhaled the invigorating scent of saltwater as she reached for her shorts. One thing was certain—she would miss this place.

Get this business over with, Jenna. And the sooner the better.

Jenna put her shorts on. Fully dressed, she felt somewhat less vulnerable. What she'd really like to do was go to the bathroom and shower, but that would mean spending more time here. And right now, that wasn't an option. Trey didn't appreciate that she needed time to think, but she did. Here, she was under the influence of their memories and his charm, and much more inclined to think with her heart. She needed to think with her head.

She would head back to her hotel, shower there, and take care of Ruby—and not necessarily in that order.

"How do you want your eggs?" Trey called from the kitchen.

"Actually . . . I'm not very hungry." The truth was, Jenna was starving. But if she stayed here, she would be tempted to indulge her carnal hunger, and that would get her nothing but more heartache.

"No?"

"No. I'll, um . . . just . . . head back to my hotel."

Trey appeared from behind the kitchen wall. He had a dishrag slung over his shoulder. "Oh."

"And pick up the agreement my lawyer drew up."

Disappointment streaked across his face.

Jenna glanced away, unable to face him. "You knew the deal when I got here. And you promised that if I spent the night, you'd sign the papers in the morning."

"I figured we'd at least talk first."

"I know, but . . . I feel . . . overwhelmed. At least look over the document. I can have it couriered here if you prefer—"

"No."

Jenna met Trey's eyes. "Trey, you gave me your word."

"Don't run away from me again. If we're going to do this, then let's not make it impersonal. You bring the papers here and we'll go over them face-to-face."

Jenna blew out a shaky breath. "I don't know . . . I just . . . it's pretty straightforward."

Trey tossed the dishrag onto the counter and marched toward her. "Nothing about this is straightforward, Jenna. *Nothing*."

The intensity in his voice shocked her. She took a step backward, but Trey advanced, placing both hands on her shoulders. "When I pledged before God to love you in good times and in bad, I meant that. When I said till death do us part, I meant those words in the deepest part of my soul. Now you want out and you expect me to make this easy for you. You're my wife, Jenna. My *wife*. Does that mean nothing to you?"

"That meant everything to me!" Jenna countered. Then she looked away. The last thing she wanted was an ugly argument with Trey. "Please, I don't want to fight about this."

She jerked when she felt Trey's palm on her face, but it was a surprisingly gentle caress. "I'm not angry, sweetheart. But I am frustrated. You're my wife—my *life*—and you want to walk away again before you've given us a chance."

"I'm confused," Jenna admitted.

"I'm a different person, Jenna. I've grown. Won't you give me a chance to show you that?"

"I came into this marriage with all the hope in the world. That hope was shattered, Trey. You don't know how much that hurt me."

"I was hurting, too."

"Then why didn't you just talk to me that day? Why get angry? Why watch me walk away and now act like you can't live without me?"

There was a flicker of something in Trey's eyes.

Jenna couldn't pinpoint the emotion. The tension built as silence stretched between them. Once again, he had no answers for her.

He finally said, "I know you blame me for the downfall of our marriage, and I'm willing to accept the lion's share of the blame. But if we're going to hash things out, let's not sugarcoat anything here. You played a role in our breakup, too. Long before the day you walked out on me."

Jenna's mouth fell open. "How can you say that?"

"You took a sabbatical from your job."

"Because—" Jenna promptly shut her mouth as his words hit home. She had taken a leave of absence for one reason only—in case things hadn't worked out with Trey.

"You have no idea how insecure that made me feel. Like you were waiting for the first sign of trouble so you could head back to New York."

"I . . ." What could she say?

"I knew I loved you, but your decision to 'keep your options open' made me realize I needed to guard my heart."

"I . . . I never thought about how that would make you feel."

"I know you didn't. You also didn't know that I'd spent much of my life guarding my heart. My father raised me because my mother didn't want me, and for a long time that made it hard for me to trust. I wanted to know that the woman I was going to spend my life with wanted me with the same kind of passion that I had for her. If you didn't want to be here . . ."

Trey's voice trailed off, and silence filled the air. After a moment he said, "Let's take a walk on the beach."

"Now?"

"You always liked to walk on the beach in the mornings. Now I know why. It's a great place to think. A great place to talk."

He was already walking past her to the bedroom. Moments later, he reappeared wearing jeans and a T-shirt. "C'mon, sweetheart."

Trey took her hand and led her to the terrace. At the side of the patio enclosure was a door and steps that went down to the sand.

There was something infinitely calming about the sound of waves lapping at the shore. Something peaceful about a seagull's early morning call. Jenna stared out at the water, as far as the eye could see. She found solace there, something she didn't find when she looked onto her tree-lined street back home in Buffalo. The sun and the sand were good for her soul, and Key West provided both.

Jenna and Trey walked hand in hand for several minutes, neither saying a word. Jenna had thought they'd end up arguing in the house, that she would end up in tears and he would emotionally shut down. But neither of those things had happened.

"That morning," Trey suddenly said, "when you asked me about my ex-wife, it wasn't that I didn't want to tell you about her. It was that your question caught me completely off guard. I was stunned that you knew about Irene. And when you said your father had found out that piece of information about my past—that's what sent me through the roof."

Jenna still remembered the shock of her father's news. He had never approved of her sudden marriage, and had been determined to prove to her that Trey was no good. The day he called to tell her what he'd learned— that Trey had been married before but had kept that from her—he'd had an unmistakable "I told you so" smugness.

Jenna had been angry with her father, and was certain he'd been lying. Making up a story so he could get her to return home. Surely if Trey had been married before, he would have told her that. Which was why, almost in jest, she had asked Trey that question the morning after an incredible night spent making love.

Trey said, "I thought, 'This woman doesn't trust me at all if she has her father digging into my past.' And that really hurt me, Jenna. More than I could deal with."

"I never asked him to investigate your past. In fact, I was angry when he told me what he'd done." In hindsight, she should have shared that with Trey, made him understand her father had acted on his own. "My father was on some mission to prove that you were totally wrong for me because he couldn't understand why I'd married you after knowing you such a short time." Jenna paused. "When he announced that you had an ex-wife, he made the fact that you hadn't told me sound sinister. And when you didn't want to talk about it, just got angry because of my questions—"

"You thought the worst about me."

"I didn't know what to think. But I knew that I couldn't live with secrets between us."

Trey nodded. "I know. And that's not what I wanted, either. I always planned to tell you about Irene at some point. But before I could do that, you were gone."

Jenna had told herself that it didn't matter, that she didn't care. But now she wanted to know. "Why didn't you tell me you were married before? Because I have to tell you, I couldn't help thinking you were still in love with your ex. That that's why you wouldn't give me all of your heart."

"It's nothing like that, Jenna. I'm not even sure I was in love with Irene. Not the way I'm in love with you."

Every time he said he loved her, her body had the same reaction. Her heart picked up speed and warmth tickled her stomach. But they were only words. Actions were what were important.

"I married Irene about four years before I'd met you."

"Was she a customer?" Trey met a ton of women at the bar, the same way he'd met her.

"No, she worked at the local grocery store. We dated for close to a year and then she got pregnant."

"You have a child?" Jenna asked, shocked.

Trey shook his head. "She miscarried. It was right after we'd gotten married. I knew we weren't head over heels in love, but we cared about each other. I thought we could make it work.

"The problem was, after her miscarriage, it seemed like everything we had in common had been shot to hell. We fought like cats and dogs. It was the only way we communicated. I had my issues, and I guess she had hers. Somehow we hung on for two years before she told me she wanted a divorce. I let her go and moved on. *That's* why I never mentioned Irene. Because our marriage had been a mistake and I didn't want to dwell on the past."

What he said made sense. Weren't there men in her past she wanted to forget she'd ever dated?

"I met you about a year and a half after Irene. I wanted you, Jenna. My heart knew instantly that you were the one for me. But I guess . . . I guess I didn't really know what it took to make a marriage work. I don't think either of us did."

Jenna blew out a shaky breath as Trey's words settled over her. He was right. She'd fallen hard for him when she met him, and in her heart wanted things to work. But there had been fear—fear that even though she'd never been happier in her life, she didn't know him well enough to spend the rest of her life with him.

"You're right, Trey. I didn't really know what it meant to be married. To be committed. I let my father's negativity influence me, and I'm sorry about that."

"It doesn't matter," Trey told her. "Not anymore. What does is that you know I still love you. I never stopped. And now that you're back . . . I don't want to let you go again. I'm ready for in sickness and in health, till death do us part." He paused. "Are you?"

"I . . ." Was she? She'd come here with such a clear plan. End her marriage officially and move on with her life. "I'd like some time to think."

"You're gonna leave?"

"Just for a little while. To clear my head."

"Will you come back?"

"Yes." Jenna stuck her fingers into the back pockets on her shorts and turned toward the house.

"With that agreement you want me to sign?"

Trey's question made her halt. "Like I said, I have a lot to think about. Plus, I need to see Ruby."

Trey nodded as he strode toward her, but didn't voice any disagreement.

"Do you have my purse?"

"It's in the house."

"I guess I'll catch a cab."

"You can take my car." Jenna opened her mouth to protest, but Trey added, "I took the day off, remember? I'd hoped to spend it with you, but if not, I'll do stuff around the house. Work out. Clean the toilets." He grinned. "Whenever you're ready, you can drive back here and have Ruby follow you in your rental car. Then we'll deal with . . . whatever you want."

Jenna's stomach dropped. Trey wasn't fighting her. Was he letting her go again?

And suddenly she was angry—angry with herself. Was she playing games with Trey, wanting him to beg her to stay? He'd already put his cards on the table. Now she needed to sort through her own feelings.

Back in the house, Trey handed her his car keys. "Take your time," he told her.

"I'll be back."

Chapter Six

Trey couldn't help smiling after Jenna left the house. He knew good and well that she'd be back. And a lot sooner than she expected.

Taking time to think was classic Jenna. Even the day he'd proposed marriage, despite the excited gleam in her eyes when he'd gotten down on one knee, she'd told him that she had to "go think about it." After a walk on the beach, she had returned in under an hour with a positive answer.

This time would be no different. Trey was sure of it.

Except that Jenna might be none too happy when she got back. Not if Ruby had lived up to her end of the bargain.

Trey would make no apologies for doing what it took to save his marriage. He wasn't going to stand back and watch Jenna leave his life like he did the first time. He had a feeling she was pushing him, seeing if her indecision would drive him to the breaking point. It wouldn't. If she truly didn't want to be with him, he would let her go—only after letting her know that she'd always have his heart.

Jenna was a fireball of passion, and he knew she wouldn't be happy when she learned that Ruby had left.

But he'd be ready for Jenna and her possible wrath. Give her a homecoming she would remember always.

Trey set about clearing the plates from the patio table. With the time it would take his wife to drive to the Sheraton hotel, park, head inside, and discover that Ruby wasn't there, she'd be back in about . . . oh, twenty-two minutes.

He washed the dishes by hand, then gathered up the candles and rose petals. At the eighteen-minute mark, he set the dining room table, complete with two tall glasses and a pitcher of orange juice. He'd keep the champagne in the fridge for now.

In the kitchen, Trey turned on a burner and placed a skillet on the stove. He'd make scrambled eggs with pieces of turkey. Nice and easy, and it had always been a breakfast he and Jenna enjoyed.

As he cracked the last of four eggs into a batter bowl, he glanced at the clock. Twenty minutes.

He added the turkey to the bowl, some milk, and a dash of pepper. He was mixing it all together when he heard the door slam shut.

One, two . . . right about now.

"Ruby's gone," Jenna announced in disbelief. "I went to the hotel, and the little twit checked out!"

"Little twit?" Trey raised an eyebrow. "I thought she was your friend."

"So did I, but clearly I was wrong. Damn her. She's got my suitcase." Jenna groaned. "The separation agreement."

"Actually . . . I have your suitcase. It's in the trunk of my car."

Jenna dropped her purse on the counter and moved toward him, her eyes full of expectation. "And the separation agreement?"

"Sorry."

"Trey!" Jenna slammed a hand on the counter. "Why are you doing this?"

Maybe now wasn't a good time to have a skillet of hot oil around. Trey moved it to a back burner.

"Damn it, Trey." Jenna's fingers closed around his arm.

"All right. So I pretty much coerced Ruby to hit the road." He shrugged when Jenna's eyes grew as wide as saucers. "I want you back, Jenna. Back in my life. Back as my wife, in the full sense of the word."

"What'd you promise her?"

"A trip back here on my dime whenever she's ready." Jenna snorted.

"Ruby seems to think you're still in love with me."

"Ruby is a sentimental nut."

Trey winced at the insult. "Wow."

"You know what I mean. When she gets it in her head that she's right about something, there's no stopping her. God only knows why she's certain we're soul mates."

"What if she's right?"

Jenna didn't answer. She glanced away.

"Do you still love me?" Trey tilted Jenna's chin upward, forcing her to meet his eyes. "If you can tell me that you no longer love me, then I'll let you walk through that door. No, I'll do one better. I'll call up a lawyer myself. I've been doing some research ever since I received those papers from you. I know that for you to get a divorce in New York, we have to be legally separated for a year. But Florida is a no-fault state. I'm a resident here and can file right away."

Jenna's eyes narrowed slightly as she looked at Trey. Here he was, finally offering her what she wanted—so why didn't she feel happy?

"Jenna?"

"I . . . I see."

"You don't want me to do that?"

She covered her face with her hands. "No," she answered softly, so softly she wasn't sure he heard her.

But he must have, because he looped his arms around her. Sighing softly, Jenna allowed herself to collapse against him. How long had it been since she'd had a soft place to fall?

"I'm afraid," she confessed.

"That I'll hurt you?"

"I love you so much, I couldn't stand it if we broke up a second time."

"Come here." Trey took Jenna by the hand and led her to the table. He sat on a chair and pulled her onto his lap. "You wanted some space, so I let you go, but I didn't get to finish telling you everything. I know you think I never contacted you when you left, but that's not true. I did call. I guess it was your father who answered. He told me in no uncertain terms never to call again because you wanted nothing to do with me."

"He never told me you called."

"Surprise, surprise. And before you say anything, I know—I could have called again. I wanted to. But I'm human. I had an ego, and you were crushing it. And while you were gone I accepted the fact that we *had* acted on our lust and gotten married too soon. I told myself that it never would have worked between us, but that didn't help me to stop thinking about you every day. And no matter how much I worked, I couldn't forget you. Not the way work helped me forget Irene."

"I can't believe you're actually taking time off now. I thought that bar was your life."

"No." He softly stroked Jenna's face. "You're my life."

His words stole her breath. All this time, she'd been running from him, but the truth was, she wanted this man. Wanted him more than she'd ever wanted anyone. No one had ever made her as happy as he had during the brief time they'd been together.

She wrapped her arms around him. "I'm glad I'm here, Trey. I'm glad we're talking. We haven't really talked like this before."

"Just between the sheets?"

"Mmm-hmm. Not that I'm complaining, mind you, but to make a marriage work, we need more than great sex. We need to be able to communicate."

Trey rested his chin on the top of her head. "You know what I'm happy about?"

"What?"

"That you sent me that separation agreement," Trey answered.

Jenna pulled her head back to look up at him. "You're *happy* about that?"

"You bet. If you hadn't sent it, I wouldn't have been able to force your hand and get you down here. Because I knew that sending those papers back with a nice little note would get you down here and quick. You're stubborn that way."

"Trey, I'm almost thirty. My biological clock is ticking. I needed some direction in my life . . . if it wasn't going to be with you."

"It will be with me. And I'm going to give you babies, sweetheart. Lots of them. Or at least I'll die trying."

Jenna bit her bottom lip. "Will you, now?"

"You have my word."

"Mmmm." Call her a fool, but she was getting turned on. "Sounds like you really want me to stay."

"You're damn right I do."

Jenna felt Trey's growing erection against her bottom. "And I suppose you'd like to do some of that baby-making-trying now?"

"There's no time like the present."

Jenna laughed, genuinely happy for the first time since heading back here. "You have an appetite like no one I've ever known."

"Hey, I need to keep up with you. Hopefully you won't trade me in for a younger model in two years. I *will* be thirty-five then."

"Not a chance." Jenna framed his face and kissed

him. "I love you, Trey. More than I could ever love any-body."

He squeezed her tight. "God, I love you."

A beat passed, then Jenna said, "What do you say we get to that baby-making-trying part?"

Desire flashed in Trey's eyes as he rose from the chair, lifting Jenna as he did. Then he slung her over his shoulder.

"Trey!" she protested, even as she giggled. "Trey, put me down!"

"No can do," he said. "You had a request. I'm here to fill it."

"Oooh, I like the sound of that."

"You're gonna like what I do to you even more."

"Am I now?"

"You bet."

And she did.

MURPHY'S LAW

Morgan Leigh

Chapter One

Kat Murphy felt the spark of interest as she gazed at the fine specimen of a man that had just walked down to the shoreline of the beach where she lay tanning, trying to forget her troubles. The sun was high in the sky, and her shades did little to darken her vision enough to take in the details of the man, but what she could see, her rarely used erogenous zones responded to, much as she despised herself for noticing at all. What was the matter with her? She'd come down here to forget about men. Especially ones who were attractive and totally oblivious to the things going on around them.

Sam Parrish, her former boss at the law offices of McCauley, Parrish, and Hawke, was one of those men. She'd secretly been in love with him for almost the entire two years she'd worked at the firm. But his flirtatious comments and gestures were moments of weakness to him, and he didn't seem to like letting himself feel anything for Kat. Because of that, she'd gone out of her way to make sure he never knew her feelings. If he'd shown more than a passing interest, she might have followed through on one of those hot, hungry looks, but he never did. And the surly attitude that followed those glances just hardened her resolve.

Circumstances beyond his control were the only reason she let him get away with it, but she'd finally had enough, and as of this past Monday, she was no longer employed there. She couldn't stand feeling like she was a guilty pleasure to him. One that she suspected he did personal penance for when he went into his office and shut the door on temptation.

She tipped her head curiously and continued to watch the man as he stared out at the water as if he were struggling with demons of his own. The soft foam of the tide washed the sand around his feet, and he spread them wider, taking a firmer stance.

Not a single man had been able to turn her head since she'd first set eyes on her boss, except this one. Forcing herself to look away from him, she gnashed her teeth. The stranger by the water probably had a story to tell, but Sam's story had been hard enough to cope with. She wasn't interested in learning anyone else's. From what she could see, this man was attractive, but men were scratched from her list for a long time. Her heart drummed a constant ache in her chest because of a man. She wasn't up to dealing with another one for a while. Not Sam, not some unknown stranger. No one.

The only man she felt any generosity toward at the moment was Jonah McCauley, Sam's partner and best friend. He was engaged to her best friend, and he went out of his way to shower Camelot with the love and respect she deserved. Well, she snickered to herself, that, and when she told Cam about her plans to quit her job and get away for a while, he'd offered the use of his beach house, no questions asked. She needed refuge and Jonah provided it. He was a good man.

Sam was a good man, too, she admitted grudgingly to herself. He just had more suffering in his life than any man ever should. His wife Patti had been killed in a horrid car crash two years before, and Kat had signed on with the firm just a few short months afterward. If

Kat could've helped it, she'd never have fallen for a man carrying so much emotional baggage. But her heart hadn't let her decide. She'd tumbled head over heels in love with him from the start.

She'd managed to protect her secret, though. His grief was so hard to watch, but she'd become one in his circle of friends who got him through the rough spots in his road to recovery. But when it was clear that he wasn't ready to start any new relationship, she'd cultivated a reputation as a wild child and party girl. If he thought she was a free spirit, he wouldn't have the added pressure of worrying about come-ons and advances. She'd sometimes wished she'd been brave enough to take that leap of faith, and tell Sam that she loved him to distraction and she wasn't the loose woman he believed her to be. Kat feared few things, but he was a one-woman man, and she knew if he was aware of her true feelings, their work relationship would be intolerable. Sam telling her that Patti would always be his only love would crush her heart, and it was something Kat just didn't have the guts to hear.

Her attention was drawn back to the present when the man turned to his right and walked away from her, parallel to the waves. She watched his retreating, shirtless back, and the muscles that rippled as he raked his hand through his dark brown hair, the way his bare feet sank into the eroding sand as the tide pulled it out from under him. He moved up onto the drier part of the beach and thrust his hands into the pockets of the khaki shorts that rode low on his narrow hips. If she wasn't still so damned angry for letting herself fall so hard for Sam, Kat actually might have tried to draw his attention and bring him back up the beach so she could see what he looked like from the front. But she'd come here specifically to get *away* from opposite sex. To clear her head and make some solid life plans. Men could be stubborn and so clueless sometimes; she was through trying to figure them out. And they said women were the complicated ones? *Yeah, right,* she thought.

She was powerless to ignore him altogether, but she was hurting so much from Sam's unwitting rejection that instead of desire or arousal for the masculine stranger, she felt resentment, and disgust with herself for noticing him. Besides that, the man appeared distracted, sorting out his own troubles by walking along the shore, letting it work its calming effects.

"I can *so* relate, pal," she muttered under her breath.

The man stopped abruptly and his head snapped to the right, as if he'd heard her.

He hadn't, had he? "Get a grip, Kat," she told herself, but her breath backed up in her throat when he did an about-face and started stalking back the way he'd come, only this time he cut across the sand, his feet kicking it up like spray as he closed the distance between them. As he got closer and closer, her eyes went to his hard chest, covered with light brown hair that tapered to his narrow waist and disappeared into those low-slung shorts. Kat was shocked that she actually licked her lips when her gaze followed the path down. What *was* the matter with her?

"If you were a man, Katrissa Murphy, I'd say you had some huge balls to leave me the way you did."

Kat's eyes froze on the fly of his shorts. No, it couldn't be! His voice was so low, it hissed through clenched teeth that only she and the few others near them heard.

She squinted from the sun in her eyes, not quite behind him. She turned her head a fraction until it was completely blocked by his broad shoulders and she could see him clearly through her sunglasses.

No, no, no! The words drummed in her head as she realized that it was Sam towering over her. And *he* sounded pissed at *her.* Who did he think he was? The nerve of the man! She glanced at the other sunbathers

and beachcombers as he looked down at her like he
could throttle her.

How many times did she have to have her heart broken? It was hard enough leaving her resignation on his
desk. And she'd made sure he wasn't in the office. She
wouldn't have been able to stand the awkwardness if he
demanded an explanation and she had to give her reasons just then. She'd needed time to pull herself together when they finally had that confrontation. And
now she was going to have to make the break all over
again? Damn, why didn't he just accept it and move on,
like she was trying to do? Her nerves were raw, and bitterness curled her lip.

"I quit my job, Sam. Period. We'd have to have personal contact for me to leave you," she muttered deri-
sively. "And there are children running around within
earshot. Leave the vulgarities for your clients." Her stomach was tight with dread, but she tried to keep her voice
low and succinct, letting him know that his sudden appearance wasn't welcome. "You shouldn't have come
here," she said, standing her ground. *While lying flat on
your back,* she thought ironically. A twist she certainly
hadn't anticipated.

She assumed that when she finally had to go home
and face Sam's wrath, she'd be toe-to-toe with him.
"How did you find me, anyway?" she asked. Her heart was
pounding like a jackhammer, from surprise or dread,
she wasn't sure which. She just needed a minute to
shore up that weak spot—the one that Sam could get
through. She had to tell herself that this man was the
enemy. Well, not the enemy exactly, but definitely a danger to her heart.

She was in a skimpy, zebra-striped strapless bikini, lying
on a lounger with tanning oil smeared all over her
body. And the way he was looking down at her, she
might as well have been naked. It irked her even more
that he'd notice her now, when every day she'd been in

that office, working her tail off, he'd quashed every glance of hunger, every hint of lust. Of course, his attentions weren't of the amorous kind at the moment. But not even the scolding he was delivering could hide the passion that burned in his eyes, and Kat felt it right down to her toes.

"Before I was a partner, Kat, I *was* an investigator," he said dryly. "But a word of advice, sweetheart? Never tell your best friend where you're going when she's sleeping with *my* best friend."

Her mouth dropped open. "Camelot told you?" she asked, outraged that her friend would betray the sacred bonds of the sisterhood.

"No, she told Jonah, who in turn told me. Her way of getting around the 'don't tell Sam where I'm going' pledge that she says you nearly made her sign in blood." His mouth formed a straight line, obviously not happy that she'd gone to such extremes.

Kat groused, "Remind me to include fiancés in that oath next time."

"Maybe if you'd given two weeks notice, I wouldn't have had to go around your *girl rules.*"

She scoffed, "Would you have let me go?"

"Hell no, but at least I would've had fourteen days to talk you out of it. Instead I had to get on a plane and come find you. Do you know I've been on this beach for over an hour looking for you?" he yelled, and jammed his clenched fists onto his hips.

He looked as menacing as a sentencing judge, expecting her to be contrite. *Fat chance,* she thought. She slapped her palm over her heart. "Oh, my! A *whole hour,* Sam? I'm so touched to know that I'm worth sixty minutes out of your busy schedule. I suppose I should be grateful you didn't bill me for your time," she said sarcastically. "In fact"—she tipped her head and pointed up at him—"I'll tell you what, Counselor. Go ahead and bill me for your services, and then we'll consider our association terminated. You can just hop back on that plane and get on with your life." She squinted her eyes in annoyance now. "And I can get on with mine."

"Stop being ridiculous, Kat. I'm not going anywhere."

She growled in her throat. "Me? Ridiculous? What's ridiculous is that you think coming down here would get me to change my mind. And you're a lawyer, Sam. There's a name for your behavior. It's called stalking, and last I heard, that was illegal." People were beginning to stare, and though she'd never shrunk away from attention, she didn't like being chastised.

Sam's brows furrowed, disbelief marring his features. "You don't really believe I'm stalking you, Kat."

She lowered her voice, this time really contrite for thinking it. "No," she admitted. "You'd never lay a hand on me." *Much to my disappointment,* she thought wryly. "And you'd never do anything to frighten me." But she sighed and her eyes burned in frustration. "But I left for a reason, and don't ask me what it is because I won't tell you. It's personal." He was scowling down at her, eyes drilling into hers, and Kat was hotter than she'd been for the last two hours, basking in the sun. She might try and force herself to bury her feelings for Sam in anger or derision, but the sensations just a look could evoke still burned white-hot. Her skin felt scalded under his piercing gaze. Damn the man!

He gave her one of his "I'm not amused" looks, and waited for an explanation nonetheless. *Well, he can wait until the sun goes down, and comes right back up,* she thought to herself. She wasn't about to give it to him! Not without betraying what was in her heart. And Kat didn't want it broken on some stretch of beautiful beach. She would save the anguish for the real world, thank you very much. Her emotions had taken quite a beating these past months because she'd honestly believed that there was something there, and if she waited him out, Sam would see that he had a second chance at happiness if he'd only let himself feel again.

She tipped her head and the sun beat down on her face, but she could see Sam's eyes stray downward to the way her breasts moved when she squinted and shadowed her eyes with her hand. He might have his hang-ups, she mused, but he was still a typical, red-blooded male. A little bit of bouncing flesh, and his mind wandered. She almost called him on it, but hunger replaced the frown on his face, and he seemed to forget what he was standing there for. His libido was actually working to her advantage.

"Go home, Sam." Her body was betraying her in ways she didn't want him to see. She was hot and aroused under his gaze, and that was so wrong. She'd had to talk herself up to walking away from a job she loved and a man she couldn't make love her. Now she wanted to be alone and wallow in misery for a while. It was her pity party, and he was ruining it.

His rigid stance softened; like a lawyer, he changed tactics. "I told you, sweetheart. I'm not going anywhere. And I don't have to be in court again for a week, so I'm free for a while. But then, you know that, don't you? Before you pulled your Houdini act, you left me my schedule for the next month."

"I did, didn't I?" she grumbled, wishing she'd picked a week that he was swamped in work and couldn't get away. But somewhere deep inside, she wondered why she *had* chosen to quit when she knew that there wasn't anything stopping him from tracking her down.

Her heart sank. Oh, no! Did she bring this on herself? Did she secretly hope that Sam would come and drag her home? *No!* she thought. She wouldn't wish this hurt on her worst enemy. Well, yes she would. Maybe her *worst* enemy, but not on herself, Dammit! Her doubt made her angry. "Never say I wasn't an efficient assistant, Sam Parrish."

His lip curled. "Your work performance isn't why I'm here. I think you know that."

Okay, that threw her. What was he—? No! She wouldn't let him *do* this to her again, pulling her in, just to turn his back at the last minute. No more! "You just hate not having the last word, that's all this is. I quit without giving you a chance at rebuttal. I told you, Sam. It's personal." She chose her words carefully because it had *everything* to do with him. "It's *not* your concern."

"Everything about you concerns me, Kat," he said quietly, and she felt that shiver race up her spine at his voice, like a caress along her skin. Damn! She was sinking all over again. She could spar with any man with one hand tied behind her back, but when Sam talked to her in that low, intimate tone, she melted like butter.

As much as she wanted to just crawl into a hole and hibernate until spring, forget how wonderful he looked standing over her, his chest and broad shoulders covered with a sheen of sweat, Kat saw that Sam wasn't going to let her sidestep the issue here. From his guarded look, he wasn't any happier than she was to be discussing private business with an audience watching the drama. And even though she wasn't sure how to take that last statement, it would be emotional suicide to be alone with him. She'd say things that she'd been so careful to keep hidden. She couldn't spill her guts now. Better to be in a public place, where there were plenty of people around and the arousal that always gripped her when he was near would be tempered.

He cocked his hip and crossed his arms. "You might as well just come talk to me, Kat."

She pressed her lips together, not ready to concede yet. She still had some fight left in her.

"All right then. We'll do it here. But I can guarantee you won't like what I have to say."

Her eyes shot to his. "Like what?" She was the wounded party here. She hadn't done a thing but love a man who couldn't love her back. *Gimme your best shot*, she thought.

He smirked. His lip curled and she knew she'd made a grave mistake in underestimating this man.

"Oh, I don't know . . . maybe we should talk about your penchant for flirtatious behavior in the workplace."

Kat's mouth dropped open. She was actually speechless. The blood drained from her face. He didn't actually believe that *she* was guilty of that, did he? Her eyes burned again, holding his gaze as she finally found her voice. "Don't do this, Parrish. You won't like where it leads either."

He met her challenge, one brow raising. "What have ya got, sweetheart?"

"*I'm* not a tease."

If they weren't so angry at each other, Kat might've laughed at the way he went rigid, furious and offended. He actually staggered back like he'd been struck. "*I'm* a tease? You've got to be kidding," he said. "If it wasn't for you, I wouldn't be in a constant state of—"

Kat scrambled up off the lounger and slapped her hand over his mouth. She took her cue from the state of his arousal and stopped him before everyone within shouting distance could hear him finish that sentence. She was glad to know that she wasn't the only one who suffered from those hot, hungry looks, but enough was enough. They'd embarrassed each other enough.

"Okay, okay. Uncle! You win. We'll talk in private," she muttered through tightly clenched teeth. Touching him in any way was delicious, and Kat fought the pull, chanting to herself that he'd just played dirty pool and she wasn't going to forgive him for it.

Her hand stayed clamped over his mouth as she

looked around again. Great. They were making a spectacle of themselves. Not that she usually gave a damn. She just didn't like doing it so scantily clad.

She gasped, clapping her eyes on Sam when his tongue flicked out and tasted the soft pad of her palm. His normally slate blue eyes were as dark as a brewing storm now, and his nostrils flared as he breathed. He was still coiled tight as a spring, but Kat recognized that look, and it wasn't anywhere near annoyance anymore. She swallowed hard, feeling the weight of that stare wash over her.

He reached up and tugged her hand away from his warm lips. "Oh yeah," he said huskily. "We *definitely* need some privacy right now."

He let go of her hand and she curled her fingers around her damp palm.

Bending down, he stuffed her book, tanning oil, and wrap into her bag. He literally tossed it to her as he folded her beach chair and set out her sandals for her to slip into. "Better put them on. When you step off that towel, you'll feel how hot the sand is."

She dutifully did his bidding as he scooped up the towel, too, shaking it gently, starting up the beach. "Let's go, Kat. I've come a *hell* of a long way to have this . . . *discussion.*"

She wasn't sure how to interpret the way he put the emphasis on the last word. She'd said all she was going to say about the job, and if it was anything else, well then, he'd had ample opportunities before, and he'd always been the one to call a halt. But she supposed that she should let him have his say. The sooner they were alone and he understood that she was through with the games of cat and mouse, the better. Unless of course, he threw her down on the bed and made passionate love to her. She snickered silently. *You're the weak one, Kat. Not him,* she thought. She let Sam think she was easy.

He still loved his late wife. Even the need for physical satisfaction wasn't enough for him to indulge in a one-night stand.

More's the pity, she mused, her gaze following him as he marched up the incline toward the boardwalk. She didn't realize she'd sighed in delight until he turned, saying, "Are you coming, Kat? Or are you going to stand there and admire my backside the whole day?"

Kat felt the flush travel up her neck and cheeks as she straightened her shoulders and stomped down on the arousal that had pushed its way past her resistance. She looked up at his face. She wished she could deny it. But she *had* been staring at it. "On my way, Sam," she chortled loud enough for his ears, but under her breath, she murmured, "You arrogant jerk."

Chapter Two

Sam felt the blood pumping through his veins as he waited for Kat to reach him on the boardwalk. He'd been searching for over an hour on the beach, but when he almost gave up, discouraged that he'd never find her, he'd heard her voice, clear as day. And when he'd turned, there she was, up on the sand, watching him. He'd felt her eyes on him. He couldn't believe that was *his* Kat in that incredibly enticing teeny bikini. She was reclining in a lounger among the hundreds of sun-soakers blanketing the sand.

He'd had the sun to his advantage; it was at his back, and she'd had to squint when she looked up at him. And when she realized who was standing over her, well, her expression was priceless. But even as he railed at her for her desertion, he'd suppressed a shudder, envisioning how she'd look under *him* in that same position.

But now, as he watched her trudge up the incline, he didn't feel as in control as he had when she was peering up at him from the beach chair.

She had this seductive sway to her walk, though he knew it wasn't meant for him. It was just part of everything about her that brought out all things male in him.

The breaths she took pushed her full breasts against the skimpy bathing suit top. They weren't overlarge, but they bounced slightly as she made her way toward him. She was doused in tanning oil; beads of perspiration rolled down between her slight cleavage, and he wanted to hustle her along, away from the crowd on the beach. Her appearance, along with the enticing coconut scent and her own sweet essence, aroused him more than he would've imagined. Sam felt like he was drowning in desire for her.

Christ, but she was a dangerous woman. It was a good thing he liked that about her. His only regret was that he didn't know before she quit her job just how daring she wanted to be with *him*. She'd have been under him months ago. He was here to make up for lost time, and he didn't want to waste a single second. Kat Murphy *would* be his lover before they ended their little vacation—and his wife before they got back to the city. Thanks to her best friend, he had inside information. Whatever flimsy excuse she came up with wouldn't hold any weight with him. He knew better.

She reached him on the boardwalk and boldly stood too damn close, her green eyes shining brightly from the dark tan of her face as she tipped her chin up to meet his gaze. Her barely covered breasts brushed his chest, and he fought the urge to wrap an arm around her and make full body contact. He grinned at her silent challenge. But his eyes went only as far as her full lips. Even those had been treated with some kind of balm; Sam ached to devour her mouth, and keep *on* kissing her until his lips were coated, as well. *Her taste would linger, too,* he thought hazily.

Sam stepped back, wisely compartmentalizing his emotions and denying her the evidence of his cock responding to her close proximity. Letting her think she was in control would be a mistake, but the raised brow and sly grin she flashed told him that she thought she had it when he retreated. *You've met your match, lady,* he conveyed with his matching stare.

Impatience still gnawed at him, and he snagged her hand, nearly dragging her along the boardwalk. "Which hotel is yours?"

"None of them. I'm staying at Jonah's beach house down the way."

He stopped abruptly and turned to her. "Then why are you up here when you could have the beach all to yourself?" he asked. Then his eyes raked over her entire form. "Ah."

"What do you mean, 'ah'?" she asked, but she knew what he was thinking. And from the way her jaw dropped and her eyes shot fire at him, she didn't like him assuming what he had, either.

He raised a brow, giving her the once-over again as he let go of her hand and gestured with his. The muscle in his jaw clenched, not particularly pleased with his own conclusions. "It means that I get it; not many men have access to that private section of beach, and who would you have to flaunt that next-to-nothing suit at if you were sunbathing alone?"

He took her hand again and started off, but she yanked back hard and pulled it away. He turned around, annoyed that she was taking offense to what was completely obvious.

"Is that what you think, Sam? That I like to be ogled, the object of some pervert's fantasy?"

Sam used his advantage of over six feet of height to crowd her, but she didn't budge. She just tilted her head farther back. His control was slipping, and not from the thread of conversation, though he knew he could very well be lumped into the pervert category. She was driving him crazy in that getup! "No. I think you like to be a little bit wild and unconventional. And *that*, my dear, will get you into trouble one day. You can bet on it."

Her hands came up between them and she shoved him hard. Sam was unprepared for it and he stumbled back, but he stayed on his feet. He always knew she had an Irish temper, but he'd never been on the receiving end of it. She was spitting mad, and if he was right, wounded at his accusation.

Her voice dripped scorn. "I'll have you know that it's not safe for a woman to sunbathe alone on a deserted beach. Add to that, the dress Camelot chose for me to wear as her maid of honor shows a lot of skin, and I'm in this outfit so I don't have ugly tan lines when I walk with *you* down the aisle, since you're Jonah's best man."

Sam was almost ashamed that he'd jumped to conclusions. Almost. He couldn't concentrate when her breasts heaved with every deep breath she took to lash out at him. How could he be sorry when even her wrath dramatized her sexuality? He couldn't.

His erection was growing by embarrassing leaps as he stared, and it didn't help matters any when she looked down at his fly. She was insulted that he wasn't apologetic, but instead was becoming aroused from her dressing down.

"Typical." She sneered at him. "If we weren't in a public place with so many kids around, I'd tell you exactly what I think of *you* right about now, buddy."

She turned and stalked down the boardwalk, past the hotels and shops that lined the strip, her tight curvy ass clad in nothing but that tiny bikini bottom, swaying as she walked at a brisk pace to widen the distance between them. Sam shamelessly enjoyed the view. *Whew, she's a firecracker!*

He yelled after her, "Aw, c'mon, Kat! I'm sorry, all right?" But he stayed rooted to the spot when she turned her head and shot him a nasty scowl as she stormed off. If looks could kill, he'd be six feet under right now. As it was, he knew it rankled that she couldn't flip him the bird. He grinned as he saw her hand curl into a fist, forcing herself to not give in to her ire in front of the very children whose ears she'd refused to corrupt.

He didn't say another word. He knew where she was headed. Better to let her work off some of that fury he'd provoked.

He used her lounge chair to hide the evidence that her sassy walk and tantrum had stirred in him. How was he expected to think clearly when the sight of her body and her insolence matched every fantasy he'd ever had of her? He was a man, after all. "It's your fault, Kat," he muttered to himself.

An hour later, Sam stepped onto the porch of the beach house and spotted his bag sitting beside the chair there. Before he'd headed off to look for Kat, he'd put it just inside and relocked the door. *She thinks she's going to put me out, does she?* he thought. "Like hell," he said aloud.

He tried the doorknob. Locked. Sam rolled his eyes, fished the key that Jonah gave him from his pocket and let himself inside.

Kat was in the foyer, leaning against the wall, ankles crossed and arms akimbo, staring at him as he picked up his suitcase. She'd showered and slipped into a pretty, loose-fitting sleeveless dress while he was gone. She was decently attired now, but the shift was short enough that he could see her luscious, tanned legs from midthigh down. He felt the fire in his belly ignite and begin to burn.

"Breaking and entering now, are we, Sam?"

He lifted his gaze to her face and held up the key. "No, sweetheart. I was invited to stay here when I learned where you'd taken off to. What puzzles me is why I wasn't informed that I'd have a roommate."

She let out an exasperated breath and dropped her

arms. "Damn Camelot and Jonah and their meddling. They should've left well enough alone."

"And you think walking away from your job and your friends was well enough?"

"I didn't walk away from them. I walked away from you, Sam."

"Yeah. No kidding," he grumbled, his gaze sliding from hers. He was glad she'd admitted it, when she'd denied it down on the beach, but he let the subject go without further comment. There would be plenty of time for *that* talk soon enough. For now, he wanted to get settled. Maybe get a drink. He hoped Jonah kept the bar stocked. He'd need one or two to dull his senses enough to concentrate on Kat herself, not what her body and scent were doing to him. She still smelled faintly of coconut oil, and her skin looked silky smooth.

Sam shut the front door with more force than was necessary, but he was battling to shut out the images that played in his head of her body sliding against his. He shook his head and hefted his suitcase, passing her as he strode down the hall.

"Just where do you think you're going with that?" she asked shrewishly, following close behind him.

"Well, Sherlock, I think I'm going to stow my things in the bedroom."

"Ah, no, Parrish, I was here first. You'll take the sofa."

She collided with him when he halted in the middle of the bedroom and dropped the luggage. He turned around and she stood so close, Sam could swear an electric charge arced between them.

He advanced; she had no choice but to retreat, stepping backward. Reaching a hand past her shoulder, he swung the door shut and kept going until he had her pinned against the hard wood with his body. He touched his forehead to hers and closed his eyes.

He was tired, Sam realized. Tired of going round in

circles. Of waiting until the time was right. *Well, this is it,* he resolved.

Murmuring low, his voice almost soundless, he said, "No one is sleeping on the sofa, Kat."

Always a wild thing, he thought, opening his eyes when she stiffened, trying to work up some bluster.

Kat did indeed have Camelot as a best friend. Sam had gone to her for help in finding out why Kat quit and where she'd gone. She wouldn't say much, but what she *had* revealed was enough for him to fill in the blanks. It was why he was convinced that Kat was exactly where she wanted to be, and whether she wanted to admit it or not, he wasn't going to back off until she did.

He wedged a leg between both of hers before she could muster enough indignation, his hard thigh lifting and pressing against her cleft. Her breath whooshed out and her eyelids lowered. *Yeah,* he thought. *We're both exactly where we need to be.*

He braced his forearm against the wood by her head and leaned into her, his other hand sliding around and cupping her bottom. His lips brushed over hers. "I want the truth now, honey. Do you really *want* me on that sofa?"

Kat's eyes closed. Sam didn't like it. It gave her time to build a wall of defense against him. He wouldn't allow that anymore. His thigh flexed and pressed upward. "Kat?"

"N-no," she stammered, and her heavy lids lifted.

"Good answer," he rasped, and captured her mouth with his own. He pulled her close and tangled his hand in her hair, his leg continuing the teasing friction. The smell of her shampoo, skin, and *God,* her growing arousal was like a drug to him, dragging him under.

His tongue flicked at the seam of her lips, and she opened readily for him. He groaned and drove in, fully engaging her in their first kiss as lovers.

He kept on kissing her as both hands moved down,

cupping her buttocks and maneuvering himself until both of her legs wrapped around his waist. His strength supported her against the door and he ground his growing erection against her center.

Breaking the heated kiss, his breathing ragged, his lips grazed along her cheek, then lower to her throat. He was getting drunk on the feel of her, the delicious taste of her!

She whimpered through swollen, moist lips as her fingers dug into his shoulders.

Sam had barely whetted his ravenous appetite and already his cock had throbbed to aching thickness, needing to be sheathed and surrounded by her warmth. He launched a full-out assault on her senses, and she cried out, her body jolting as his lips closed over the cord at the curve of her neck, sucking her there. He delighted in his discovery; she made the most erotic sound in her throat when his tongue flicked relentlessly over the sensitive spot. "Oh, yeah, Kat. Purr for me," he growled.

He slid one hand up her ribs to cup her swollen breast through her clothes, plucking at the hard nipple as his teeth nipped at the vulnerable area on the column of her neck.

Her fingers felt like claws on his shoulders as her back arched, and her head rolled against the door as she tipped her chin, urging him on. He held tight to her, stimulating her senses, and she mindlessly reached for the climax that he knew was fast approaching.

She squirmed, thrashing against him as he rocked into her, the two of them all but fucking were it not for the clothes that prevented their union. She finally shattered, screaming out her pleasure. "Oh my God! Sam!"

It was the sound of the sweetest surrender. "That's it, baby, let yourself go," he groaned, slowing his movements and reveling in her gratification.

She was wracked with prolonged shudders as he nuzzled her gently. She panted, trying to catch her breath, becoming boneless in his arms, her rushed climax leaving her weak and pliable.

Sam's gut was tight with restraint and need. Having her this way and evoking her responses had driven him to the very brink, but he was just short of crashing over. He was still hard as a diamond.

Her sexual appetite was something that Sam had been dying to experience, but he'd always denied himself before her fiery glances could pull him in. She was dazzling in her sensuality.

His breath was harsh as he leaned back to look at her. Her curly black hair, tousled and so sexy, had fallen over her face when she rode her climax. Her lips were puffy from their hard, hungry kiss; he wanted to take her fully right there, against the door, but Sam knew if he gave in to the excitement, he'd become a slave to it. And he wanted more than just her desire, seductive as it was. He wanted her to admit her feelings for him. Needed to hear the words. And he would. Soon.

"Tell me where you want me, Kat," he commanded huskily, his hips still pinning her to the door, and his hands slid along her bare thighs, tipping the scales in his favor.

She whimpered and bit her lip.

She closed her eyes again, only this time, Sam didn't compel a response. He didn't need to. She was past the denials, past everything but the passion. She clung to him with what little strength she had.

"Deep, Sam," she moaned. "I want you deep. Just one night—"

Sam wasn't any too steady when she gave voice to her desires. But if he had his way, they'd have more than just one night. They'd have a lifetime. He'd convince her that they were a perfect fit.

Her hips rolled and he couldn't concentrate on anything anymore but the way their *bodies* fit perfectly, even through his shorts and her panties. *Tomorrow,* he told himself. *We'll talk tomorrow.* Tonight they'd succumb to nothing but the pleasure they both craved.

Chapter Three

Kat's heart and common sense waged a war inside her. But the way her body felt wrapped around Sam was winning whatever conflict she was having. How he'd made her come apart in his arms simply from kissing and teasing a place on her neck was unbelievable! She'd never known that pleasure point existed until his lips had closed over it and she felt like she'd been electrified.

When he'd turned those bedroom eyes on her, any protest she might have made died on her lips. She'd only ever gotten glimpses of what he was so boldly demonstrating now: desire, hunger, and a look she'd always longed to see—possession, even if it *was* rooted in passion.

His hands cupped her bottom and she slid her arms around his neck, her fingers playing at the hair that was perhaps a little too long for a conservative lawyer, but on Sam it was roguish, sexy. His eyes, normally slate blue, had turned dark and stormy as they focused on hers. She'd told him what she wanted, and *sweet Jesus*, he was going to give it to her! He'd already made her climax, but she was afraid to break the fragile connection of their gaze.

Always before, when an intense moment presented itself at work, she'd get her hopes up, but he'd look away and the moment would pass. And each time it happened, Kat lost a little bit more of her heart to a man who seemed determined to refuse it. She wanted all the minutes in the night before he inevitably came to his senses in the morning and let this encounter pass, too. But she'd have gotten her one night. And that was all she could allow herself to hope for.

"Hold onto me, Kat," Sam warned. Pushing away from the door and turning, he carried her to the bed.

Her eyes still steady on his, her meaning double-edged, she whispered, "Don't let me go, Sam."

His body went still and he stopped, staring into her eyes as if searching her soul. Kat held her breath. Had she just blown the one night she was going to allow herself with this man?

She wanted to breathe a sigh of relief when he finally relaxed, grinning seductively, saying roughly, "Only long enough to get you naked."

Sam deposited her in the middle of the bed and followed her down, kissing her so slowly, lingeringly, Kat felt cherished. Her body was lazy from her recent orgasm, but she was eager to continue their play.

His mouth made love to hers, sending his tongue deep and luring hers back into the hot furnace of his own. She tasted his passion as it built, and his hard angles brazed against her soft ones, his chest making the sensitive nipples yearn for the feel of his mouth. She tingled and pulsed, already climbing again and wanting him in ways she'd only dreamed of before. Kat ached to tell Sam how much she loved him, but she kept those words locked inside. She'd already avoided one near catastrophe.

She moaned in protest when he lifted his weight from her and swept his hands along her body as he got off the bed.

She stared unabashedly as he unsnapped his shorts, then slid the zipper down. He pushed them off, along with his boxers, and a sigh escaped her lips, her eyes devouring him as bent to his suitcase. Oh wow. That trail of hair her eyes had followed down his chest ended in a springy patch around his arousal. And he was hard, thick and heavy between those powerful thighs that had supported her when he'd brought her to such heights. Sam was magnificent in his nudity.

She came up on her elbows as he went about searching for something inside the case. She was impatient for her fingers to feel their way over his washboard abs, his narrow hips, and when he turned slightly, Kat couldn't wait to feel his tight butt when she dug her nails into the smooth flesh there, making him thrust deep. Her body hummed with anticipation.

He pulled some condoms from a compartment, tossed them on the bed, and joined her again on the mattress, spreading her legs and kneeling between them.

He didn't say a word as he lifted the dress over her head and she lay back on the bed, his fascinated gaze on the rise and fall of her breasts. He brushed his knuckles along the damp panel of her panties, and his eyes lowered, following the movement.

Kat reached her hand down and gripped his wrist, suddenly self-conscious.

His brow furrowed in question as he looked up and tucked a curl behind her ear. "What's going on in that pretty head of yours, honey?"

Kat felt her belly clench in uncertainty. "Please tell me you were a Boy Scout, and 'be prepared' is forever your motto."

He tipped his head, not following her. "What do you mean?"

Her other hand picked up one of the foil packets. "No woman likes to be a foregone conclusion, Sam." She hated to think that she'd been that transparent. She'd tried so hard to keep her feelings to herself when it became clear that he wasn't interested beyond hot, hungry looks. Her trepidation was so unlike her, but this was Sam. She didn't want him to think she really *was* a tramp and would sleep with anyone who came equipped with protection. She knew he hadn't been with a woman since Patti died. Those condoms could only be for her.

A smile split his face, but it was gentle, understanding. "No man in his right mind would ever *assume* such a thing with a woman that he wants to make love to, sweetheart. But we sure as hell can hope for those things," he said, leaning down and kissing away her worry. His tongue plunged into her mouth, his late-day beard deliciously abrading her chin, but he ended the contact sooner than she would've liked. She could kiss Sam all night, and she wouldn't utter a single complaint.

He kissed the tip of her nose before sitting back on his heels. "And FYI, I was an Eagle Scout, babe. I went all the way. Sometime I'll show you what I can do with knots," he said, winking at her and grinning mischievously.

Kat sighed and flushed, her mind imagining it. She settled back and soaked in the sight of him devouring her with his eyes and it chased away her apprehension. She wanted to know *everything* about Sam, but that would only hurt more when they parted ways. She already knew what a sensitive, caring man he was or he wouldn't have been hit so hard when Patti died. Kat could never come back to work for him, but she didn't want to cause him pain either. He'd already lost one woman who was important to him. Kat had become important in a different way, but she couldn't go back to being his assistant after tonight. He still loved his late wife, and Kat wouldn't play second fiddle to anyone. Not even a ghost.

I'll tell him tomorrow, she thought. She was being selfish, but she couldn't deny herself this one indulgence of having him as hers, even if it was only for one night.

He licked his lips as he stared at her breasts, then his eyes burned a path down the length of her body, at her legs sprawled wide on either side of his hips, her panties her only article of clothing. "I could make a meal out of you, Kat," he said huskily.

Not even having her heart's desire could stop her smart-ass retort. "I suppose you expect me to tell you to 'eat me'?"

He barked a laugh, but it was strained in his condition. He shook his head. "I was thinking more along the lines of 'bon appetit,' " his voice lowered, gravelly and rough. "But I like your answer better." His pupils darkened, looking black instead of blue as he pinned hers in his gaze.

He plucked the packet from her hand and dropped it away. *But not too far*, she noticed. Linking her hands with his on either side of her head, he lifted himself until he leaned over her, his sex so hard it jutted out and brushed against her stomach. Pre-come pearled at the tip, leaving a trail on her heated skin. The sensation was too exquisite; her belly sank inward as her breath caught, but Kat lifted her hips, needing to feel it again. She gulped a whimper and clutched his hands tight; his sensual torment was more than she could bear, even having had the edge taken off earlier from her first climax.

He shifted his body down, trapping her beneath him, and his head lowered to her breast.

"Ohhhh!" she sighed loudly, and he groaned in reply. He suckled hard, and his tongue batted at her sensitive nipple. Shivers ran down her spine as he brought her body to life; nerve endings clambered for his attentions. Kat didn't know how much she could take before he went where she so desperately needed him to go. No man had ever enjoyed her, thrilled in her responses so much. He made pleased sounds as she undulated beneath him, grinned with every moan that caught in her throat and reverberated there. "Oh my God, that's so good, Sam," she breathed.

"I know, baby. For me, too."

His hot mouth, tongue, and beard stubble were a triple threat. His lips released the pressure, and when her plump, swollen breast settled back, his tongue flicked and laved it until she was writhing, could hear herself begging for him to take it in his mouth again. He ignored her pleas, but continued his sweet torture, sliding his rough chin to the other peak. Sam gripped her fingers tighter, and Kat could tell he was on the ragged edge, too.

"How long are you going to keep this up, Sam?" she panted.

He chuckled and lifted his head. "Just as long as *I* can stand it, sweetheart."

Kat closed her eyes. "I just hope I'm still conscious when you finally reach your breaking point," she whispered, and ground her pelvis against his torso. He was driving her insane, rocking her world with the meticulous delight he took in her body. Her tongue darted out, licking her dry lips, the gloss she'd applied long gone.

She opened her eyes, and she saw the muscle in his jaw jump. Whatever his comeback might have been, it was forgotten as he watched her mouth.

She grinned, thinking again how typically male he was. She tugged on his hands, but he held firm. "Let go of my hands, Sam. I want to touch you, too." And she emphasized her meaning by biting down on her bottom lip, her white teeth sinking into the soft flesh.

Sam shuddered, his eyes never leaving her mouth.

His Adam's apple bobbed as he swallowed hard, and he did let go of her hands, but only to breeze down her form, his fingers hooking in the elastic of her panties, dragging them down her legs. He bent her knees, tugged the skimpy material off one foot, then the other, and she sighed when he crushed the white lace in his fist and brought it to his face, closing his eyes as he breathed in her scent. She never thought the gesture could be erotic until Sam did it. She felt like squirming.

He sat back on his heels and her thighs were draped over his knees. Her hands were free, but she couldn't move. She was dazed, and more aroused than any man had ever made her. She was completely open and exposed to her lover, but she'd never felt more secure than she did in that moment.

Before she could gather her wits and take advantage of her freedom to touch, Sam opened his eyes. His burning gaze was like a hot stroke to her skin as it raked down her body until it settled at the juncture of her thighs, and the patch of tight, sable curls there. That feral look was back, and Kat groaned when his tongue passed over his lips, like she was a succulent morsel on display for him.

He pushed her up on the mattress, keeping her legs open, and she gripped the wooden slats of the headboard, needing something to hold on to if Sam was going to torment her the way she suspected he was about to. She looked down her body, past her swollen breasts, her flat belly, and there he was, his eyes staring up into hers and his mouth so close to her center, she could feel his hot breath on her flesh. Kat knew that the torment had only just begun.

Sam's cock pulsed with the agony of waiting, but he knew the moment he sank into her body, he was done for. And he wasn't ready for that yet. He'd been too hungry for her and he wasn't going to rush their first time together.

He still had a few personal demons to conquer, but he couldn't be happier that he finally had Kat where he wanted her, her eyes pleading with him to take her, her body so responsive and eager. And before this night was finished, she'd be pleading with that *mouth* that constantly drove him to distraction with her saucy remarks and sexy grins. But Lord, did she know how to kiss! He'd had to pull away from her earlier. Her tongue had tangled with his and he'd felt it straight to his groin. Damn, how he wanted to be buried inside her! But it could wait. His insatiable urge to taste her couldn't.

He settled his shoulders between her lush, tanned thighs, and he wanted nothing more than to plunge his tongue into her warm, delicious depths, but the whimpers and anxious mewling sounds were driving him insane. He wanted to take his time, hear more of them.

His hand petted her, softly fluttering over her damp curls, then went lower, his fingertip brushing her slick, wet lips. He blew on the silky skin and inserted one long finger into her, sliding deep. She shuddered, a ragged, animal-like cry tore from her lips, and she gripped his finger tight. Knowing how his cock was going to feel there made Sam shudder as well.

He stroked in and out of her passage. "You are so wet, Kat," he murmured, and her hips rolled, her body arched, communicating without words what she wanted.

He pulled his finger free and slid both hands under her warm buttocks. He tilted her hips up and lowered his head to the sweetness that awaited him.

She wailed, thrashed, and bucked against his mouth, but he wouldn't surcease. He feasted on her, his tongue lapping at her honeyed richness as he took his fill of her.

"Ah, yes! Oh, Sam! Yes," she cried out, one hand reaching down and tangling in his hair. Holding him to her, she writhed under him.

He had to fight his own climax! He felt seduced by her passion.

He shifted, and plunged a finger in again. The combination of sensations inside and out were turning her into a wildcat. His lips closed over the swollen bud of her clitoris and gently suckled. She screamed so loud, Sam loved it, but he shifted again and brought his other hand to her mouth, stifling her cries of pleasure as his own mouth and fingers brought her from one pinnacle to the next, pushing her past each one.

He registered the strain in her muffled pleas, the tight grip on his hair, and with one final, delicious lick, he lifted his mouth away, his hand lowering from hers. Her body went from bowed and rigid to liquid and limp as she dropped back onto the mattress, her breathing shallow and her eyes closed, and Sam worried he'd gone too far. Except for the spasms that still shook her body, she didn't move.

He crawled up the bed, lying next to her and tucking the curls that had fallen over her face behind her ear. He wiped a tear from the corner of her eye. "Kat? Are you okay?" he asked worriedly.

Her eyes opened slowly, sleepily, but they shined, sated. Regardless of his painful condition, he smiled down at her, relief filling him.

She curled her body into him, and reached down to close her soft hand around his aching erection. "Have you reached your breaking point yet, Sam?" she murmured lazily.

He sighed and groaned, stilling her hand. "I got greedy, baby. I wore you out. Sleep now."

He held her hand immobile from moving up and down, but she squeezed him so blissfully that he feared he'd come in her hand. She kissed his collarbone, her tongue licking along the bone, and slid her slick body down to their joined hands. "Sleep? Now? No way!" she breathed into his skin, sounding renewed as her mouth moved to its goal.

He hissed, and his eyes rolled back as her tongue flicked the swollen tip of his sex. "Oh Christ, Kat!" He jerked and groaned in ecstasy when her mouth sucked the bead of fluid that pearled there, and both their hands tightened around the thick shaft. Just one taste and Sam was already so close to coming.

He let go of her hand, but she kept stroking him, tasting him, moaning and enjoying the turnabout. His hand shook as he reached for the condom.

He gently pushed her off him, sheathing himself quickly, and she lay back, licking his essence from her lips, watching his hurried movements. He rolled and settled himself between her thighs once again.

Staring into her beautiful green eyes, so full of passion and excitement, he said, "I'm at the breaking point now."

Her hands gripped his biceps. "So I gathered." She grinned, but when he pushed her legs high and wide and surged into her, embedding himself to the hilt, her mouth opened on a gasp. They both stilled, holding their breath, savoring the mutual possession.

She broke the spell, but wrapped them in another. "Ah, yes. This is where I need you, Sam."

Sam's eyes closed. "Yeah," he growled. He was exactly where he needed to be, too—deep, surrounded by her warmth, his cock full and pulsing inside her.

And then he began to move.

He concentrated hard on keeping his strokes slow and steady, even when Kat wrapped her legs around his hips, tilting her own, trying to rush them along. She wanted it fast and hard, but he couldn't give in to her. He'd make sure neither of them would ever forget a single moment of the experience.

His rough hands cupped her face as he rocked into her, and she sighed into his mouth when he lowered his head and kissed her tenderly, his lips taking possession of her as surely as his body was. God, he loved her!

Ripples of sensation assailed him as her hands slid along his rib cage and around to his buttocks. He reared up and sucked in his breath as her nails bit into his skin. It was more than even he could stand.

"Here we go, babe," Sam rasped. Reaching up and gripping the slats, he started them on the breathtaking climb, together this time. He thrust deep, but even that was too slow now. Harder and faster he drove into her, the friction of their tight fit sending licks of flame along his already raw nerves.

He was covered in sweat as he pumped into her, dropping his hands to the bed and leaning low, needing the full body contact as his downstrokes ground against her swollen, sensitive clitoris. "Come for me, Kat," he urged, his voice rough as sandpaper in her ear.

She careened over with edge with a scream of completion, her warm passage seizing around him. Her teeth sank into his shoulder and he roared her name, letting his own climax take him as the blinding pleasure slammed into him.

He pulsed inside her, and they both groaned, shuddering with the long ride. She stayed with him every step of the way and welcomed him into her arms when the last of the tide ebbed and he collapsed onto her, exhausted and replete.

When he could gather the strength, Sam slipped free of her and disposed of the condom in the trash under the nightstand, then rolled back over to pull Kat's relaxed, slack form into his arms.

With her tucked to his side, her swollen, well-kissed breasts pressed to his ribs, he stroked her head, his fingers tangling in her soft, wild curls. She still trembled, feeling the echoing swells of her freefall.

Finally settling in, she draped her arm possessively across his chest, whispering groggily, "Perfect." Her voice drifted off as she sighed, "Night, Sam."

He dipped his head, watched her eyes drift close in exhaustion. He smiled; he *had* worn her out. He stared for a long time, then brushed his lips softly over her brow.

"Good night, Katrissa. I love you," he said quietly. But she didn't hear, Sam knew. She'd already drifted off to sleep in his arms.

Chapter Four

Kat awoke to the sound through the open window of the surf crashing upon the beach. And it only took a moment for her to remember that she'd fallen asleep to a warm body and a heart beating a steady cadence under her ear. She was cold, despite the blanket Sam had tucked her in. But she wasn't lying next to him anymore. His body heat was gone. She was alone. And it was nearly three A.M.

That rolling and pitching feeling in her belly was back, but she beat it down, hoping, praying she was being silly and Sam just got up for a glass of water or to use the bathroom.

She slipped out of bed, and the cool breeze sweeping in from the window chilled her naked skin. Sam's suitcase was open in the middle of the floor and she took a T-shirt from the pile that looked liked he'd thrown all his clothes in haphazardly. Pulling it on over her head, she went in search of him.

He wasn't anywhere in the house. She peered through the sliding glass door in the living room that let out to a sprawling deck, but she didn't see him there either. Then something caught her eye down by the shore.

A man was standing at the water's edge. Kat's heart drummed in her chest; even if she didn't recognize the broad shoulders in the white shirt that stood out in the dark of night, her hormones did. That was Sam down there on the beach. Only this time, he wasn't looking for her. He'd left her side and sought solitude in the waves.

Kat thought she might be ill.

"Don't cry, dammit. You brought this on yourself," she berated herself, turning and going back to the bedroom. She curled up on the bed in Sam's T-shirt, the scent of him surrounding her, the memory of their love-making all around her. She'd never been so sad to learn the truth about anything in her life.

The sight of him down at the water's edge was the answer to the question she'd been too afraid to ask: he wasn't over Patti. She'd suspected as much anyway. That was why she'd quit her job. For months, she'd thought Sam was recovering from the loss, that his heart was healing. She'd even nearly gotten up the nerve to tell him that she wasn't what he thought she was, but then she saw the invoice from the florist. An arrangement was to be delivered annually to the cemetery and the plot number where Patti was laid to rest. That confirmed for her that Sam wasn't past the grief, that he might never get past it. She'd done the only thing she could; she'd decided to make a fresh start, and that meant quitting her job. She needed a place where her heart wouldn't hurt every time she turned around.

But he'd come after her, dammit! He shouldn't have done that. And when he did, she should have been firm and made him sleep on the sofa. At least then she wouldn't know what she was missing. Now she forever would. And the memory of his lovemaking had ruined her for any other man. Damn it all!

She heard the door slide shut, and she knew he was back. He didn't come into the bedroom right away, and by the time he did, the bitterness had left her and she was physically and emotionally drained. The bed dipped as he slid in beside her. *When he's back asleep,* she resolved, *I'll leave first thing.*

Sam spooned up behind her, his arm going around her, pulling her against him. Kat choked back the sob that rose in her throat. She was hurt that he couldn't love her, but even more disappointed that she'd allowed herself to be vulnerable. It wasn't Sam's fault, but this feeling of regret was exactly what she'd tried to avoid by coming down here.

The rhythm of his breathing as he settled into sleep calmed her, but she started to like it a little too much. She had to get out or she might not leave at all. What little dignity she had left gave her the impetus to slide out from under his arm, and tuck a pillow there in her place.

Sam rolled and clutched the fluffy pillow to him; the muscles in his broad back rippled and flexed, and Kat fought the almost overpowering urge to crawl back in that bed. But her pride stopped her cold. She'd already compromised it so much. This *had* to be the end of the line. She wanted every part of Sam, and not just his body, sexy as all get out that it was. But if he couldn't give her his heart along with it, then she had no choice but to sever their association for good.

She turned her back on the temptation before she could talk herself into yanking that pillow out from under him and making room for herself against his warm, powerful, sleeping body.

Quiet as a mouse, she quickly dressed and packed her small suitcase. She tiptoed through the house and sat down at the table in the dining room to leave Sam a note, telling him *not* to follow her this time. This was good-bye.

She propped the paper on the hutch and left the small light on so he'd be sure to see it, then took one last look around. Not a trace of her was left behind. Well, except her heart, of course. Sam completely had that now.

She sighed and unlocked the door, wondering how long the hurt would last, if it would *ever* pass.

"Halt!" Sam's voice boomed from the hallway.

Kat jumped nearly a foot. He'd scared the hell out of her. *Murphy's Law,* she thought. If something could go wrong, it would. And it always did.

Her fright spurred her temper, and she turned around, her face screwing up as she stared at Sam, standing naked in the archway. "Halt? As in 'Hark, who goes there?' " She shook her head and shrugged her shoulders. "Who says that?"

Sam ignored that blatant sarcasm. He leaned against the archway, crossed his arms, and tipped his head. "Where ya going, Kat?"

Think. Think hard. Think fast. Her eyes darted around the room. "Since you're staying here, we'll need more food?" *You are so bad at this, Murphy,* she thought.

"What? The local Shop-N-Bag run out of paper and plastic? You use your suitcase to haul your groceries home now, do you?"

She shrugged, and looked at anything but his face—and the rest of him.

"Get back in the bedroom, Kat," he said coldly in that lawyer voice of his, and she knew he meant business.

Unbelievable! Her mouth dropped open. "You don't really expect us to—"

"Oh, ho ho," he chuckled, but his face went deadpan except for the daggers his eyes shot at her. "Don't flatter yourself, sweetheart."

Kat's brow furrowed, certain she'd just been insulted.

"I don't go in for angry sex, and right now? I could

tear the New York City phone book in half, I'm so pissed at you."

Kat stood at the front door; the image of him tearing into that impossibly thick book made her fight a grin. That was mad, all right!

Sam's voice was full of scorn and it drew her attention back to him. "I don't trust you not to sneak away again like a thief in the night, and I need to put some clothes on." The muscle in his jaw flexed and his lips were drawn back over his teeth.

Kat shook her head, her shoulders slumping in resignation now. "Why do we have to do this, Sam?"

Sam threw his arms up in the air, gesturing wildly, shouting, "Because I love you, you *crazy* woman!"

Her eyes nearly bugged out and she stood frozen. Not only had he shouted at her again, but Sam was as shocked as she was at what he said.

He recovered first, cursing and expelling an exasperated breath. He was obviously upset that he'd spoken before thinking. But her failure to close her mouth or come back with a snappy retort made him grin. "Took the wind right outta your sails there, didn't I, honey?"

Boy, had he! But he hadn't meant to say it, and dammit! Saying it didn't prove it. She *had* proof that he was lying through his teeth. She felt cornered, torn between lashing out at him and still caring too much to call him a liar to his face. She addressed the last part of his outburst instead. "You don't have to resort to name-calling, Sam."

He folded his arms again, and took that damnable casual stance, leaning against the wall. "Can we go back in the room so I can get dressed and *then* we can talk?" He tipped his head; his brows rose as he looked down at his morning erection. "Unless you'd rather I stay right here like this . . . parts of me standing at attention?"

Oh, he was annoyed at her! More so than yesterday,

she guessed. He was resorting to being crass again. Well, two could play at that game. Her head gestured to his throbbing penis as she approached. One eyebrow arched. "I didn't know you could actually make that thing jump on command."

He cast her a dull glance. "It's got a mind of its own where you're concerned, sweetheart."

She snickered, but as she came abreast of him, he lifted an arm and barred her passing. She looked up at him, confusion creasing her brow. "What now?" she asked, her resentment clear.

Sam turned his hand up. "My keys please, klepto?"

She wasn't used to seeing Sam behave like this. He was always in control. But time and again since he'd arrived, she'd pushed him beyond his tolerance. Banter was one thing, even the sexual tension she'd dealt with. But this provoked attitude was something entirely new. They were walking a fine line with each other, and any misstep was going to do damage to them both.

"Okay. Jeez," Kat grumbled, but dropped the keys into his palm. "That'll teach me to take a cab from the airport." Now she was stuck here until Sam decided they were done.

He chuckled humorlessly and followed close behind her as she continued down the hall and into the bedroom. If she didn't know better, she might think he was enjoying himself, in spite of his agitation.

He grabbed the shorts he'd taken off when he came in from the beach and put them back on. "I want some answers, Kat. I want to know why you were taking off again, but I have a more important question."

"Which is?"

"Do you have *no* reaction to the fact that I told you out there that I love you? Or"—he grinned wickedly and wriggled his eyebrows, another sign that he wasn't quite as mad as he'd let on—"did the sight of my naked body distract you that much?"

"Oh yes, Sam. That's it exactly." She preened, then rolled her eyes as she dropped into the chair. The heat rose up Kat's neck to her cheeks. She really, really didn't want to have this conversation. But they needed to or he'd just keep chasing her, and that wouldn't do. She looked up at him. "Sex isn't love, Sam. And I know for a fact that you aren't in love with me."

"First of all, I *love* having sex with you. But I do know the difference, Kat. And I wouldn't have taken you to bed if I didn't love you."

Kat felt her anger rising. *Liar!* she wanted to shout, but the lump in her throat was back and she had to think about that more. She wouldn't cry, dammit! She remained mute, but she focused her gaze on the springy hair on his chest as he stood over her, his hands on his hips.

"I'd also like to know why you let me believe that you were promiscuous."

Kat almost choked. *Oooh, busted,* she thought. Here she was, silently condemning him for being a liar, when that's exactly what she was. He had some tough questions! Ones she wasn't ready to answer yet. Instead, she went on the offensive, saying, "I saw the invoice, Sam."

He took a seat on the end of the bed, facing her. She was distracted by his spread legs as they bracketed her knees, the soft hair on his thighs tickling hers and making her remember the feel of them sliding along hers in the bed. *Too close,* she thought. But he smelled so good; she'd been wrapped in the subtle, spicy scent of his cologne when she'd worn his T-shirt. And she hated that the memory of his beard stubble made her skin tingle and tighten. She didn't like feeling aroused when he obviously had himself under control. He appeared gentle, encouraging, but determined. She could see it in his eyes and in the position he took. They were going to finish this, one way or the other.

"What invoice?" he asked quietly.

She drew a deep breath as she met his direct gaze. He was troubled, but she didn't know if that was from her second attempted vanishing act, or the truths she was about to reveal. Now that they'd gotten this far, there was no turning back. She was going to spill everything, and hope that they could at least remain friends when it was all over.

"For the flowers for Patti's grave. I know I shouldn't have, but I didn't know what it was, and everything comes through me first at the office, but that invoice hadn't. So I read it." She justified her actions while hiding her shame for looking at something he obviously hadn't wanted her to see. She understood that it was personal and didn't have anything to do with her, but it didn't make her feel any better. He nodded, but something else he said made her curious. "And how do you know I'm *not* promiscuous, Sam?"

His voice was menacing, like a rumbling volcano ready to erupt, but he kept it capped, saying, "Camelot told me you haven't had a date in six months, when every morning you'd come in, telling me about some man or other who'd shared your company the night before. Things started to fit together after that. I've been confused and frustrated, trying to figure you out. The party girl you told me you were didn't gel with the woman I know." His eyes were accusing, judgmental.

She shot right back, fueled by his rising ire. She told him how much it hurt every time he'd look at her like he wanted her, then in the next minute he'd have his poker face on, and she felt cheated. "That was why I let you think I was a wild child. At first, it was that stupid policy that Jonah made you and Elliot sign. I was so angry. He had no right, legal or otherwise, to tell you whom you could and couldn't date within the firm. So I rebelled a little. And I don't know if you noticed, but I gave you names of men who work there, I just didn't specify with last names because I didn't want them to get in trouble for my bluff. I just let *you* believe I was dating every man I saw, and frankly, I was running out of employees! But you didn't seem to care. You know Elliot's assistant, Summer?"

He simply nodded, not uttering a word as she picked up speed. He'd broken the dam, and he was letting the deluge rush free.

Well, he asked for it, she thought. "She told me I was playing with fire, but I told her that Jonah was wrong, and so were the both of you for going along with it." She couldn't stop her damn blabbering mouth. She was exposing herself for the fraud she was. "But then I started to see you for the kind, loving man that you are." Her throat was tight with emotion, thinking back to the man she had watched emerge from a black hole of despair. "Oh, you had a chip on your shoulder those first months after I got there, but I knew it was because of Patti's death. That wasn't the real you. Not from what Jonah told me."

She glanced at him briefly, feeling her belly tighten in knots, his focus was pinned on her. She dropped her eyes to her hands in her lap, not able to maintain eye contact. "Those looks, Sam, the ones that made me breathless and excited. They gave me hope that you were getting past the pain. But before you'd follow through, you'd look away and pretend they never happened. That's when I decided to let you believe I wasn't such a good girl. I couldn't stand the guilt in your eyes after every one of those lusty glances. I wasn't going to be responsible for you feeling like you'd been unfaithful to Patti by wanting me, even if it was just a physical reaction." She finally met his gaze, tipping her head up, hoping he could see her compassion. "And then tonight, I knew for sure." Her voice sounded pitifully weak to her own ears; her throat was dry and her lip quivered. This was taking it out of her more than she thought it would.

"Tonight?"

She sighed and closed her eyes as she nodded. Giving her his undivided attention made her long for the attention he gave her earlier. But she drove her point home instead. "What man would leave the bed of the woman he'd just made love to, unless his heart wasn't in it and his guilt drove him from it?" Her lashes were heavy with tears. The hurts that had been eating her alive these past months were exposed now. Maybe someday it wouldn't make her feel ill to recall that image of him down at the water. But her mouth had been like a runaway train, speeding along, not even seeing the trouble up ahead.

Sam's face had drained of color as she poured out her reasons for quitting her job; she'd even unintentionally answered his question about why she'd pretended to be something she wasn't. But he simply sat there listening, his hands finding their way to hers as they rested on her knees. His thumbs circled her palms, having a calming effect on both of them.

But it didn't last.

He squeezed her hands, making sure she had no avenue of escape. "You *are* a crazy woman," he growled at her, his brows lowering over his eyes.

"So you said," Kat replied dryly, wondering how he got her to switch gears from sadness to annoyance so fast. She'd just bared her soul and he was calling her crazy? Again? She was glad at least she hadn't come right out and said she loved him. He might call her certifiable.

Sam sighed, swiping his hand down his face. He dropped his head. "Ah, Kat, I'm sorry. For so much, I'm sorry. I didn't mean that. You've been carrying the weight of the world on your shoulders, haven't you, honey?"

She shrugged when he looked up at her, then lowered her eyes. He was incredibly masculine and gentle at the same time. She wanted him to soothe her, but how could he do that when he was the one causing the pain?

"I'd never hurt you intentionally, honey."

She shrugged again, but his hand cupped her chin.

"Never, Kat," he said, bringing her face level with his. She couldn't avoid his direct stare. "But we've been dealing at cross purposes here, and I need to make a few things clear to you, okay?"

He looked too resolute for her to do anything but nod in agreement. It wasn't like she could go anywhere anyway.

Sam took her hands again and stared down at them. "I loved Patti, Kat. I've never made a secret of that."

She nodded. "Yeah," she whispered. This hurt, dammit! Whether it was intentional or not, hearing him say it was so hard for her.

He went on. "Just because she's gone doesn't mean that she should be forgotten. In fact"—his head lifted and his gaze pinned hers—"I don't want to forget her."

Kat bit her lip. Okay, she hadn't expected him to come right out and say *that*. She considered taking back her thoughts that he was gentle and kind. This felt cruel and unusual. But she forced herself to keep her mouth shut. The sooner he finished, the sooner she could get away and lick her wounds. They were gaping right now. She closed her eyes and fought back the tears. She so didn't want to cry in front of him, but it didn't seem like she was going to have much of a choice.

"Kat, look at me."

Figures, she thought. *Never easy*. She slowly opened her eyes, and her heart squeezed. He looked so good sitting there in nothing but his shorts, his dark hair tousled, looking like he'd run his hands through it, his blue eyes staring into hers. He wanted her to understand, and she did. In fact, if she weren't in love with him, she'd find it terribly romantic that not even death could stop him from loving Patti. But *she* was in love with him, too, and from where she was sitting, it sucked. But when he spoke, she got the shock of her life.

"The invoice on my desk was one of the steps I've taken to move on with my life. The flowers are paid for. They'll be delivered to Patti's grave every year on her birthday. Please understand, Kat. She deserves to be remembered. She was a wonderful, loving wife. But I didn't think that it was fair to you to keep going there."

Fair to me? She looked sideways at him, not sure she'd heard right.

"That's right. You, Kat. You're the woman for me now. The one I love. And as for going out on the beach tonight . . ."

She watched him struggle to find the right words. She wanted to comfort him, but he was on his own. That last revelation threw her for a loop, she felt paralyzed, coping with trying to breathe. He'd said he loved her. And he didn't look like his head was ready to explode this time. He looked relieved that she was stunned silent again.

The rough, gravelly timbre of Sam's voice was distracting; it didn't matter what he said, he could make it sound sexy. She valiantly ignored the shivers racing up her spine as he said, "I've been carrying my wedding ring around in my pocket since the funeral. And I swore to myself if I ever told another woman I love her that I'd get rid of it. Patti didn't have any family, and we didn't have children, so there was no one to give it to."

Kat saw what might be regret in his expression at the mention of not having any children, but it passed quickly and he held her hands tighter.

"A wedding ring is a symbol of an unbroken bond, and though I'll always love Patti in a special way, she's gone. She died as my wife, but when I die, it won't be as *her* husband." Sam tipped her chin up, his thumb caressing it gently as he told her, "She'd be happy that I found love again, Kat. I'd wish the same for her if things were reversed. And the only guilt I feel is for what I've put you through all these months, that you made up a persona to protect yourself. And that I didn't see through your ruse."

Oh, that was so romantic, so sentimental, and so . . . tear-jerking. She couldn't help that they were welling in her eyes. Kat didn't like herself very much at the moment.

"Sam, you didn't say you loved me until you caught me trying to leave." *Prove him wrong,* she thought. *Go on the defensive.* She was still so reluctant to believe all that he was saying.

His lips turned up in that sexy grin, and he tucked a curl behind her ear. "I exhausted you with my lovemaking, and you fell asleep in my arms before you heard."

"I did?" Her hands covered her mouth, but hope bubbled up inside her—she could barely keep it contained. He was teasing her, though it was true. He *had* exhausted her. She wanted to believe him more than anything in the world. And she wanted to curse that she hadn't heard it when he was holding her, soothing her heated body. There was a regret.

"Yes, you did." He chuckled at her horrified expression. "I've loved you for a long time. It wasn't hard to take that final step, Kat. But you blindsided me when I walked into work and found you'd gone and had taken off for parts unknown. Thank God for our friends. Jonah told me where you went, and I knew when I came down here I wasn't going home without you. The only reason I held back at the office was because you seemed to go through men faster than a box of chocolates on a dateless Saturday night. I wasn't going to be just another notch on your bedpost."

Kat giggled, thinking about the double standard; if she were a man, Sam would be clapping her on the back, calling her a lucky dog, or some other archaic male phrase.

He leaned toward her, his mouth so close, her tongue

would touch his lips if it darted out. He growled, "I didn't want to take away your choices, didn't want to break that spirit. It's one of the things I love about you. But I knew if ever I found myself in your bed, Kat, no man would *ever* come after me."

Her breath caught in her throat. Could a man *be* more sexy? He was perfect, inside and out, and she didn't feel very good about herself for the things she'd assumed. "I feel so selfish. I wouldn't tell you that I love you because I just couldn't bear you telling me that you were still in love with Patti."

Sam kissed her tenderly, his hands coming up and cupping her cheeks. "I *want* you to be selfish when it comes to me. Be greedy. Because I'd give everything I've got to have you. Go ahead and quit your job, Kat, but don't quit me."

A tear tumbled unnoticed down her cheek, and her voice was shaky as she whispered, "I love you, Sam. So much. But are you absolutely sure? I *need* you to be sure."

Sam pulled her out of the chair and onto his lap, nuzzling her throat. "If I'd found a shy, quiet woman like Patti was, then I'd worry that I was just looking for a replacement. But you're the only one who can fire my blood with just a look, make me want to drag you against me and kiss you senseless in the blink of an eye, so I know it's for real."

She shivered; his hot breath on her throat was making it difficult to follow the conversation, but from what she could comprehend, it was everything she'd only dreamed of.

He leaned back, his warm palm coming up to cup her cheek. "I've fallen in love twice in one lifetime, Kat, with two completely different women. And I've been so lucky that they've both loved me back. Not many men can say he's found the love of his life . . . twice. Some will argue how that's possible, but for me, it just is."

"Oh my God, I love you, Sam," she whispered, amazed that she'd said it twice now, right to his face. She could barely breathe, but she didn't care. It felt so good to say it.

He helped her off his lap, sat her back in his place on the bed, and went to his suitcase. She grinned and shook her head as he messed up the clothes even more than they already were, and unzipped an inner compartment. Then she lost her breath altogether.

He came back over to her, knelt on the floor in front of her, and opened a blue velvet box. "Now, getting rid of the ring from my first marriage was something I had to do on my own, Kat. But I brought this one with me because when I leave here, I want you to come with me wearing it, and I want it to be as my wife."

Her heartbeat was like thunder in her ears as she stared down at the bridal set nestled in the shiny satin.

Sam smiled, then leaned up and kissed her full on the lips. She couldn't even kiss him back, she was so stunned. He pulled away and laughed. "Breathe, honey. Now."

She pulled in air through her nose and it was like a rush—she felt dizzy!

"Tell me you'd like nothing better than to marry me, Kat."

She snapped out of it, tearing her eyes from the rock in the box. "Aren't you supposed to ask me?"

He chuckled. "I figured I'd get a 'yes' while you were in shock."

"The answer would still be the same. Yes, I'll marry you, Sam. I'd like nothing better. I love you."

"Good answer," he said roughly, kissing her hard on the lips. He pulled away reluctantly, but he took the engagement ring and slid it on her finger, kissing it and sealing the bond. "You get the other one when we close the deal," he said smugly, and snapped the box shut, the wedding band secure inside it.

Setting the box on the table next to the chair behind him, he turned back to her, spreading her thighs and insinuating himself until her cleft was against his bare torso.

Kat gazed down at his handsome face, free of strain, his eyes shining with joy and passion. All she could think was, *I love this man. I love him!*

Chapter Five

Sam didn't think he'd ever be this happy again. Kat was here, in his arms, looking down at him with such love in her eyes, and she was *his*.

One thing he'd never understood was how any man could leave her bed and not beg for a repeat performance. She was hot, wild, and sometimes wicked. Now he knew that there hadn't been other men; she'd made them up, and he was glad. He would've beat every one of them off with a stick because, what he said was true—no man would ever replace him in her bed.

She'd suffered heartache to make sure his suffering was as minimal as possible. That was the kind of woman she was, and his throat tightened, knowing that somehow he'd been blessed for a second time in his life. He'd make sure she never regretted a minute of it and always knew how much he adored her.

"I love you, Katrissa," he murmured, and he heard her charming whimper as he leaned up and his lips captured hers. He groaned as she used the advantage of her position above him and took possession of the kiss, her tongue dancing and playing with his. God! She was good at this. What a lucky bastard he was.

His hand tangled in her sable curls, holding her close, ready to drag her up on the bed when the phone rang. *Murphy's Law*, he thought. "Tell me you'll change your name when you marry me," he sighed.

Kat snickered at him as she crawled up the bed to answer the phone.

Only the partners and their assistants had this number, and he'd specifically left instructions not to contact him unless it was an emergency. Sam's curiosity piqued as he looked up and read the caller ID. It was the police department.

Kat snatched it up. "Hello?"

She listened, and her worried expression put Sam on alert. Who could be calling *here* this early in the morning?

She held him off as he silently questioned who was on the phone, but said into the receiver, "Okay, got it. I'll get hold of him for you. Right. Hang in there, sweetie," she said, and hung up, her teeth worrying her lip.

Sam couldn't suppress his agitation. "Well? Who was it?" he asked.

Kat's brow furrowed. "That was Summer. She's been arrested." She shook her head. "It's a misunderstanding, Sam. She's taking care of her mother's house while she's away on a cruise, and Summer punched in the wrong codes for the alarm. They can't get through to the ship to straighten it out. Her mother just bought the house, so no one knows her there who can vouch for Summer."

Sam was confused. "Why hasn't she been released on her own recognizance? It's just a B and E."

"The police got there shortly after she tripped the alarm. She heard a noise and hid. When she saw a shadow, she clobbered it with a paperweight. She ended up putting an officer in the hospital with a concussion. Until it's all cleared up, she's been booked on breaking and entering *and* assaulting a police officer. She wants me to find Elliot. He's not at home, and I gave her this number before I left. They let her make a second call."

"Damn! That poor kid!" Sam said, taking the phone from her and punching the keypad. He waited as it rang and dragged Kat close. He knew she was worried about her friend, but there was nothing they could do from here. Besides that, Elliot had left when Sam did, but he'd gone fishing at the lake for the weekend. He told Sam he'd be on his cell, and he wasn't that far out of the city.

Elliot picked up, and Sam said, "Hey, it's Sam. Wake up and get dressed, buddy. Your assistant's in the slammer." He grinned at Kat when she socked him in the shoulder, appalled at his amusement when Summer was facing serious charges.

As he talked to him, Sam was sure Elliot would take care of things. His partner had it bad for his wayward assistant, and he was rightly in a rage when Sam relayed the information Kat had given him.

Sam hung up the phone, confident that while Summer might *need* the weekend to recover after her experience in the clink, she'd be cleared of all the charges, even the assault. Both she and the police were victims of circumstance. Her booking would most likely be the worst of the whole ordeal. Well, Sam chuckled, that or the lecture she was in for from her boss.

He pulled Kat down beside him on the bed. "Elliot's on his way back home to get her," he said, and smoothed the crease from between her eyes. "Don't worry."

She still looked concerned.

"Kat, you have to know how he feels about her, right?" Sam had seen the signs for weeks, even if Elliot wouldn't yet admit it to anyone—even himself.

Kat smiled and snuggled back down beside him. "I suppose so," she said. "But you have to admit, it was getting a little ridiculous in that office. All three partners swearing company celibacy, their assistants unwittingly testing *their* resolve, and all of us fighting the attraction. It's like an old black-and-white movie that only comes on late at night. Now that's two that have broken Jonah's stupid, *illegal* policy, including Jonah himself. I wonder if Elliot will be the holdout."

Sam chuckled and slipped an arm around her, bringing her close to his side. "It was a gentleman's agreement, sweetheart. Jonah just didn't want to lose good people . . . like *you*. But if Elliot knows what's good for him, he won't wait too long."

Kat stroked his skin, her fingers making circles in his chest hair. "I hope he realizes what he's in for, though. Summer's a shy little thing, but she's got gumption. If he backs her into a corner, I have a feeling she'll come out swinging." She laughed. "The man won't know what hit him."

Sam grinned, thinking that Kat didn't fit the mold he'd imagined of her either. But every new thing he learned made him love her that much more. He figured Elliot was in for a few surprises where his own assistant was concerned.

He pulled Kat to him and captured her lips hungrily. "Where were we before our felon called?" Sam asked, then kissed along her throat as she tilted her head for him.

"Alleged felon, Counselor. And you were just about to make passionate love to me," Kat replied teasingly.

"Yeah, that's exactly where I was." He tweaked her nose. "You'd make a damn good lawyer, babe," he said, rolling and pulling her under him, his mouth just inches from her delicious lips.

"I'd rather be the wife of one." She sighed.

Sam wholeheartedly agreed. "Mmm, I like the sound of that. Let me show you the benefits package *that* position offers." He growled, his grin wicked as he began undoing the endless row of buttons down the front of her dress.

Kat wriggled under him, and tugged it easily over her

head, leaving her in nothing but her bra and panties as she tossed it away.

"God, you're pretty, Kat. I'm an incredibly lucky man."

Her throaty laugh bubbled up and his excitement began to build as he gazed down at her. The sun was breaking over the horizon, casting a soft glow through the window onto her silky skin. Her hands stroked his heated flesh, sliding down and unfastening his shorts. "I'm the lucky one, Sam. I got you. For once, Murphy's Law worked in my favor."

He couldn't argue with that. Didn't want to. Instead, he let her slide his zipper down as he lowered his head for a kiss that was reverent, yet demanding. Her soft hand wrapped around his hardening erection and he dragged his mouth from hers, his lips brushing the shell of her ear. "For both of us, sweetheart," he breathed raggedly. "It worked for both of us." And Sam began to show her just how grateful he was.

In another wonderful Brava anthology,
BAD BOYS DOWN UNDER,
Nancy Warren has written all three stories.
Here's a sample of one of them,
The Great Barrier.

Bronwyn Spencer dragged out the photo of the man she'd be looking after for the next fortnight. Mark Forsyth. Even his name sounded wet. He was some sort of finance type, coming over to sort Crane's financial system and explain how all the taxes worked in the American market. She knew this was important, but she couldn't imagine anything more boring.

She'd tried to balance her checkbook once and found it so futile she'd given up. She'd discovered instead a wonderful thing called overdraft protection.

And after that ran out, in extreme emergencies there was always Cam. Except that he wasn't here. Off with his new lovey dove right when she most needed him.

Why did her overdraft have to run out right when the week's rent was due? Oh, well. Luckily she was a resourceful woman, and had allowed Cam to bail her out of a jam once more, even though he'd done it without his knowledge. Which wasn't her fault. He hadn't been around to ask.

She wasn't going to stand around the baggage claim area holding a sign with Mark Forsyth's name on it, so she was going to have to recognize the man. She studied his corporate photo while she drank the coffee.

Mark Forsyth gazed back at her from a corporate

head shot, earnest and dull. Black hair that would look better if it was a little longer and not so neat, serious blue eyes in a serious, narrow face. Firm lips that looked as though they never smiled at a joke, never mind told one.

Her lip curled. It was going to be a long two weeks. Already she was irritated with the man since she was on time and his flight wasn't. She could have snatched a bit more sleep. Her feet ached from all the dancing last night, and she stretched them out, noticing the coral polish on her nails was already chipped.

With a quiet chuckle she remembered that Fiona had outlasted her at the party, and seemed pretty keen on a blond surfie from Brisbane wearing a shirt of so hideous a green that it ought to be burned. She wondered how Fi was faring and pulled out her mobile. She hesitated, and then decided that if she had to be functioning at nine in the morning on a Saturday, her best mate ought to as well.

She punched in the number and after a few rings, Fiona answered. "This better be life or death."

"Did you go home with your surfie?"

A great groan met her ears. "What the bloody hell are you doing ringing me at this hour?"

"Well, did you?"

A few passengers began drifting out from the California flight. Idly she watched them, blinking with tiredness, or stretching after more hours than she cared to contemplate stuffed in a tin can thirty thousand feet above earth. Bron shook her head, she firmly believed that if God had meant man to fly, he'd have given surfboards wings.

She glanced down at the black-haired, serious and controlled-looking man in the photo and kept her eyes open while Fiona yawned and groaned.

"No," her friend said, finally. "I didn't go home with him. Now would you piss off."

A man came through the glass doors alone. Right general age and he had black hair, but he was nothing like the photograph. His hair was a mess. His face was shadowy with stubble, giving him a disreputable look. He moved slowly, but she liked the way he walked, with a kind of rolling gait, as though he were getting off a boat rather than a plane. He stood as though he were about to fall asleep on his feet, his gaze searching out someone. Then their gazes connected and she felt her heart flop over.

No photograph could have captured the blue of his eyes. They were the dark, smoky blue of a wailing sax at some bar at three in the morning, with a half drunk whiskey and a smoldering cigarette. They were so tired, and so lonely in a cynical way that she wanted to fix everything for him and kiss his hurts better. It was an odd reaction for her to have for a stranger, but he didn't even look like a stranger, she thought with a spurt of recognition.

He held a briefcase in one hand and a black suitcase in the other. She glanced back at the photo and back at him, every hormone in her body doing a victory dance.

"Oh, my God," she said into the phone. "He's gorgeous."

"I dunno," her friend said in her ear. "He was all right looking, I suppose, but that shirt! I thought he'd—"

"What are you going on about? You can't see him." She'd have to remember never to wake Fi early on a Saturday again. "I've got to go." And she ended the call, while Fiona was in the middle of something.

Mark Forsyth's gaze had paused only briefly on hers and kept going, but whew, what could happen to a person's pulse in a few seconds.

Slowly she rose and approached. Could she really be this lucky and find that she was being asked to look after just about the sweetest sexpot she'd ever seen? Taking a deep breath, she said, "Mark Forsyth?"

He looked at her for a moment and a crease formed between his brows as though he weren't quite sure what his name was. She wanted to kiss the frown away.

Please turn the page for a sizzling preview of
RETURN TO ME
by Shannon McKenna.
Available right now.

"Excuse me, miss. I'm looking for El Kent." The low, quiet voice came from the swinging door that led to the dining room.

Ellen spun around with a gasp. The eggs flew into the air, and splattered on the floor. No one called her El. No one except for—

The sight of Simon knocked her back. God. So tall. So big. All over. The long, skinny body she remembered was filled out with hard, lean muscle. His white T-shirt showed off broad shoulders, sinewy arms. Faded jeans clung with careless grace to the perfect lines of his narrow hips, his long legs. She looked up into the focused intensity of his dark eyes, and a rush of hot and cold shivered through her body.

The exotic perfection of his face was harder now. Seasoned by sun and wind and time. She drank in the details: golden skin, narrow hawk nose, hollows beneath his prominent cheekbones, the sharp angle of his jaw, shaded with a few days' growth of dark beard stubble. A silvery scar sliced through the dark slash of his left eyebrow. His gleaming hair was wet, combed straight back from his square forehead into a ponytail. Tightly leashed power hummed around him.

The hairs on her arms lifted in response.

His eyes flicked over her body. His teeth flashed white against his tan. "Damn. I'll run to the store to replace those eggs for you, miss."

Miss? He didn't even recognize her. Her face was starting to shake again. Seventeen years of worrying about him, and he just checked out her body, like he might scope any woman he saw on the street.

He waited patiently for her to respond to his apology. She peeked up at his face again. One eyebrow was tilted up in a gesture so achingly familiar, it brought tears to her eyes. She clapped her hand over her trembling lips. She would not cry. She would not.

"I'm real sorry I startled you," he tried again. "I was wondering if you could tell me where I might find—" His voice trailed off. His smile faded. He sucked in a gulp of air. "Holy shit," he whispered. "El?"

The gesture tipped him off. He recognized her the instant she covered her mouth and peeked over her hand, but he had to struggle to superimpose his memories of El onto the knockout blonde in the kitchen. He remembered a skinny girl with big, startled eyes peeking up from beneath heavy bangs. A mouth too big for her bit of a face.

This woman was nothing like that awkward girl. She'd filled out, with a fine, round ass that had immediately caught his eye as she bent into the fridge. And what she had down there was nicely balanced by what she had up top. High, full tits, bouncing and soft. A tender, lavish mouthful and then some, just how he liked them.

Her hand dropped, and revealed her wide, soft mouth. Her dark eyebrows no longer met across the bridge of her nose. Spots of pink stained her delicate cheekbones. She'd grown into her eyes and mouth. Her hair was a wavy curtain of gold-streaked bronze that reached down to her ass. El Kent had turned beautiful. Mouth-falling-open, mind-going-blank beautiful. The images locked seamlessly together, and he wondered how he could've not recognized her, even for an instant. He wanted to hug her, but something buzzing in the air held him back.

The silence deepened. The air was heavy with it. She didn't exclaim, or look surprised, or pleased. In fact, she looked almost scared.

"El?" He took a hesitant step forward. "Do you recognize me?"

Her soft mouth thinned. "Of course I recognize you. You haven't changed at all. I was just, ah, surprised that you didn't recognize me."

"I didn't remember you being so pretty." The words came out before he could vet them and decide if they were stupid or rude.

Based on her reaction, he concluded that they were. She grabbed a wad of paper towels from the roll on the counter, wiped up the eggs and dropped the mess into the garbage pail. She dampened another paper towel. Her hair dangled down like a veil. She was hiding.

"What's wrong, El?" he asked cautiously. "What did I do?"

She knelt down, sponging off the floor tiles. "Nothing's wrong."

"But you won't look at me," he said.

She flung the soggy towel into the garbage. "I'm called Ellen these days. And what do you expect? You disappear for seventeen years, no letter, no phone call, not so much as a postcard to let me know you weren't dead, and expect me to run into your arms squealing for joy?"

So she hadn't forgotten him. His mood shot up, in spite of her anger. "I'm, uh, sorry I didn't write," he offered.

She turned her back on him. "I'm sorry you didn't, too." She made a show of drying some teacups.

"My life was really crazy for a while. I was scrambling

just to survive. Then I joined the Marines, and they sent me all over the map for a few years while I figured out what I wanted to do with myself—"

"Which was?" Her voice was sharp and challenging.

"Photojournalist," he told her. "Freelance, at the moment. I travel all the time, mostly war zones. By the time I got things in my life more or less straightened out, I was afraid . . ." His voice trailed off.

"Yes?" Her head swiveled around. "You were afraid of what?"

"That you might have forgotten me," he said.

**Don't miss these other great summer reads.
Available right now!**

I LOVE BAD BOYS

They are the men of our wildest dreams. With just a look, they can jump-start our deepest desires. So, crack open the cover . . . and discover men who can't be tamed . . .

HER CRAVING
by *New York Times* bestselling author Lori Foster

Shy Becky Harte has decided to explore her wicked side. Being spotted in a sex shop by her secret object of desire, George Westin, was not part of the plan. George is intrigued at her purchases, and he'd love to teach the blushing Becky a thing or two about surrender. But when fantasy becomes reality, it's the not-so-innocent Becky calling the shots.

NAUGHTY BY NIGHT
by *USA Today* bestselling author Janelle Denison

Since they were teenagers, sparks have flown between Chloe Anderson and Gabe Mackenzie. Now, Gabe is back in town, and a friendly poker game is turning into a game of seduction. The stakes: their wildest desires. Leave it to the irrepressible Chloe to turn the poker tables on Gabe. Now she has him at her mercy for four nights—and they've got six years of pent-up passion to make up for . . .

. . . AND WHEN THEY WERE BAD
by *USA Today* bestselling author Donna Kauffman

For Cameron James IV, a vacation at the private Caribbean club Intimacies is his chance to find his inner wild man. In real life, Allison Walker is a computer nerd with a successful firm, but at Intimacies, she's in over her head—until she meets Cam. And though Cam is looking to shuck his nice guy image with a wanton woman, it's the nice girl he's just met who's about to bring out the wickedness in him . . .

BAD BOYS TO GO

Hot. Tempting. Irresistibly decadent. These are some of the most mouth-watering dishes ever to satisfy a woman's sweet tooth . . . and make her want to go back for seconds . . .

BRINGING UP BABY
by Lori Foster

Gil Watson has always been the soul of responsibility . . . apart from that wild night that resulted in a daughter he didn't know he had. Now that the little girl's mother is gone, Gil wants to do the right thing, even if it means a marriage of convenience with the woman who's been raising her. Anabel Truman is sarcastic, free-spirited, and totally wrong for him. But the sensations she rouses feel very, very right . . .

THE WIILDE ONE
by Janelle Denison

Untamable, sexy, and a complete rogue, Adrian Wilde has agreed to pose for Chayse Douglas's charity beefcake calendar—if Chayse is willing to take those pictures at his cozy mountain cabin. It promises to be one provocative weekend . . . and as the nights turn steamy, Adrian finds that sweet, sensual Chayse is the only woman who can tame his wild heart . . .

GOING AFTER ADAM
by Nancy Warren

Private investigator Gretchen Wiest has met her share of tough guys, but she's never had one kidnap her—or leave her weak with attraction. Adam Stone is a whistle blower on the run from two hit men in Vegas. Now, Gretchen and Adam are posing as a couple on their way to the chapel. But in the city of sin, it's hard to resist temptation . . . and even harder not to fall for their own masquerade . . .

BAD BOYS NEXT EXIT

Forget the straight-and-narrow. When it comes to the uncharted off-ramp of desire, these sexy bad boys can show you exactly where to get off . . .

MELTDOWN
by Shannon McKenna

Jane Duvall wants to bag a big account for her head-hunting firm, even if it means stealing an employee from under sexy hotel CEO Michael "Mac" McNamara's nose. To find out what game the luscious Jane is playing, Mac's going to give her a private tour of the hotel's finest suite, where she can take whatever she wants from him—and he'll give everything he's got in the process . . .

EXPOSED
by *USA Today* bestselling author Donna Kauffman

It's Christmas Eve and Delilah Hudson is on a train stranded by a blizzard. At least she can snap a few pictures . . . if she can elude the gorgeous passenger who claims to be interested in her "equipment." Something about Delilah has photographer Austin Morgan feeling hungry for more. And once they're alone, Austin can't wait to see what develops . . .

PURE GINGER
E.C Sheedy

Ginger Cameron is a P.R. pro who has wasted too much time on the hey-baby, great-sex, see-ya kind of guy. From now on she's a serious woman who sleeps alone. Cal Beaumann wants to hire Ginger, and he's convinced there's more to her than orthopedic shoes and industrial-strength underwear. And if anyone is skilled at penetrating defenses, it's Cal . . .

Put on your blinker, and make the turn toward sheer temptation . . .

BAD BOYS ONLINE
by Erin McCarthy

Take a little time to reboot, 'cause these sly guys give a whole new meaning to on-site tech support . . .

"Debut author Erin McCarthy pens a sizzling anthology that triples our reading pleasure! She superbly combines wicked humor with red-hot passion."
—*Romantic Times*

HARD DRIVE

Mack Stone can't believe he's just walked in on the delilcious Kindra Hill in *computer flagrante delicto* in her office. When Kindra claims to prefer an online affair to the complication of a relationship, Mack convinces Kindra to grant him twelve hours to turn every erotic e-mail into a hot reality and prove that there's no substitute for the real thing . . .

USER FRIENDLY

Computer guru Evan Barrett can solve any tech problem, but the sight of Halley Connors's lovely head pasted onto some woman's nude body—courtesy of a hacker determined to derail her catering Web site—has him in a cold sweat. Now, as they work overtime to save the business, Evan realizes that not every fire needs putting out so quickly . . . and some require very little stoking to catch . . .

PRESS ANY KEY

To Jared Kinkaid, the only way to keep his mind—and his hands—off his luscious co-worker Candy Appleton is to insult or ignore her at every turn, until his boss signs them both up for online counseling. But when they mistakenly enroll in sensual couples counseling instead, Jared and Candy's shock turns to pleasure as they each deliver some hands-on therapy of their own . . .

Contemporary Romance By
Kasey Michaels

__Can't Take My Eyes Off of You
  0-8217-6522-1 $6.50US/$8.50CAN

__Too Good to Be True
  0-8217-6774-7 $6.50US/$8.50CAN

__Love to Love You Baby
  0-8217-6844-1 $6.99US/$8.99CAN

__Be My Baby Tonight
  0-8217-7117-5 $6.99US/$9.99CAN

__This Must Be Love
  0-8217-7118-3 $6.99US/$9.99CAN

__This Can't Be Love
  0-8217-7119-1 $6.99US/$9.99CAN

Available Wherever Books Are Sold!

Visit our website at **www.kensingtonbooks.com**.